MW00936652

Books by Richard Helms

Geary's Year
Geary's Gold
The Valentine Profile
The Amadeus Legacy
Joker Poker
Voodoo That You Do
Juicy Watusi
Wet Debt
Paid In Spades
Bobby J.
Grass Sandal
Cordite Wine
The Daedalus Deception
The Unresolved Seventh
The Mojito Coast
Six Mile Creek
Thunder Moon
Older Than Goodbye

RICHARD HELMS

CORDITE

WINE

Copyright © 2005, 2019
by Richard Helms
All Rights Reserved
No portion of this book may be reproduced in any form,
whether mechanical, electronic, or otherwise, in any
language, living or dead, without the expressed written
consent of the author.
This is a work of fiction. No events or persons in this work
of fiction are intended to represent actual persons, living or
dead, or actual events of the past or future. Any depictions in
this book which appear to represent actual persons or events
are purely coincidental.

For Elaine

The stuff that dreams are made of

ONE

Asa Corona sat across from my desk, dabbing at his eyes with the tissue I'd handed him. He'd been weeping for five minutes, as he tried to get his story out. He was in his early thirties, with thick dark hair, a gym-built athletic frame, and a dark secret.

"It's just weakness," he said. "I get this urge, and I can't resist. It's like my mind shuts down, and the next thing I know I'm on my knees in some tawdry bookstore. I can't explain it."

I could. Asa didn't want to hear my explanation, though.

"Who have you told?" I asked.

"Nobody, Mr. Gold. I've been in the closet for years. I suppose it's no big deal anymore, for most people. In some circles, it's even fashionable."

"But your family wouldn't understand."

"Hell, no. Especially my grandfather. He'd call me eight kinds of pervert and then cut me off without a cent."

There it was. As usual, it came down to the money.

Asa Corona was the fourth generation in his family of winemakers. Corona Farms covered five square miles of prime Napa Valley real estate, produced two hundred thousand gallons of California varietals each year, and raked in several million after expenses. They'd been at it since before Prohibition.

You do the math.

"Tell me again how you were approached."

He snuffled, blew his nose into the tissue, and stared at me with crimson-lidded eyes.

"It came by email," he said. "There was an attachment, a picture. Someone had managed to take a photo of me, at a bathhouse. It was... explicit."

"Could you identify the bathhouse?"

"Yes."

"We'll get the address later."

"The person who sent the email said they'd destroy the pictures if I paid them money."

"Pictures. So there are more?"

"I don't know how many. He told me how to pay the money, and said I'd regret it if I didn't. He said he'd send the pictures to everyone in my family. To prove it, he included their names and addresses."

"The blackmailer had done his research," I said.

"It seems that way."

"How were you to pay?"

"Through an online bill-paying service called PayMaster. It's one of the programs you use to pay for auctions and stuff like that. I would simply indicate that I wanted to transfer ten thousand dollars to the account of this guy's screen name."

"It's clever. No drop, no chance to nail him when he does the pickup. And he avoids raising any red flags at the IRS."

"Huh?"

"The easiest way to catch a blackmailer is to go ahead and pay him, which usually means making a blind drop somewhere, like in a secluded area. It's almost always someplace where he can scope you out from a distance, make sure there's nobody waiting. If you can get there earlier, and hide yourself better, you can catch him when he picks up the money. The way your guy is doing it, there's no drop."

"He seemed to know what he was doing."

"He also knew that any deposit in his account totaling more than ten thousand dollars would trigger an automatic report to the IRS. So, he's no dope. What did you do?"

"I paid him, of course. Ten thousand was nothing compared to what I stood to lose."

"And after you paid, he wrote you back, demanding more."

"Can you help me, Mr. Gold?" Asa asked.

I thought it over. The odds were in my favor on this one. The fact that the blackmailer was using so much anonymity meant he wasn't particularly bold. He was clever, but probably not very dangerous.

I like them that way.

"Extortion is a felony, Mr. Corona," I said. "This is really police business. Even if I catch the guy, I'm not a cop. I can't charge him or put him in jail. What is it you want?"

Corona started weeping again.

"I just want it... to... stop." he said.

I waited for him to pull things together.

"Let's get something straight," I said. "I'm a detective. I find things. I find people. I gather information. That's it. I'm not hired muscle, and I don't settle scores. I find this guy, the best I can do is maybe jam him up a little, tell him if he doesn't lay off I'm going to turn him in to the police. Maybe he'll stop."

"And if he doesn't?"

I shrugged.

"I don't like making threats I can't back up," I said. "But at least you'll know who you're dealing with."

"And so will he?" Corona asked.

I nodded.

"That too," I said.

TWO

Heidi Fluhr and I were having dinner at an Italian place in North Beach. I was eating spinach ravioli with roasted garlic and sundried tomato pesto. Heidi had ordered what appeared to be an elephant smothered in linguini and alfredo. We were halfway through our second bottle of sangiovese.

Heidi isn't exactly my girlfriend. That would imply some sort of long-term commitment. We're more like close friends who screw a lot, but otherwise try to stay out of each other's lives. It's a convenient arrangement, which has not yet bored me.

Heidi is a whole lot of blonde northern European woman, with a healthy appetite for just about everything. She stands just under six feet, which means she can stare me right in the chin, and her build would probably be referred to as 'big-boned'. That's deceptive because, while she's soft and fluffy in all the right places, she's also strong and muscular where it counts. A romp with Heidi is like going seven rounds with Mike Tyson wrapped in throw pillows.

Fortunately, I'm a pretty tough guy. I can keep up with her.

Heidi runs the art gallery just underneath my second-floor office near Hyde Pier in San Francisco. She carries a lot of the usual stuff – some Thomas Kinkade and other popular representative artists – but she also caters to the more esoteric collector crowd.

San Francisco is the capitol of Esoterica. Heidi does all right.

"I give up," I said. "The world's becoming just too electronic."

"How so?" she asked.

"I can't say much – confidentiality and all – but I got this client. Blackmail case. This kind of thing used to be easy. You set up the drop, wait for him to grab the cash, and nick him. This joker wants to be paid through an online service. How in hell do I trace that?"

"Oh, I love those services," Heidi said. "A man in San Diego was looking for a low-numbered Erte' print, which I just happened to have, and we did the whole deal over the Internet. I just set up a merchant account, he transferred the money to me in about five minutes, and I had the print FedExed out the door an hour later."

"How hard was it to set up the account?"

"Not hard at all. All you need is an Internet screen name and a bank account. If someone wants to pay you, he just lets the service know, and they transfer the money from his account to your account."

"How do they make their money?"

"They take a percentage of the payment. I don't mind. It's so convenient, and there's no hassle with waiting for a check to clear."

"So, in order for my client to pay the blackmailer, both of them would have to be members of this service."

"As far as I know."

"That would mean the online bill paying service would have a record of the blackmailer's name and bank account number."

"They'd almost have to."

"Seems too easy, doesn't it?"

"How do you mean?"

I stared at her. We'd been bumping up against each other long enough for her to see things from my perspective.

"Oh, I get it," she said. "The blackmailer wants to remain anonymous. Giving his name and bank account number to the bill paying service kind of defeats that purpose."

"On the other hand..." I said.

"He *is* a criminal."

"If he's willing to blackmail, what's to keep him from opening a bank account under an assumed name?"

"I thought banks had ways of protecting against that. Safeguards."

"It wouldn't be very hard to do," I said. "There's an entire underground industry out there dedicated to helping people set up false identities."

She ate a little more while I thought about the problem.

"You know what I think?" she said, as she reached for her wine glass.

"What?"

"I think you're up against a pretty smart cookie."

THREE

The main office for PayMaster was a post office box in a mail center off Stockton Street in Chinatown.

I suppose I could have gone to their website, emailed customer service, and waited for someone to get back with me. That would have been easy enough, and Asa Corona was paying by the hour.

On the other hand, I had the scent of this blackmailer in my nose, and it wasn't going to go away while I was waiting.

I picked up the telephone and called Kevin Krantz.

Kevin works for the business desk at the *Chronicle*. We knew each other in high school, where we both worked on the school paper, and we've tried to stay in touch ever since. I was an usher at his wedding, and I was a pallbearer at his wife's funeral. It's that kind of relationship.

"Krantz," he said, picking up the telephone.

"Did you hear the one where Bill Gates, a rabbi, and a kangaroo walk into a bar?" I said.

"No, lay it on me."

"Bartender took one look and said, '*What is this, some kind of joke?*'"

Kevin laughed. Hard. It was good to hear, after what he'd been through. A couple of years earlier, his wife had noticed this lump in her breast during a shower. That was just about the end of the happy part of their marriage. He was due a little laugh.

"What can I do for you, Eamon?"

"I could use some information on a company called PayMaster."

"Internet startup. Dot-commer. Handles paperless payments for people doing online auctions, that sort of thing."

"This much I know. Who runs it?"

"Hold on."

He put me on hold and subjected me to the easy listening version of *Our House* by CSN.

I reflected on the decline of western civilization.

Mercifully, he came back before the tape could segue into some string quartet rendition of *Do You Think I'm Sexy.*

"Okay, looks like the owner is a guy named David Eudy. His resume is pretty much your basic Silicon Valley stuff— undergrad at Stanford, then graduate work at Cal Poly, nothing out of the ordinary. He's a computer geek."

"Any idea how I'd contact him?"

"Sure. I have a main company address here."

He read off the name of the mail center on Stockton Street.

"That's no good," I said. "It's just a mail drop."

"How about a telephone number?"

"Lay it on me."

I wrote down the number, spent a few minutes catching up, and then racked the receiver.

I immediately called David Eudy's number.

It took a few minutes to work my way through several operators, but each time, when I identified myself as a detective, it was like saying *Open Sesame.* Finally, Eudy came on the line.

"I'm sorry. Is there some kind of problem, Detective?" he asked.

Sometimes people hear *detective,* and presume they're talking with the police. I let them presume. I am not responsible for their guilty consciences.

"Perhaps. I'd like to ask a few questions about your operation. Would it be possible to meet you at your office?"

He gave me an address in San Jose. I wrote it down. We arranged to meet later that afternoon.

My house in Montara was on the way to San Jose, so I grabbed an early lunch and dropped by the beach house to do a little work on a dreadnaught guitar I was building as a present for a friend. I started building musical instruments as a hobby shortly after I went private. It's relaxing and relatively non-intellectual, so I have time to think things through while I'm sanding or shaping or carving or whatever.

The dreadnaught was made from some pre-CITES injunction Brazilian rosewood I'd bought from a dealer in Healdsburg, and a creamy sitka spruce top. The rosewood was worth, easy, five hundred dollars. Bending the sides had been an exercise in controlled terror. Splitting a side during bending would have been tragic, since this stuff is so hard to come by nowadays.

I had finished the body, and was working on the neck, which I was carving from a nice quartersawn piece of mahogany. The headstock veneer was a leftover piece of the rosewood from the sides.

I had decided to carve a nice grape-leaf relief pattern in the heel of the neck, and that was my project for the early afternoon. It wasn't all that hard. I just drew the pattern on the wood with a pencil, and then carved the relief with my knives and miniature gouges, but it was tedious and time-consuming. It also took my mind off the rest of my life for a while.

Before I knew it, it was two in the afternoon, and I had to drive down the coast.

An hour later, I parked in front of a row of cookie-cutter offices in a park of cookie-cutter buildings, straightened my tie, and walked into the PayMaster office. The receptionist gave me the twice-over.

I checked her out a couple of times myself.

A few minutes later, David Eudy greeted me in the lobby. He was just shy of six feet tall, but soft and pudgy in the way that sitting behind a desk bathing in cathode rays can do to you after a decade or so. His complexion was copy-paper white, except for his cheeks, which glowed with this rosy blush that portended a short but well-fed life.

"Come on back to my office, Detective," he said. "Would you like some coffee?"

I declined, and he led me past a warren of cubicles toward his modular office in the back of the building. Like everything else at PayMaster, it was a functional space that was never going to make the cover of Architectural Digest. The furniture was mostly plastic and tough fabrics, with not one ounce of solid wood in sight. The desk was fiberboard covered with a photographed veneer, made to look like Oregon redwood but without any semblance of having ever been a part of nature.

The rest of the office was filled with computers.

When Kevin Krantz had told me Eudy was a computer geek, he had neglected to mention that he was their King.

"What can I do for you?" he asked.

"I just have a few questions."

"Is this in regards to some… crime?"

I smiled.

"An ongoing investigation. If I understand correctly, sir, your service is used for individuals to send money to each other without using paper?"

"That's a good description. What actually happens is that a person wanting to send money sends a request to us, indicating whom he wants to receive the money, and how much. We already have his bank account information on file, and by asking us to send cash he is authorizing us to debit his account by this amount, and then deposit it in the bank account of the payee."

"So, you have all this bank account information stored away?"

"Yes, after a fashion. If you take a look at the bottom of your checks, Detective, you will see a series of numbers. These are routing numbers, and every account has a unique number. We match client information and routing numbers."

"Can you retrieve this information on any specific account?"

"Of course."

"I don't want to give away any particulars," I said. "Ongoing investigation and all. But let's try a couple of hypotheticals. Let's say that you wanted to conduct a drug deal with a guy in, say, Long Beach. You contact one another via email, using some kind of pre-arranged code, and decide how much stuff the guy in Long Beach will part with for, say, a thousand dollars. Then, you arrange for PayMaster to deduct a thousand from your account and place it into the payee's account."

Eudy seemed to blush even more.

"I would hate to think that our service was being used that way, but of course it is possible."

"Then each person in the—uh—transaction would have to be a member of your program?"

"Not at all. If you are a member of PayMaster, you can send money to anyone anywhere, as long as they have an email address."

"How does that work?"

"Quite simply. Let's say you want to send – we'll use your example – a thousand dollars to this fellow in Long Beach. You are a member. He isn't. After you send the authorization, we would deduct the thousand from your account, and inform the payee via email that we are holding these funds for him in escrow, as it were. The payee can contact us, again by email, and inform us where to deposit the funds. Or, at his request, we can simply write a check for the amount and send it to him via the postal service."

"A real check?"

"As real as the one in your checkbook."

"But, to do that, you'd need his name, right?"

"Certainly."

"Suppose he didn't want to give his name?"

Eudy stroked his chin for a moment.

"Well, in that case, if he could provide us with a routing number for a bank account somewhere, we'd be able to just deposit the funds there."

"Any bank."

"Yes."

"Anywhere."

"That's the way banks work, Detective. It's all about routing numbers and transfers of funds. No real money changes hands, you see. It's all electronic."

"Just so I understand," I said. "Let's say this guy in Long Beach doesn't want anyone, even the buyer, to know who he is. Now, let's say he's managed to open a secret numbered account in a bank in—say—the Cayman Islands. You could still take my thousand and transfer it into his account, and nobody would ever know who received it?"

"I suppose that's possible. I'm sorry, but I'm not sure I see where this is going."

"Me either. One last question, sir. Let's say the police got wind of this transaction and wanted to stop the drug deal before it was completed. Now, let's also say everything else was as we have just said—the receiver wants to remain anonymous. How could the police access information on the receiver from you?"

"They couldn't," Eudy said. "Not without a warrant."

"Confidentiality and all."

"Absolutely. It's one of the reasons people use PayMaster. We provide safe, secure money transfers. If the police wanted information on one of the people we serve, they'd have to get a court order for us to release it. Not only that, but because we move money across state lines, and for that matter across international borders, it would have to be a federal warrant."

"I see," I said. "So, if I suspected that a person had used your program to – for instance – receive ransom money in a kidnapping case, you'd require a federal warrant just to release his email address, let alone any other information."

"Absolutely."

I wasn't going to get any more information out of Eudy, and certainly none about Asa Corona's blackmailer. I was going to have to try another avenue.

FOUR

I called Asa Corona and had asked him to meet me at my office with some information.

"We're not going to get anywhere with PayMaster," I told him. "The owner's straight-up, and he's not going to give us dick without a federal warrant. I'm not sure it would help, anyway."

"Why?"

"The guy blackmailing you sounds smart. He's developed this sophisticated process for juicing you, so it stands to reason he's found some way to hide on his end too. My guess is that he opens a phony bank account somewhere, and he just drains it as soon as a deposit is made. Probably writes a check out to "cash", waltzes out of the bank, and that's it. Did you bring the stuff?"

He slid a manila envelope across the desk to me. I opened it.

Inside were the pictures he had received from the blackmailer, and copies of the email that had been sent to him.

The pictures, as Corona had implied, were explicit. They showed Corona hunched over a kneeling man, cornholing him furiously, sweat dripping off his face and chest. I could see the other guy's face clearly. He looked, maybe, twenty-five, California blond surfer type, hair halfway to his shoulders. He wasn't grimacing or frowning, so I figured he had done this kind of thing before.

"Who took the picture?" I asked.

"It was a bathhouse," Corona said. "There were, like, thirty guys in there. Could have been anyone. I didn't notice. I was busy."

He sounded petulant, almost irritated. He acted as if I was trespassing in his territory.

"What's this guy's name?" I said, pointing to Surfer Boy.

Corona just stared at me, his mouth set in a pair of thin, white lines.

"You don't know, or you're not saying?" I asked.

"It's a bathhouse," he repeated. "It's not the kind of place you go with your steady."

"So you don't know. Tell me something, Asa. How does this work? You just walk around in this place until some guy gives you the high sign, and then you just go at it right there?"

"Crudely put, but it's an accurate description."

"Doesn't the idea of disease bother you?"

"Between sessions, yes. Like I said before, though, I get these… urges, and when they come over me I don't think about anything but getting off. I can't explain it. If it makes you any more comfortable, I always remember to use a condom."

I looked over the pictures again. The kid Corona was shtupping made a good picture. I figured I could probably identify him if we crossed paths.

"I need to keep these," I said. "I want to make some copies, show them around."

Corona looked panic-stricken.

"I'll crop them, keep you out of the picture. I want to see if anyone can identify this kid."

"Why?"

"He might be in on the blackmail scheme. Most confidence games include a shill and a stinger. The kid shills you into having sex, the stinger takes the picture. Later they split the take."

I placed the pictures aside and looked over the emails. The writer had used the screen name *BathBoy* and had sent it by an email service that proudly advertised itself as being free, if you could stand the ten pop-up advertisements on each screen.

I fired up my computer and accessed my own Internet account.

"What are you doing?" Corona asked.

"Saving myself some time," I said.

I pulled up my email and wrote a message to BathBoy. I hit the "SEND" button and waited for a couple of minutes.

My computer announced that I had mail, and I checked my mailbox.

"Sure enough," I said. "BathBoy's out of business. He's deleted his screen name from this service."

"Why?"

"Because it was a trail to him. Email, like everything else on the 'net, is sent in packets of information that are reassembled on the other end. The packets can go through a number of convoluted paths. All that gobbledeegook at the bottom of the email indicates the paths taken. It will be different every time, but eventually everything winds up in the same place. My guess is you'll receive a new demand from a new screen name later today, if you haven't already. Like I said, this guy's smart."

"What will you do now?"

"What you paid me to do. It's time to go back to old style detecting."

FIVE

The WaterWorks Bathhouse was located in SoMa, several blocks south of the Tenderloin. Formerly a dreary area filled with warehouses, tenements, and more crime than you can eat on a cracker, it had recently begun to fall prey to the same gentrification that had hit most of the peninsula. Gay Urban Professionals had started to flow over from the Castro district, and the natural direction of their flow was north. With them had started to migrate trendy clothing stores, bars, and music halls, along with the occasional glitter disco. They had also brought bathhouses.

At one time, in the early 1980's, bathhouses had been threatened with extinction. After researchers discovered that AIDS wasn't just God's judgment against gays, Public Health decided one way to cut down on transmission was to eliminate indiscriminate sex between members of the highest risk group at that time. The city issued an order closing bathhouses and the like. Folks down at the Civic Center realized shortly just how powerful the gay voting bloc was, and after a 'reasonable period' some clubs were allowed to—quietly—reopen. Some of them kept heaping salad bowls of foil-wrapped condoms at the front desk, free for the taking. It was once again Party Time on the Barbary Coast.

I opened the door to The Waterworks and was hit by a humid wave of chlorinated air. Like most of these places, there was a sort of airlock at the front that you had to pass through before getting to the real action, and this one was guarded by a former San Francisco 49ers fourth string defensive back named Chris Driscoll.

Driscoll and I had never met, but I had spent several seasons watching him warm the bench at Candlestick before it changed names. I didn't feel superior. I'd never made it to the bench, after seeing my career end with a knee injury in college.

"You're Chris Driscoll, aren't you?" I said, as I pulled out a business card.

"Yeah," he said. His voice was surprisingly high and raspy.

"Always wondered what happened to you after you quit playing."

He smiled and shook his head.

"Some people say I never *started* playing."

He looked at my card.

"What's this about?"

"Wonder if I could talk to the boss."

"Hold on."

He picked up the telephone and hit a speed-dial button. While he spoke, I pulled out the cropped picture I'd made of California Blond.

"He's on his way down," Driscoll said.

I put the picture down on the counter.

"Know this guy?"

He looked at the picture for a second.

"He looks familiar, but you know how it goes. Hundreds of guys in and out."

"And in and out and in and out..." I said.

"No shit, man. After a while though, they all sort of blend in together. This kind, we must see fifty a day. All of them want to look like Brad Pitt. Probably why Pitt cut his hair and spiked it."

A door next to the desk opened, and a redheaded man about my height stepped out. He was wearing a yellow *WaterWorks* embroidered pullover sport shirt, a pair of khakis, and sunglasses. His biceps were very freckled and as big around as a football. He looked like he could do ten reps lifting me over his head while eating a sandwich.

He extended his hand.

"Gary Chiklis," he said.

I watched my reflection in his sunglasses reach out and take his hand as I introduced myself.

"Why don't we step up to my office?" he asked.

I followed him up a short flight of stairs to a small but nicely decorated room, with a leather couch on one side, and a walnut desk with matching leather-covered chairs on the other. There was a picture window on the wall between them, which I figured was the watching side of a one-way mirror.

Remembering what went on in this place, I declined to sit on the couch.

Chiklis sat behind his desk.

"How can I help you, Mr. Gold?"

I placed the pictures down in front of him.

"I can't provide a lot of details—confidentiality. I'm trying to find this guy, though. I know he's been here, but I thought he might be a regular."

Chiklis placed his sunglasses on the desk and pulled a pair of reading glasses from his desk drawer. He looked at the picture for about three seconds.

"What's he done this time?" he asked.

"Signifying recognition?"

"His name is Ty Cannon. At least, that's what he calls himself. I think it's a stage name."

"An actor?"

"A wannabe. Is he missing?"

"I don't know. That's not why I'm looking for him. He may be mixed up in a case I'm handling. I'd like to ask him some questions."

Chiklis placed his reading glasses back down on the table and slid the pictures back to me.

"Mixed up how?"

"That's where the confidentiality comes in. I can say, however, that my client has… um… been involved with Cannon."

For the first time, Chiklis smiled, and then he chuckled.

"Man, you can't get much more confidential than that. I'd like to see three fags in this city haven't been up Ty's ass, me included."

"He gets around?"

"He gets around. Yeah, that's an understatement. He's careful, though. Ty never allows the other guy to take responsibility for the rubber. He makes sure it's on. Nobody gets a piece of this guy without a raincoat. I figure he's clean, but it could be because he doesn't want to spread anything around."

"Have you seen Ty here lately?"

Chiklis thought about it for a moment.

"Not in a week or two. That's not unusual, though. He gets out-of-town gigs sometimes, maybe a month at a time. He always comes back to roost. He'll show up in a week or so."

I picked up the pictures and started to put them back into the envelope.

"I don't suppose you have his address," I said.

"It's not like we exchange calling cards around here. I never dated Ty. Never date any of the guys that come here. I just get out into the spa once in a while, pick off a quickie. Have you been here before?"

"No."

"Come here."

He stood up and walked over to the picture window. I followed him.

"It's called a bathhouse, but it's more like a big heated indoor pool with a bunch of hot tubs scattered around. We have some dressing rooms off the main pool house. What we run here is more technically called a sex club. Real bathhouses have private rooms for rent."

"You don't?"

"The narrow-minded city fathers won't allow it. They think private rooms lead to AIDS transmission. They figure if our customers can't get it on behind locked doors, they will simply stand around and ogle each other."

"And they don't."

"Of course not. You can drive across the bay to Berkeley and go to a real bathhouse, but here in the city you have to get down and get funky with an audience."

"I see," I said, looking out over the pool area. It was only one in the afternoon, but there were already ten or fifteen guys lounging in the pool area, most of them naked.

"It's a little early for things to heat up," Chiklis said. "Most of these guys are out-of-work actors or they work nights. Some of them just drop by on a long lunch hour to relax. Come back after dark, and it's wall-to-wall meat. We turn on the mirror ball, play a lot of Euro disco. Once the bar cranks up, it's open season."

"How does it work? Do you just pay a cover charge, or do you sell memberships?"

"Either way. Technically, everyone here is a member, but you join for the cost of a day pass—seven dollars—or you can pay by the month."

"How does Ty Cannon pay?"

Chiklis scratched his chin.

"I don't know. Let's check."

He returned to his desk and opened a file on his computer.

"Tough luck," he said. "Looks like Cannon's a day player. I should talk to him about that next time he comes in. He'd get by a lot cheaper with a monthly membership, frequent flyer like him."

"Does he seem particularly close to anyone? Possibly someone with a membership?"

He thought about it a little.

"Maybe... hold on a minute."

He clicked through a few spreadsheets, and then stopped.

"You could check with this guy. He's also a regular. I don't know how well he knows Ty, but I've seen them hooked up a few times down by the pool."

He scribbled a name and some information on the scratch pad next to the computer, and then picked up the telephone.

"I'd rather clear it with him, first, if you don't mind," Chiklis said. "It's just good manners. I don't want my customers to start thinking I'm selling mailing lists."

He dialed a phone number, and after a few seconds spoke.

"Hey, this is Gary down at WaterWorks. I have a guy here looking for Ty Cannon. He'd like to talk with you. Is it okay if he comes by?"

He nodded a couple of times.

"Thanks, man. Treat this guy right, I'll let you off the hook for a month, okay? Thanks."

He racked the receiver and handed me the scratch paper.

"Name's Tom Schuyler. He's okay. A regular."

I pocketed the slip and extended my hand.

"You've been a big help," I said.

"No problem. Would you like a pass?"

"Beg pardon?"

"You know, try it out one night?"

"You got Coed Swim?"

"No, but... Hey, that's not a bad idea. Straight, huh?"

"Sorry."

"No problem. Some of my best friends are straight."

"Sure, but would you let your sister marry one?"

"No way. My sister's a lesbian."

I opened the office door to leave.

"And they say it isn't genetic," I told him, as I left the office.

He grinned and waved goodbye.

I walked down the stairs, where Chris Driscoll was still guarding the entrance to the bathhouse. He nodded at me as I hit the bottom step.

"You into this scene?" I asked.

"Naw," he said. "It's a little too... I guess the word is *direct* for me. Besides, it's risky. All the steroids I took for all those years, my immune system's already a little messed up. Why take chances?"

"So you just check 'em in and out?"

"That and the occasional bouncing. You might not believe it, but these guys can get pretty rowdy. Hey, you ever play football?"

"San Francisco State, years ago."

"You look pretty big. What happened?"

"Blew out my knee."

"Bad tackle?"

I shook my head.

"Artificial turf."
He shook his head.
"Stuff's a bitch, man."

SIX

Tom Schuyler lived in the Marina district, in a three-story apartment rebuilt after the '89 Loma Pietro quake. The neighborhood was clean, the sidewalks were swept, and Schuyler's doorknocker shone like a ship's bell as I rapped on the striker plate a couple of times.

The door opened almost immediately.

Schuyler was about thirty. His dark brown hair was cropped almost to the skin, except for a little fringe right at the front that was an inch long and bleached bright yellow. It made him look like a cockatiel. He was in the late five feet range, lanky and sinewy. He wore a crew-neck sweater and tan khakis. He was barefoot.

"My name's Eamon Gold," I said. "Gary Chiklis called about me."

"Of course," he said. His voice was surprisingly deep, without any trace of the stereotypical sibilance I had expected. "Please, come on in."

He led me into a room he'd apparently ordered directly from page fifty-seven of *Arts and Crafts Bungalow* magazine. It was all Mission-style chairs and settles, mostly ammonia-fumed quartersawn white oak.

I approved.

"Have a seat," Schuyler said, pointing toward the settle. "Can I get you anything to drink?"

I pulled a picture of Ty Cannon from my jacket pocket and handed it to him.

"No thanks. Is this guy Ty Cannon?"

He picked it up.

"Where'd you get this?" he asked.

"Guy I know. Can't tell you more than that. Sorry."

"Looks like Ty's taking it up the Hershey Highway."

"How can you tell?"

"Because that's how he looks when he's getting fucked. He gets this dreamy, peaceful look on his face. Sometimes I watch."

"What can you tell me about him?"

"Not a lot. He's an actor. You've seen him, commercials and shit like that. He did that one for Soilite detergent last year. Mostly, though, he does cruise ships, Vegas and Reno gigs, short term stuff like that."

"When was the last time you saw him?"

"Just before he took off for a month to do a dinner theater gig in Tahoe. Let's see. That would be about two weeks ago."

"You know which dinner theater?"

"Lord, no. We weren't that close. He told me he'd landed a part in a show out there, and he'd be gone for four or five weeks."

"You don't remember the show, do you?"

"No...Wait. Maybe. Seems like he told me. Damn, don't you just *hate* it when you can't remember something?"

I gazed at him, trying to figure out whether he was fishing for a payoff. He didn't seem the type, but you never know.

"I've got it!" he said. "It's a musical version of *The Importance of Being Earnest.* Ty was supposed to play Reverend Chasuble."

"I suppose I could track that down pretty easily. So you haven't seen him in two weeks?"

"He was supposed to leave two weeks ago, so he spent the evening before driving out to Tahoe at WaterWorks. We didn't hook up that night, but we talked a little at the bar."

"I don't suppose you have his address," I said.

"Not even a phone number. He was a little squeamish about giving out stuff like that. Guess he liked his privacy at home."

"Guess so," I said.

SEVEN

It took about ten minutes to find out that *Earnest In Love* was playing a four week engagement at the Washoe Dinner Theatre. I thought about calling out there but decided it would be better to confront Cannon in person. If he was involved in the blackmail scheme against Asa Corona, calling might scare him off.

I decided I'd done enough for one day, so I dropped by Heidi's gallery and convinced her to close up shop early. We went to dinner at a little place off Montgomery over in North Beach.

She'd had a good day, selling about ten thousand dollars' worth of paintings and sculptures. She told me about it, and then I told her about my day

"Go on," she said. "You mean they walk around all nekkid and if they like each other they just... *do it* right there?"

"That's the way it was described to me. I didn't actually see anyone hook up."

"Hook up? You sound like some seventh-grader."

"I'll bet no self-respecting seventh-grader has said that in a year or so. Once it filtered up to the grown-ups, it was *so* over," I said, grinning. "Two different guys used that term today, though. *Hooking up.* Guess it's the code these days."

"What time are you leaving for Tahoe tomorrow?"

"Early. If I'm lucky, I can make a day trip out of it, maybe get back in time to follow up on whatever I find out. Unless

I'm wrong, my client is going to get another email demanding money tomorrow or thereabouts."

"Your client's a rich guy?" she asked.

"I can't go there," I said. "Confidential."

"He must be rich, if he can dole out thousands of dollars a pop. Think maybe you can steer him my way once this blackmail mess is cleared up?"

"I'll mention it to him."

We were finishing our meal, and I ordered a chocolate bread pudding for dessert. We took turns spooning off portions, until the plate was cleaned off.

Heidi dropped her spoon into the plate and sat back in her seat. Her face was slack, the way she often looked when delightfully sated. It reminded me of what Tom Schuyler had said about Ty Cannon's face while he was getting reamed.

"Too early to call it a night," she said, looking through the restaurant window. We were high on a hill, as Tony Bennett put it, and we could see the lights of the Bay Bridge in the distance.

"What would you like to do?"

"We could catch a movie. I've been dying to see that new Tom Cruise flick."

"And after?"

"We'll see," she said. "Maybe we can hook up…"

EIGHT

The Washoe Dinner Theater by daylight was a dreary, two-story barn-like building with a corrugated tin roof and ancient thready redwood siding. It looked a lot like Dorothy's barn, after the tornado. The parking lot was gravel, which crunched under my tires as I parked my car in the very first unmarked space.

The inside smelled like a thick roux of musk, cleaning fluid, and garlic. As I walked in the front door, I could see the dining area, a raised platform ringing a twenty by twenty stage on all four sides.

Down a short hall, I heard a typewriter clacking away, maybe twenty words a minute.

"Hello?" I called out.

A feminine voice said, "Right with you!"

The typing went on for a moment though, before stopping abruptly. Seconds later, the door at the end of the hall swung open. A young woman walked my way.

She was twenty, maybe, dressed in a rock band tee shirt and jeans. She was just to the healthy side of slender, and her breasts bounced around unfettered under the rock band logo as she walked my way. Her nipples poked at me as she spoke.

"Can I help you?" she asked.

"My name's Eamon Gold," I said, handing her my card. "I've driven up from San Francisco looking for a kid named Ty Cannon."

She glanced at my card, and then at my face. She bit her lower lip, as if deciding whether to jump my bones right there.

Or maybe that was just my imagination.

"Come on back," she said.

I followed her to her office. It was little more than a large closet, with the desk jammed into one back corner. There were posters lining the wall, announcing shows dating back as much as ten years or more.

She sat at the desk and offered me the only other chair in the room, one of the dinner chairs from out in the theater.

"A private eye, huh?" she asked.

I nodded.

"That is so cool."

"It's why I became one."

"Huh?"

"The cool factor. Ty Cannon?"

I pulled a picture of Cannon from my pocket and handed it to her.

"Asshole," she said.

"Beg pardon?"

"This guy's on my shit list."

"Why's that?"

She seemed to collect herself and offered her hand.

"Shelley Proulx," she said, introducing herself. I shook her hand, as I'd already told her who I was. "I'm the managing director here."

"You direct the shows?"

"No, that's Brad Zukowski. He's the artistic director. My boyfriend."

"A real Mom and Pop operation," I said.

"Oh, puh-lease," she said, rolling her eyes. "Brad directs the shows, I run everything else—reservations, hiring the kitchen and wait help, managing the house on show nights. It's like being a crisis counselor."

"And Ty Cannon was a crisis?"

"Big time. Brad cast him to play Reverend Chasuble in the show that's running now. Have you seen it?"

"Only the non-musical version. I know who Reverend Chasuble is."

"Well, Brad offered it to this guy Ty Cannon. Cannon accepted the part, but he never showed up when we started rehearsals. I tried for two days to reach him, but he never answered the phone or his messages. We had to call five other guys before we could find someone who had time to take the role. Between you and me, he isn't as good as Ty, but what can you do?"

"What indeed? So you never heard from Cannon?"

"Not a peep. We figured he'd taken another job, maybe a movie or something, and didn't have the balls to call and cancel out on us. Creep."

"When was he supposed to start work?"

She pulled a day planner from her top desk drawer and riffled through it.

"Umm, rehearsals started two weeks ago today. We open tomorrow night."

Two weeks. The same time Ty was last seen by Tom Schuyler.

The same time, roughly, that Asa Corona had made his first payment on the blackmail. Maybe Ty had taken another gig – one that paid a lot more money.

"Do you still have Cannon's address and phone number?" I asked.

She turned and opened a side drawer on the desk. It turned out to be a file cabinet.

"Somewhere... here it is. We file stuff here by shows, and I haven't started cleaning out the file yet. I'll get you a copy."

She disappeared back down the hall for a moment, and then reappeared. She handed me a sheet of paper.

The picture was Ty Cannon. He was better arranged and more professionally photographed than in the one I was carrying. It was a headshot, the kind actors tote around by the ream to hand out at auditions. On the back, he'd listed his address, telephone number, email address, and his acting credits. I noted the Soilite commercial among them.

"Can I keep this?" I asked.

"Sure. He'll never work in this theatre again."

She smiled at her turn on the showbiz phrase.

I smiled back, mostly being polite.

"How did he seem when you met him?" I asked.

"Very high-strung. That was why Brad wanted him for Reverend Chasuble. Brad wanted the character to be nervous, fidgety. Cannon was like that. Nice guy, though, at least at the audition. What an asshole..."

I thanked her for the picture and the information and started to stand.

"A detective, huh?" she said again.

I smiled at her.

"Got a gun?"

"Not on me. In the glove compartment. I don't have much call to use it."

"You kill anyone?"

"Not in the last month. You want me to plug Ty Cannon for you when I find him?"

"Please do," she said. "And send me a picture. We'll use it as a warning for other actors."

NINE

Not finding Ty Cannon had made for a short day, so I phoned Asa Corona from the car on the way home and asked him to meet me at the office around four.

I also tried Ty Cannon's telephone number, though I had no intention of speaking with him. I just wanted to see if he was home. The number was disconnected.

Curiouser and curiouser.

Corona arrived about ten minutes after I settled in behind my desk.

"Kid in the picture is named Ty Cannon. Mean anything to you?"

"No. I never got his name."

"The manager at WaterWorks says he gets around, has sex with lots of people. You'd never seen him there before?"

"Well, sure, we'd seen each other. We just never met, at least until that night..." he pointed at the picture.

"Do you know anyone else he had sex with?"

"I don't know. I might. Why?"

"Because if he was the shill in a blackmail scheme, he might be pulling the same game on some other WaterWorks patrons. It would be nice to develop a pattern."

"How would you go about finding out?"

"I could hang down at WaterWorks for a couple of nights, ask around."

"I don't think so, Mr. Gold. No offense but..." he stopped.

"I don't register on your gaydar?"

"Sure, but not as... well, you come off pretty straight."

"It would be hard to take any WaterWorks customers into my confidence."

"I don't think they'd talk to you."

I played with a pen on my desk, waiting for the kid to bite. It took him a while.

"Maybe I could ask around," he said.

"You don't want to get too enthusiastic about that," I said. "You don't want to sound like you're pumping people."

"Hell, Mr. Gold, you don't know what it's like in there. Guys are asking about other guys all night long. I had one guy ask me about a fellow across the room while I was... you know."

"Too much information," I said.

"You want me to ask about this Ty Cannon?"

"Sure, if you're going to the baths. Don't push it. Just ask around, see if anyone else has seen him lately. Make it look like you want to hook up."

"Hook up?"

"It's a thing I heard lately."

He smiled at that. Asa Corona had a nice smile. I could see why he was popular at the baths.

"Another thing," I said. "You should be getting another email demanding money in the next day or so. It will come from a different screen name."

"What do I do?"

"Stall them. Tell them you're working on it. Only pay if you absolutely have to. I'm going to say this one more time. This really is a police matter. You'd stand a much better chance of catching these guys with the cops helping."

"Then I'd have to explain why I was involved with the cops to my family, wouldn't I?"

"It could go down that way. Maybe you underestimate them, kid. Maybe they wouldn't be so bent out of shape."

He stared past me, out my back window, at Alcatraz.

"I'm not ready to find out," he said. "Let's keep trying to find these blackmailers the way we're going."

"It's your nickel," I said.

TEN

I was at the Montara house, doing some more work on the dreadnaught guitar. It was Sunday, and I had a Giants game on the radio. I don't have a television at the beach place, because I go there for solitude. I'm not a monk, on the other hand, and it's nice to have some background noise.

I had just finished gluing the neck to the body and was tightening the clamps to hold it in place to dry, when my cell phone rang.

"Mr. Gold, this is Asa Corona. I did like you said, asked around at WaterWorks."

"Any bites?"

"Nothing. Several of the people there know this guy Cannon, but nobody's seen him in a couple of weeks. What do you think?"

"I think it's suspicious. You make a big payment, and Cannon goes missing."

"What do you do now?"

"Good question. Did you happen to recall any names of guys you've seen with Cannon?"

"I made a list."

He ran down a list of names. I wrote them down.

"I don't suppose you got any phone numbers?"

"You said not to push."

"So I did. Okay. I'll follow up from here. First thing tomorrow, I'll check out Cannon's place in Pacifica. I guess you haven't received any more demands."

"Not yet, but I haven't checked my email today."

"Check it and call me back."

I started cleaning up, and had just about finished putting my tools away when the phone rang again.

"Mr. Gold? They wrote again."

"What's the email address?"

He gave me another address at the free site. I didn't doubt it would be shut down in a day or so. No way I could check it out on a Sunday anyway.

"What do I do?" Corona asked.

"Write them back. Tell them it's Sunday, and you can't get to the bank before tomorrow. Tell them... I don't know... tell them you have to transfer money into your account before you can send it via the pay site."

"Won't they be suspicious?"

"You already paid them once. These guys, once they have you on the hook they can get pretty bold. They probably won't suspect anything until you've put them off a couple of times."

"I can't afford to have them send those pictures to my family."

"If you feel like you absolutely have to pay, then go ahead. Maybe if I find these guys I can squeeze it back out of them."

―――――――

It started raining that evening, and the Weather Channel maps indicated the showers would stick around for a couple of days. The next morning, I parked my car half a block from Ty Cannon's house in Pacifica, about two blocks back from the beach. I was on a hill and had a good line of sight straight down at Cannon's front door.

I had brought a couple of books, and a sandwich, ready to settle in for a long siege.

By noon, I was getting pretty creaky from sitting in the car. Somehow, stakeouts had been a lot easier five years earlier. The older I got, the more I wanted to be moving.

I pulled out my binoculars and scanned the house again. The shades were drawn, and the single garage door was closed. There was a pile of newspapers lying on the front stoop.

That wasn't encouraging.

Around two that afternoon, the mailman arrived. I watched through the binoculars as he opened the box and tried to stuff the mail into it. It was practically full.

An hour later, I spotted the shadow.

I'd been so absorbed in watching Cannon's place, I'd failed to notice that someone else was watching it too. He sat in a plain jane green Ford, in a driveway four or five houses up the street from Cannon's place. There was a *For Sale* sign in front of the house, and the grass had grown ragged along the driveway, so I guessed the house was empty. If someone came along and asked the guy in the Ford what he was doing, he could always plead that he had been stood up by the agent.

I couldn't make out the guy's face, because the glass was tinted too dark to get much more than an outline. From the height of his shoulders in relation to the seat back, though, I imagined he'd be about my size, somewhere over six feet and change. He had the car backed into the driveway, so I couldn't see the license plate.

I was confused.

Maybe, as I'd considered, Cannon was in on the blackmail scheme, and one of his other marks had come across him the same way I had. It was also possible the guy in the Ford was in on the scheme, and Cannon had taken off with more than his own share of the take. Maybe this guy was waiting for Cannon to show up so he could cop his share, and maybe teach Ty a lesson in the process.

While I chewed on all the possible configurations, the Ford's lights came on, and the driver pulled out onto the street. He turned left, going away from me, and I yanked up the binoculars to get a glimpse at his tags.

He was too far away, though, and all I got was a couple of numbers, before he cruised around a corner and disappeared down the cross street.

"Now what?" I said to myself.

Cannon hadn't shown his face all day. Odds were he wouldn't materialize in the next several minutes.

On the other hand, I had what amounted to a clue.

I started my own car and took off after the Ford.

If I had seen him, it was a reasonable guess that he had noticed me. On the other hand, he hadn't done anything menacing or suspicious, at least no more suspicious than I was, sitting out on the street all day staring at Cannon's house.

Even so, I really wasn't all that crazy about letting him know I was tailing him.

It was times like these that I wished I had a partner. Tailing someone is a black art. Doing it right takes a little help. There wasn't a chance in hell I was going to be able to creep up on his bumper without being noticed. My best bet was that he might stop somewhere, so I could read the tag without him knowing.

First, though, I had to catch him. When I turned onto the same street he'd taken, though, I couldn't see him.

Great.

I juiced the gas a little, taking care not to go too much over the limit, and put my wipers on high so I could see further ahead. Nothing.

Then, shortly after passing a side street, I glanced in my mirror, and there he was.

Tailing me.

Writing something on a pad attached to his dash.

After half a block, he peeled off and headed up another street, toward the Pacific Coast Highway. By the time I did a sloppy three-point turn and gave chase, he was long gone.

I realized he'd wanted to know who I was every bit as much I wanted to know who he was. He'd driven off specifically to make me follow him, and then had waited, parked, on a side street until I passed, so he could pull out behind me and jot down my license number.

Some detective.

Boy, did I feel stupid.

ELEVEN

I shook off my embarrassment and drove back to Cannon's house. I was tired of pussyfooting around, so I parked right in Cannon's driveway, and decided to have a look around.

The mailbox was attached to the side wall of a small front porch—not much more than an alcove for the front door. I flipped up the hinged lid and riffled quickly through the accumulated mail. It was mostly bills, some junk political ads, and several offers for low-rate credit cards. I didn't see any personal letters.

I jabbed at the doorbell, more in frustration than anything else. I didn't think Cannon was home, but at this point I was willing to try just about anything.

A couple of minutes later, I jabbed it again. I could hear the chimes ringing inside the house, but there were no footsteps or other noises inside.

I walked around to the back of the house, my Reeboks sloshing on the soft, sandy soil. The shades were drawn in the windows on the side of the house. The back was fenced in, to provide Cannon with some small amount of privacy, I supposed, but the gate wasn't locked. I glanced around quickly, to make sure I wasn't being watched—again—and I flipped up the latch and opened the gate.

The back porch was a redwood deck, about ten by ten, accessed by a set of French doors. My guess was the French doors led in to the breakfast nook, which would be next to the kitchen.

I stepped up onto the deck and put my face up against the windows on the French doors and squinted to get a glimpse inside. What I saw made my stomach clench, and I started breathing heavily.

I pulled out my cell phone to call the cops.

As soon as I got off the phone with the Pacifica police department, I called Asa Corona.

"We have a problem," I said, when Corona answered.

"What is it?"

"Cannon's dead. I just creeped his house, and I saw him through the back window."

"Are you sure he's dead?"

"The way his cat was lunching on his face, either that or he's a really sound sleeper. I've called the cops. They're on their way. Look, Mr. Corona, I'm going to be straight with you. I'll have to tell them why I was here."

There was a long silence on the other end.

"Can you keep me out of it?"

"I can try. The homicide detective here in Pacifica is a guy named Crymes. We've known each other for years. He's kind of a hardass, kid. He might want details. I need to let you know, if he demands your name, I have to give it to him. If I don't, it's obstruction. He could have my license."

"Oh, Jesus…" I could hear him starting to cry on his end.

"I'll explain the situation to him, try to get him to keep your name quiet. The police, though, they don't have any obligation to protect your privacy. Understand?"

"Why in hell didn't you call me before you called them?"

"Because, at some point, they might subpoena my phone records. It wouldn't look good if I called you first. Might look like I was trying to cover something up. I'm sorry, but I had to do things this way."

I could hear the sirens several blocks away.

"Look, Mr. Corona, I have to go. I'll call you when I know more, okay?"

I stuffed the phone in my pocket and walked back around to the front of the house.

TWELVE

I sat in the front seat of the police cruiser, watching all the pretty red and blue lights, when Crymes opened the driver's side door and slid in beside me. He pulled a handkerchief from his pocket and wiped away the Vap-O-Rub from under his nose.

"Now, that's dead," he said, shaking his head. "There's dead, and there's *dead.*"

"Any idea how long he's been there?" I asked.

"Quite a while."

"Nobody's seen him in about two weeks."

"Sounds about right. After we bag this guy, they're gonna have to rip up the floor to get all the stuff out of there. You ever seen anyone's been dead two weeks, Gold?"

I had, but I didn't say so.

"Awful mess. Body wasn't made to hold all that liquid in for long. So, you wanna fill me in on this thing? What's your involvement?"

"Look," I said. "Before I start, I want to let you know. I wasn't hired to find Cannon or anything. For all I know, he isn't even involved in my case. I have this client. He's gay, but his family doesn't know. He'd like to keep it that way."

"Tough shit," Crymes said.

"A little compassion, okay? Here's the deal. My client did the hokey-pokey with this guy Cannon in a bathhouse over in SoMa, and someone took pictures of them. They've been blackmailing my client with the photos."

"Should have come to the police."

"That's what I told him. He'll back me up on that. He decided to handle it privately. He hoped to keep his secret from his family. There's... there's a substantial amount of money involved."

"Client's rich?"

"He stands to inherit a bundle. If his family finds out, though..."

"I get the picture."

"My client didn't even know Cannon's name until two days ago."

"You said he and Cannon were sex partners."

"In a bathhouse, Crymes. You know how that works. My client never got Cannon's name. I got it from the bathhouse manager."

"Which bathhouse?" Crymes asked.

"WaterWorks."

"Never heard of it."

"Manager's name is Gary Chiklis." I spelled it for him.

"And this manager, Chiklis, is the one who ID'd Cannon?"

"From the picture."

"You get me a copy of that picture, okay?"

I fished one out of my jacket pocket and handed it to him.

"Nice lookin' kid. Sure don't look that nice now. So, besides bangin' him at this bathhouse, your client didn't know Cannon?"

"He'd never heard the name until Friday."

"You think maybe Cannon was the shill in this blackmail scheme?"

"It worked for me."

Crymes nodded.

"Me too. Maybe I'll follow up on that. Wouldn't be the first time a coupla crooks had a falling out. I can reach you at your office?"

I handed him my card.

"What's your client's name?"

"Is there a scenario in which I don't have to tell you?"

"Sure. In that same scenario, I trot you downtown and sweat you in a tiny, cement-block room for day or two."

I told him.

"Tell you what," he said. "Right at this moment, your client looks in the clear. I'll do what I can to keep him out of the picture. I might still have to talk with him, though. If I call you, you can arrange to bring him down to talk with me?"

"I'll see to it."

An ambulance drove up, its lights flashing, but without a siren.

No real hurry, I guessed.

Two attendants hopped out and headed for the house. One was carrying a black body bag.

"Hope they brought a bunch of sponges," Crymes said, reaching for his tin of Vap-O-Rub.

THIRTEEN

I'm not certain why I'd decided not to tell Crymes about the other guy watching Cannon's house. Maybe I was embarrassed about the way he gave me the slip. Maybe I was hoping I'd run across him myself, get a chance to even the score.

Besides, the guy in the green Ford probably had no more to do with Cannon's death than I did. I had a hard time figuring the percentage in staking out a dead guy's house, unless you didn't know he was dead in the first place.

With Cannon dead, I was left without much in the way of leads.

I thumbed Asa Corona's number on my cell phone and waited six rings before his voice mail answered. I didn't leave a message. It might be hard for him to explain to anyone overhearing why a private cop was calling.

I was halfway back to the City when I caught a glimpse of the green Ford in my rearview. If I hadn't been as good at the tailing game as I was, I'd never have noticed him. He was good at it, too.

He was staying about two hundred yards back, making certain he was well blended with the traffic. A couple of times, I caught him voluntarily getting himself hemmed in between cars, just to look natural.

The way he acted told me he'd done this shadowing thing a lot. That meant he was either a cop or a private eye, or maybe some kind of spook.

I checked my gas gauge. Half full.

Just for kicks, I decided to see just how far and how long this yahoo would follow me. It was times like this that I wished I had a partner. It would have been easy to raise him on the phone, tell him where I was headed, and have him ready to put a tail on the tail.

I didn't have a partner, though, so I called Heidi.

"Jefferson Street Artworks," she said.

"I could use some help," I said.

"Eamon?"

"There's this guy, he's following me around. I'm going to lead him by the art shop in about fifteen minutes. I was wondering if you'd step outside and see if you can catch his license number."

"Cool. Sure. I could use a little fresh air. Fifteen minutes?"

"Thereabouts. He'll be five or ten cars behind me, a green Ford Taurus. Got it?"

She told me she'd be ready.

I set the phone back down and plotted the course that would take me by the office. I drove through Union Square, and took Columbus up through North Beach and Chinatown, making a big loop around to the Embarcadero, which would intersect with Beach Street near Pier 39. I spent half the time watching where I was going, and the other half checking the rearview for the Ford. I hoped I wasn't being too obvious, since after a while it would take a real dope not to know he'd been made.

Or maybe this character just didn't care.

Keeping that in mind, I opened the glove compartment and took out my Browning nine. I clipped it to my belt and stuffed my concealed carry permit in my jacket pocket. If my tail didn't care whether he'd been made, maybe he wouldn't mind messing with me a little.

I don't like to be messed with. I figured it wouldn't hurt to be ready for him.

It took a little more than a quarter hour to make the distended circle around to my office. Heidi was standing outside, sipping from a big cardboard soft drink cup, trying to look nonchalant. She winked at me when I drove by her and headed up the hill toward Fort Mason.

I watched in the rearview as the Ford cruised by her. Then I stopped the car in the first parking space I could find.

As I expected, the Ford dodged up the next open road to the left, to avoid running right by me.

I didn't bother following. If Heidi had gotten the license number, I didn't have to.

I made a quick illegal u-turn and drove back to the office.

Heidi was waiting for me when I walked into the gallery.

"That was fun," she said. "What are you doing for the next hour or so? Detective work makes me hot."

"Simmer down. Did you get the number?"

She handed me a slip of paper.

I was gratified to see the two numerals I had gotten at Cannon's house in the tag number. It's always nice to find out you haven't completely lost it.

Never one to spend too much time patting my own back, I reminded myself that ten years earlier I'd probably have gotten the whole number myself.

"What do you do now?" Heidi asked.

"This is when it pays to have buds down at the DMV."

I gave her a big, sloppy thank-you kiss and a promise of more to come, and dashed up to my office on the second floor.

Shirley Jones was at her desk at the Clerk of Courts office in the Civic Center when I called.

"I'm still waiting for those football tickets," she said, almost as soon as I said hello.

Months earlier, I'd promised to take her to a 49ers game in return for helping me get some information on a case I'd been working.

"The guy that got killed in my office the next day had them in his coat pocket. They became evidence."

"Excuses, excuses. What do you want this time, goldbrick?"

"Just wondering whether there are any wants on this tag number."

I read off the number Heidi had given me.

It took her a couple of minutes, but I knew she'd come up with something. If the guy in the green Ford was a private cop, he was sure to have picked up some parking tickets. You don't go long in this business without violating some minor road statute. It comes with the badge and the gun.

"Your lucky day," she said. "He got popped by an automatic camera running a red light about a month ago. They mailed him the citation, but he hasn't paid it. What's his name worth to you?"

"C'mon, Shirley. This is important. The guy's been tailing me."

She sighed.

"His name's Sheldon Moon. The car's registered in his name. Want the address?"

She read off an address in Pacific Heights, and a phone number. I wrote it down.

"So, who's this young piece of fluff I've seen you with around town?" she asked.

"You mean Heidi?"

"Heidi? That's her for-real name?"

"I didn't give it to her."

"Jesus. She's cute, though. You know, I go both ways. Maybe we could all go out together."

San Francisco. You meet all kinds.

FOURTEEN

The address Shirley Jones gave me was a drab, two-story office building on Presidio Avenue. I cased the parking lot to assure that there were no green Fords parked there and left my own car in a space two buildings down the street, nose out.

I walked into Moon's building, just as the canned music kicked in with a studio cover of Conway Twitty's *Happy Birthday, Darlin'*. I contemplated the impending apocalypse, and studied the directory hanging in the hallway.

Full Moon Security.

I was right. The guy in the Ford was another private eye.

It was possible this piece of news rendered him somewhat less harmful. On the other hand, I know plenty of detectives who hire out as muscle, and the word *Security* implied something more than tailing errant spouses.

Besides, I was strapped aplenty, which probably made me feel more confident than I should have. I took the elevator to the second floor and entered the Full Moon Security office.

At first, I thought I'd taken a wrong turn, and wound up in some lawyer's digs, or maybe a stockbroker's den. The walls were solid walnut wainscoting, and the ceiling was coffered. All the chairs were upholstered in real leather. A woman wearing a severe business suit and a perpetual scowl sat behind an ornate solid myrtle wood desk in the center of the waiting room.

"Can I help you?" she asked. Her expression made it clear she didn't want to.

"Sheldon Moon?" I said.

"I'm sorry, sir. Mr. Moon isn't expecting appointments this afternoon. Would you like to schedule one for later this week?"

I pulled one of my cards from my pocket and slid it across the polished top of her desk.

"Courtesy call," I said. "Tell him it's about Ty Cannon."

She excused herself and walked through a pair of doors behind her. I shifted from foot to foot and waited. I entertained fantasies of building guitars out of her desk. I desperately hoped for a major malfunction in the canned music system.

She returned after a couple of minutes.

"Would you follow me, please, Mr. Gold?"

I did. She led me down a short hallway to an end office. The door was already open.

Sheldon Moon wasn't the driver of the green Ford. When I walked in the door, he twirled his wheelchair around and rolled it toward me. He stopped and extended his hand.

"Mr. Gold?" he asked.

I shook with him, and he gestured for me to have a seat.

"One of your employees is driving around town in a car you own," I said, handing him a slip of paper with the tag number. "Normally, I wouldn't mind, but he seems very interested in me. I'd like to know why."

"You mentioned Ty Cannon," he said.

"The *late* Ty Cannon."

"That's disturbing news. I understand you and my... *employee* were both watching Cannon's house."

"I know why *I* was, but I'm a little confused as to your interest."

"Perhaps we could share information. We might both be working on the same problem."

"Not without my client's permission."

"How about hypotheticals, then?"

I waited.

"All right," he said. "I'll just say one word, and you tell me whether it has anything to do with your case. How about... *blackmail?*"

"Tell me more," I said.

"I'm sorry but, like you, I have to protect my client's confidentiality too. We are both working on blackmail cases, though, aren't we?"

"Okay, no ethical problems so far. Sure. It's blackmail."

"You suspect that Ty Cannon is involved or knows something about a conspiracy to extort money from his... casual acquaintances."

"I knew enough to want to talk with him, yeah."

"So did we. My operative, Jack Delroy, was confused when you staked out Cannon's house. He wanted to know who you were."

"So he followed me all over town?"

"While we checked you out, yes. Once we discovered you were in the business, he lost interest in you."

"And now Cannon's dead."

"An unfortunate roadblock."

"*Full Moon Security.* Strange name for a private investigation agency."

"We had to call it something."

"I'm talking about the *Security* part. Just what kind of stuff do you do?"

He deftly spun his wheelchair and pulled a brochure from a Lucite box on his desk.

"We're a diverse company," he said, handing the brochure to me. "We handle a wide variety of assignments. Some rock star comes to town without his own retinue of bodyguards, we can put together a small army for him. We provide anti-terrorist support for Silicon Valley billionaires. We also handle fraud investigations for companies who want to keep their dirty laundry out of sight. We can handle background checks, divorce investigations, and even the occasional criminal case when the victim doesn't want his name splashed all over the front page of the *Chronicle*.

"I've been working this city for almost twenty years," I said. "Funny I never heard of you."

He smiled. He didn't look very amused. It was the kind of smile I saw a shark make once at SeaWorld.

"We keep a very low profile," he said. "We have a small client base, and they pay us a remarkable retainer to step in at any time to protect their interests."

"I suppose that explains your interest in Ty Cannon," I said.

"How's that?"

"This guy seemed to only go after people with really deep pockets. Your kind of clients, for instance."

"Yes. Which also tells me something about *your* client."

I stood and folded the brochure, to place it in my jacket pocket.

"So, I suppose your interest in me is satisfied?" I said, extending my hand.

"Rest assured," he said, grasping it with a strong, even somewhat boastful grip. "I'm sorry to have alarmed you. It seems we just crossed paths headed toward the same destination. If your client is willing to share information…"

"I'll ask him about it," I said, as I let myself out.

FIFTEEN

I punched Asa Corona's number on my cell again when I got back to the car. This time he answered.

"I had to give Crymes your name," I said.

"Is he going to want to talk with me?"

"I don't know. He'll call me first, to set it up. That way we can meet at my office, if we have to. Did the blackmailer write back?"

"There's a new note today. He's still demanding the money. Does that mean Cannon wasn't one of the blackmailers?"

"I don't think it means anything one way or the other. Sometimes, though, when the money starts rolling in, these guys decide to find a way to keep from divvying it up. Cannon hasn't been seen since about the time you made your first payment, until I found his body today. Maybe he just became expendable."

"Should I pay the money?"

"With Cannon dead, I'm going to have to start over. I suppose I'll run down some of these names you gave me, people Cannon knew. Maybe I'll come up with a new lead. In the meantime, I don't have a clue who's squeezing you, Asa. The way I see it, you have two choices. You can pay for now, or go to the cops."

"I'm not ready to go to the cops," he said.

There wasn't much I could tell him, after that. I said I'd call later and broke the connection.

———

I sat in my office, trying to figure out what to do next, when my telephone rang. It was Crymes.

"I need to talk with your guy," he said.

"What's wrong?"

"We have a slight... complication. The M.E.'s still got the body from Cannon's house, but we already know something important. The body wasn't Ty Cannon."

I had been sitting with my feet up on the desk. Now I swung them off and straightened up in my chair.

"Tell me more."

"Cannon had a couple of soliciting beefs two or three years ago, so we had prints on file. The body you found didn't match."

"Did you get an I.D.?"

Crymes didn't say anything.

"Aw, c'mon Crymes," I said. "If I have to drag Corona in here to talk with you, I ought to get a little something out of it."

"Can you let me meet with Corona tomorrow morning, say eight-thirty?"

"I can call him and find out. Who was the guy in Cannon's house?"

"We don't know much about him yet. His name was Anthony Luft. He had a sheet, too. Looked a lot like Cannon's."

"So, this guy Luft gets killed in Ty Cannon's house around the same time my client starts paying off on blackmail demands. What's the chance Luft was actually doing the extortion, and we just had it backwards before? That would still make Cannon part of the game, and points toward him as the killer."

"We're already working that angle, Gold. You'll call your guy?"

"Yeah. I'll call him."

I hung up the phone and immediately lifted the receiver again to call Asa Corona.

"You know a fellow named Anthony Luft?" I asked.

"We call him Little Tony. He's a regular at WaterWorks."

"Not any more. It turns out he was the dead guy at Ty Cannon's house. That mean's Cannon's still out there somewhere."

"Tony's dead? Man, that's awful. He was a really nice guy. Everyone liked him."

"Someone didn't. Crymes wants to meet with you, Asa. Tomorrow morning. Here in my office. You'll be here?"

"Is he going to insist on investigating the blackmail?" Corona asked.

"I don't see how he can avoid it. It probably got this Luft kid killed. I don't know how much longer we can keep you in the closet, kid. Maybe you should start thinking about how you're going to break it to your family."

There was a long silence.

"I can't do that," he said.

I didn't argue the point with him. He was still in denial. Corona wanted to keep dipping into the WaterWorks trough, without getting his face wet. He was due for a major collision with reality. I had a feeling it would come any day.

"You made the payment?" I asked.

"Yeah. I forwarded it through PayMaster. This really sucks, Mr. Gold."

There wasn't much to say about that, either. I had a feeling Corona had spent most of his privileged life hidden from responsibility. His family had probably bailed him out of every jam he'd gotten himself wedged into. He was like a thirty-year-old teenager, and his first reaction to being held responsible for his own behavior was to complain that it sucked.

I reminded him to be at my office by eight-thirty and hung up.

The list Corona gave me had five names on it. The first was Harold Stamey. He had a number listed in the phone book, so I gave him a ring.

He had a *basso profundo* voice as he answered the phone, and his enunciation was perfect. He sounded like he was broadcasting the Glenn Miller Orchestra from the Penthouse Suite at the Waldorf Astoria.

"My name is Eamon Gold. I was given your name by one of my clients. I'm trying to locate a kid named Ty Cannon," I told him.

Like everyone else, Stamey hadn't seen Cannon in about two weeks.

"How about Anthony Luft?" I asked. I figured news of Luft's killing hadn't filtered out yet.

"Little Tony. Sure, I know him. Funny thing—I haven't seen him in a couple of weeks either. You think maybe he and Ty have gone off together?"

"It's a possibility," I lied.

"They'd make a stunning couple."

"Had you ever seen them hanging out together?"

"Oh, Jesus, yes. They had a business arrangement."

"What kind of arrangement?"

"Well, you know Ty's an actor. These actor fellows, they're just slaves to fashion. Every time styles change, they have to get a completely new set of photos for their portfolios. It's like an obsession of some kind."

"And Tony?"

"He's a photographer, silly."

I pulled out the head shot Shelly Proulx had given me and checked the back of it again.

At the bottom was a stamp reading *Anthony Luft Photography.*

Some detective I was.

"Could you do me a favor?" I asked. "If you see Cannon or Luft in the next couple of days, could you give me a call?"

I gave him my number and hung up the phone.

Tony Luft was a photographer. Asa Corona was being blackmailed with photographs of him and Ty Cannon. Luft had turned up quite sincerely dead on Ty Cannon's kitchen floor.

I called Crymes and filled him in.

"Sounds like we really need to find this Cannon kid," he said.

"That's the way I see it. Any word on how Luft was killed?"

"It's all preliminary. M.E. says it was probably blunt trauma, something big and heavy laid up against the back of Luft's head. Probably shut him off like a light switch."

"If I were an enterprising cop," I said, "I'd get me a warrant and go check out Luft's place. Might find a lot of incriminating photos there, maybe a box full of candid bathhouse shots."

"If you were an enterprising cop, you wouldn't be spending all your time outside motel rooms pulling your pud," he said. "As it happens, I *am* an enterprising cop. I have a couple of guys checking out Luft's place even as we speak."

"Is there any way we can keep my client's name quiet?" I asked.

"Hell if I know. We don't know yet how he fits in. We'll talk about it tomorrow morning."

"There's something else," I said. "I didn't mention it earlier, because I didn't see how it mattered. Cannon's place was being staked out by another guy, fellow named Jack Delroy. He works for Full Moon Security."

"Sheldon Moon?"

"Yeah. How come I never heard of him?"

"Because you're a bottom feeder. Moon's client list reads like the Society Pages."

"He's legitimate?"

"Depends on whether you want your own private police force. We've had some beefs over the year from guys who told us Moon's people worked them over, sometimes pretty good."

"Why?"

"Some of them were paparazzi trying to get shots for the tabloids. Others were just gawkers who got too close to some hot commodity in a club or a restaurant."

"So Moon's guys took them outside for a talking to?"

"Strange thing. You get bounced off the sidewalk once or twice, and it chills you out a little."

"Anything ever come of these beefs?"

"Now that's the funny thing. Every time we'd assign the case, the complainants would just sort of gloss it over, like getting their asses kicked wasn't so bad after all. How do you read something like that?"

"Like I don't care to cross Sheldon Moon?"

"There you go. Every time I give up hope on you, Gold, you go and say something that makes me think you aren't a total waste product. So Moon's goon was watching Cannon's place?"

"Yeah."

"Wouldn't you like to know who their client is?"

"They sure wanted to know who mine was. Moon told me they were following up on a blackmail scam themselves. See you tomorrow morning."

SIXTEEN

Heidi and I were in my Russian Hill house, where I'd grilled a couple of ahi steaks and some silver queen corn. We sat my table, from which we could see both the Golden Gate and Bay Bridges. Between us sat the second bottle of Corona Farms chardonnay we'd opened. It was half empty.

Heidi had pulled one of the unused dining chairs out and had her feet propped up in it. She twirled her glass and watched the amber wine refract the candlelight into tiny prisms of color.

"Roy G. Biv," she said.

"Pardon?"

"An acronym I learned in school. Doesn't matter how you bend light, it always comes out Roy G. Biv."

"Okay."

I picked up her plate and mine, and deposited them next to the sink.

"All right, I give," I said. "What's it mean?"

"Red, orange, yellow, green, blue, indigo, violet. Spectral colors, Gold. *Roy G. Biv.*"

"I get it," I said, sitting down. "Tell me, did you ever let anyone take pictures of you naked?"

"Hell yes," she said.

"Really?"

"I was in college. One of the photography students needed a model. He paid nicely."

"I mean, besides a modeling gig. Something more... I don't know... *candid.*"

"Hard to say. I'm sure I have. Hasn't everyone?"

"What about... you know? Sex pictures."

"Why, Eamon Gold, you old goat. Are you getting kinky on me?"

"No!"

"I don't mind, you understand. You want to pull out the ol' video camera while we go at it, it's all good, you know?"

"That's not what I..."

"Of course, you have to give me a copy."

"You'd want a copy of something like that?"

"Mutually assured destruction," she said.

She took a sip of the wine and lowered it about half an inch from her lips. She gazed at me over the glass. Her eyes were bright, and not entirely from the alcohol.

"Okay," she said. "I can be honest with you. Sure. I've had lovers videotape me in the act before. I imagine just about everyone has, anymore. It's just so... *tempting,* don't you think? You've got the camera right there, and you're going to be doing it anyway. Why not take a picture? It'll last longer. Though, in your case..."

She leaned over the table and kissed me, hard, her tongue flitting across my lips as she separated.

"You don't mind it that somewhere out there some guy might be showing a videotape of you doing the horizontal mambo at some bachelor smoker?" I asked.

"Not really. Ain't no such thing as bad publicity."

I shrugged, and poured out the rest of the chardonnay, taking great pains to see to it that both glasses were level.

"Is this about your case?" she asked.

"Maybe a little."

"Look, I'm proud of all this," she said, running her hands down her body in a way that made my man stuff get all jumpy. "I'm not ashamed of anything I do. Maybe it's because I was born and raised in Europe. Things are a lot looser over there."

"Looser than San Francisco?"

"Hell, yes. This is one straight-laced, tightly-wound, uptight country you got here. Half the people in the U.S. run around acting like they never get hard or wet, or at least are ashamed to admit it. I've never understood why some guy can sit around in a bar bragging about how he screwed a customer in a business deal, but he won't dare admit he screwed his wife on the kitchen table the night before. Weird standards, man. When I lived in Paris, I knew five or six guys who had wives *and* mistresses. Everyone knew about it. Nobody cared. Hell, one of these guys died, and his wife and mistress rode to the funeral together. You think he could have been blackmailed?"

"I guess not."

"You get blackmailed for doing something you're ashamed of. If you're ashamed, it's because you've been *taught* to be ashamed."

I sipped at the wine. Heidi seemed to have come to a resting place in her diatribe.

The lights on the Bay Bridge twinkled in a light fog that had rolled across from Marin.

I had to meet with Crymes and Asa Corona in about nine hours.

"So," Heidi said, lifting her glass to me, "Are me gonna make a movie, or what?"

SEVENTEEN

Asa Corona didn't show for the meeting at eight-thirty.

When he hadn't arrived by nine, I called. His phone rang several times, and the voice mail picked up. I didn't leave a message.

At ten, Crymes pulled out his two-way and asked Pacifica Dispatch for the phone number for the Napa Police.

"You going up there?" I asked.

"Looks like. I need to talk with your client. He doesn't seem very interested in talking with me. Up to now, it's been friendly. Guess it's time to make it official."

"Can I ride with you?"

His eyes narrowed, as if he were trying to look right down into my soul.

"Suit yourself," he said.

He called the Napa cops on the way out to the Golden Gate Bridge. They asked him to check in with them before driving out to the Corona estate, but otherwise gave him complete freedom to operate in their space.

Corona Farms was set about a mile down a winding two lane road that emptied out into the main drag in Napa through a couple of stone columns connected by a fancy wrought-iron arch. Halfway down the drive, we ran into a guardhouse, and had to stop.

Crymes flashed his shield and told the guard we were there to see Asa Corona.

When the guard retreated to call up to the office, I turned to Crymes.

"You notice the patch on his shirt?" I said.

"You mean the one that said *Full Moon Security?*"

"Yeah. How do you feel about coincidences?"

"Hate 'em."

The guard walked back to the car and handed Crymes a photocopied map.

"You take the right fork about three hundred yards up. Left fork will take you to the winery. You want the manor house. There's a little rise just past the fork. Just over the rise you'll see the house. They're expecting you."

He waved us through, and Crymes gunned the throttle.

"Manor house," I said.

"Impressive. Think maybe we went into the wrong business?"

"Every morning."

It took less than a minute to get to the manor house, a rangy Tudor with a circular brick drive and two more Full Moon Security guards standing watch at the main entrance.

"You think they're expecting trouble?" Crymes asked.

"Maybe they're just worried about a possible onslaught by thirsty oenophiles."

He looked over at me.

"Wine connoisseurs," I said.

"Where in hell do you pick up all this shit?"

"Not much to do on stakeouts but read."

He nodded and parked the car.

The guards escorted us into the house after Crymes did the badge thing again. The interior was cool, the way old houses get, and there was an ancient smell you can't buy in a can about the place.

I had expected we would be taken to an office, but the guards led us to a parlor about the size of my entire Montara house. They told us someone would be with us shortly, and left.

"You grab the ashtrays. I'll snoop around for a couple of Faberge eggs," I said.

I actually saw Crymes smile, for the first time that day.

We heard footsteps coming down the hall. A moment later, a man about seventy years old strode into the parlor. He was wearing a tapered-fit western shirt and a string tie, with a new pair of jeans and snakeskin boots. His hair was shock white, to match the moustache and thin goatee. His eyes were black—not just that really dark brown that some people have, but more like there was nothing but pupils. I'd seen the same effect on some speed freaks.

The man went directly to Crymes and extended his hand.

"Daron Corona," he said, in a voice that sounded like gravel rolling around in a cement mixer. "Detective Crymes?"

"Thank you for seeing us," Crymes said. "This is Eamon Gold, a private investigator. We were hoping to see Asa Corona."

Daron Corona shook my hand. He kept his eyes on Crymes, though.

"I wish I could help you, Detective," he said. "I haven't seen my grandson since late yesterday afternoon. He didn't show up for dinner last night, and maid tells me his bed wasn't slept in."

"Has this happened before?" I asked.

"Asa is almost thirty years old, Mr. Gold. I stopped holding him to a curfew a long time ago. May I ask what this is about?"

Crymes stopped writing in his flip pad, and said, "There's been a murder down in Pacifica. The victim was found in the home of an... acquaintance of Asa's. We just want to ask him a few questions."

"And Mr. Gold?" Corona said, nodding in my direction.

"Eamon was working for your grandson, sir," Crymes said. "He's cooperating with the investigation."

For the first time, Corona addressed me directly.

"You were working for my grandson? As a private detective?"

"That's right."

"In what capacity?"

"I'm sorry, but I can't discuss that without his permission."

"Have you discussed it with Detective Crymes?"

"Of course, but I had Asa's permission to do that."

"Is my grandson in some kind of trouble?"

I glanced at Crymes. He didn't seem very interested in bailing me out.

"Please accept my apologies," I said. "I really can't discuss it."

For just a second, I thought Corona was going to pitch a nutty. I could tell he didn't like to be stonewalled, especially under his own roof. The wave of fury seemed to pass quickly, though, and he sat in one of the tightly stuffed wing chairs. He motioned for us to sit also.

"It hasn't been easy with Asa," he said. "His father was killed when Asa was only fifteen. A racing car accident. We are a family of risk-takers, gentlemen. Probably my fault. I encourage it. I believe it builds character. Anyway, I've had to be both controlling father and doting grandfather to the boy."

I had a suspicion he was pretty controlling in both roles, but I didn't say so.

"I've noticed," Crymes said, "that you have a rather large security force here. Have you had problems?"

"We're a very wealthy family. There are dangerous, desperate people about who wouldn't mind trying to relieve us of some of our wealth. Terrorists, kidnappers, just plain criminals. It's a precaution. Better to be prepared, don't you think?"

"Did any of your security force see Asa leave the property yesterday?" Crymes asked.

"Yes," Corona said. "Around five-thirty. He took the Boxster. I called the main guardhouse to ask when Asa didn't show up for dinner."

"How many cars does Asa have?" I asked.

"Five. The Boxster, a Saleen Mustang, the Catera, a Mercedes, and the BMW Z3."

"He likes hot cars," Crymes said.

"We all do. His father did, especially. He collected vintage racing machines, raced them at Sears Point. He was driving a mid-60's Cooper Climax there when he was killed."

"I'm sorry for your loss," Crymes said. Before Corona could respond, he said, "Would it be possible to see the garage where the Boxster is kept?"

For another brief instant, Daron Corona seemed confused. Then he stood.

"Before I answer, I have to know. Is Asa suspected of having anything to do with this murder in Pacifica? If so, I intend to call our attorney before I answer any more questions."

Crymes folded the flip pad and stuffed it in his pocket.

"The murder took place almost two weeks ago, as far as we can tell," he said. "While your grandson may have known the victim, and had encountered the owner of the house where the victim was discovered, there is no reason to believe that he was involved in the killing."

"I take it you haven't been able to find the fellow who owned the house."

Crymes and I glanced at each other simultaneously.

"I see," Corona said. "So Asa isn't a suspect?"

"Not at this time," Crymes said. "May we see the garage?"

"Of course. Please follow me."

Corona led us through the main hallway of the house, to a back portico leading to a courtyard ringed by eight-foot-tall hedges. There was a brick walkway leading from the portico through an opening in the hedges, and Corona took us down the walkway to a long line of connected brick garages.

"Asa keeps his cars in that wing," he said, pointing to his left.

The garage doors were open. We could see the Catera, the Mustang, the Beemer, and the Merc, but there was no Boxster.

"How long have you employed Full Moon Security?" I asked.

"Several years. Before that we used an outfit from Oakland."

"Excuse me," I said.

I walked over to Asa's garage wing and knelt next to the Catera. I chose it because it had the highest ground clearance.

The floor of the garage was immaculate. I had expected no less. I slipped off my jacket and lay down on my back, looking under the car. It only took a moment to find what I was looking for. I reached up and the object pulled away with only marginal resistance.

"What are you doing there, Mr. Gold?" Corona asked.

I stood, put my jacket back on, and walked the object back over to Crymes and Corona.

"It's a GPS tracker," I explained. "I use them a lot. Most private investigators do these days. This is one of the more expensive models—a TriStar 3200. This baby runs about sixteen hundred dollars, but it's worth it. Stick it under a car, and it transmits a continuous low power signal through the local digital cellular system to an Internet node. Beats the living hell out of following someone around."

I handed the device to Crymes.

"Did you know this was attached to Asa's car, Mr. Corona?" he asked.

"No. Do you suppose they're attached to all the cars?"

"Where are your cars, sir?" Crymes asked.

Corona walked us over to another bank of brick garages. The autos stored there were somewhat larger than Asa's, but no less powerful or expensive. I took off my jacket again and slid down to look under a Lexus.

"Nothing here," I said.

We checked all the cars over the next ten minutes. We found trackers under all of Asa's cars, but none under Daron Corona's.

"You want to know where Asa's Boxster is," I told Crymes, "just call Full Moon Security. My bet is they put these things under his cars to keep track of him."

Corona stared at the box in Crymes' hand, and I saw that confused, slightly furious look on his face again. As before, it passed quickly.

"I need to call Sheldon Moon," he said. "I'll be right back."

His snakeskin boots clomped angrily as he retreated into the house.

"Okay, so fill me in," Crymes said.

"The tracking device?"

He nodded.

"Lucky hunch. I use them. Most private cops do. Old man Corona hired Sheldon Moon to provide security, but I wondered if there was more to it. Asa made him out to be this overbearing, overcontrolling son of a bitch. I had a feeling that he'd want to know what his errant grandson was up to when he'd dash off every several days."

"Corona said he didn't know the trackers were on Asa's car."

"What would you say?" I asked.

He shrugged.

"You know what this means," I said.

"Your client was being blackmailed so his grandfather wouldn't know he was packing fudge over in the City."

"And the old man had to know all along, if he was getting reports from Full Moon Security telling him where Asa was."

"You think Daron Corona might have known his grandson was being blackmailed?"

"It's a thought."

Crymes looked out toward the manor house and shook his head.

"This is going to get messy," he said.

———

Five hours later, we stood beside a pond in rural Sonoma County, watching divers' bubbles rising from the site of Asa Corona's Porsche Boxster.

Whatever had passed between Daron Corona and Sheldon Moon regarding the bugging of Asa's cars had remained between them. When Daron returned to Crymes and me, however, his face had been ashen.

Sheldon Moon had accessed the website listing the GPS tracking data for the Boxster, and the final entry coordinated on the map with this pond.

Crymes, Daron Corona, Sheldon Moon, and I had been joined at the site by the Sonoma Sheriff's Department deputies called to oversee the recovery effort.

After a quarter hour, the divers surfaced and made their way to the bank, and then trudged ashore, their flippers slapping the ground like beaver tails.

"Just the car," one of them said. "No bodies or anything. It's like someone ditched the Porsche and left."

The elder Corona seemed to deflate for a second, as if someone had hooked a vacuum cleaner to his soul. His instinct for self-control asserted itself, however, and he quickly straightened.

"Thank God," he said.

Behind us, a tow truck began to tighten the cable the divers had attached to the Boxster and started dragging the car back ashore.

Crymes and I strolled away for a moment to compare notes. Corona stayed beside Sheldon Moon's wheelchair.

"What time did you call Asa Corona yesterday to set up today's meeting?" Crymes asked.

"Around five o'clock," I said. "Right after I got off the phone with you."

"Did you tell him that it wasn't Ty Cannon we found in the house?"

"Sure.

"And half an hour later Asa leaves Corona Farms in the Boxster, which is now at the bottom of a pond."

"And Asa Corona isn't."

"You know this kid better than I do. He seem like the type to panic, take his act on the road?"

"He sure didn't want to talk with you about the blackmail case," I said.

The tow truck had the Porsche about halfway out of the water when we got back to Daron Corona and Sheldon Moon.

"We need to talk," Crymes said.

Moon and Corona looked at each other. It almost seemed as if some kind of telepathic communication passed between them.

"We can use the motor home," Moon said. "It's pretty spacious, and it's private."

One of his operatives had driven Moon up to Sonoma County in a thirty-two-foot Pace motor home, equipped with a ramp for his wheelchair.

Several minutes later, we were settled in. Moon hadn't fibbed. Not only was the motor home spacious, it was luxurious. The chairs were soft, and they reclined. The carpet was deep and thick. There was a complete home theatre system in one wall, and a kitchenette attached to the other.

"We need to get some things straight," Crymes said, after we were all seated. "This is a murder investigation, and Asa Corona disappearing has just thrown me a huge curve. Anyone lies here today, and I'm going to consider it obstruction. Understand?"

Everyone nodded.

"First question," Crymes said. "Who put the GPS trackers under Asa's cars, and why?"

Moon cleared his throat.

"That was my company, Detective. I ordered them placed there."

"Without Mr. Corona's knowledge?"

"Which Mr. Corona?"

Daron Corona swung his captain's seat around to confront Moon.

"You put one of those gadgets in our cars and didn't tell me?"

"I didn't have to, Daron," Moon said. "Asa asked me to keep it from you."

"Wait a minute," I said. "Asa asked you to put trackers in his own cars?"

Moon nodded.

"Yes. He arranged for it several weeks ago."

"Whatever for?" Daron said.

"Asa noticed that some of his cars had been adding mileage he couldn't recall putting on them. He thought maybe someone was taking them out for joyrides."

"You mean, one of our staff?" Daron asked.

"No," Moon said. "People... somewhere else. He wasn't specific. He would go places, though, and while he was there he thought maybe the cars were being used without his knowledge."

Crymes broke in.

"So he asked you to put the trackers on his car to see where they were going when he wasn't driving them?"

"That's correct."

"That means you have records of not only where the cars have been, but where Asa's been over the last month?"

"Also correct," Moon said.

"I'm going to need those records," Crymes said.

Moon started to protest.

"Don't make me get a warrant," Crymes warned.

"For Chrissake, Sheldon, I'm paying your bills. Give him the damn records," Daron said.

Moon's neck and ears were slowly turning from pink to crimson.

"I'll have the information put together this evening, Detective," he told Crymes.

"I have a question," I said. "Why did you have Jack Delroy staked out at Ty Cannon's house?"

"Same reason you were staked out there," Moon said.

He glanced at Daron, and then toward Crymes. The nonverbal message was clear. For some reason, he was trying to protect Asa Corona.

"I know why Gold was there," Crymes said. "Are you saying you were working for the same client, Mr. Moon?"

"I don't know who Mr. Gold's client was," Moon said. "I'll tell you who our client was, Detective, but not with Gold and Daron here."

Daron Corona looked angry.

I understood why Moon had insisted on privacy, and it didn't bother me.

Unless he was also working for Asa Corona.

"Was your client being blackmailed, Moon?" Crymes asked.

"Yes."

"By Ty Cannon?"

"We're not sure."

"Anthony Luft?"

"Who?"

I sat back in the chair. Moon didn't know yet who had actually been killed at Ty Cannon's house.

"Hold on," Daron said, interrupting. "Gold, you were working for Asa?"

"That's right."

"And Detective Crymes here says Moon's client was being blackmailed?"

"Right again."

"And Moon says he had this Delroy character staking out the same house as you, where this Ty Cannon lived?"

"Correct," I said.

"Are you saying my grandson was being blackmailed?"

I looked at Crymes. He didn't look back. He was letting me hang out to dry.

"I'm sorry," I said. "Unless Asa gives me permission to talk to you about his situation, I just can't do it."

"Well, I'll be damned!" Corona said, slapping the arm of his chair.

"It's confidentiality," Moon told him. "He can't tell you, Daron. Asa was paying him to keep a secret. If he tells you, he's endangering his license."

"That's just part of it," I said. "The smaller part. Mostly, I can't tell you because I told Asa I wouldn't."

"Well, I'll be *god*damned," Corona said.

EIGHTEEN

"What did you find in Luft's house?" I asked Crymes, on the way back to San Francisco.

"What makes you think I have any desire to tell you?"

"Because you never even met Asa Corona, and I might be able to help you find him."

"Making deals, here, Eamon?"

"It's an information business. I may know some things that can help find Asa. You have inside information regarding Luft and Cannon.

"Which you want."

"Which I want."

"Okay," he said. "This much I can tell you. Luft was dirty."

"There was stuff at his house linking him with the blackmail scheme?"

"Pictures. Lots of them. Apparently, he'd found some way to sneak a camera into the bathhouses and had been taking photos of the patrons."

"Let me guess. Ty Cannon showed up in a lot of the pictures."

"That would be a good guess."

"So, we were probably right all along. Luft took the pictures, and Cannon was the shill."

"We're working on that assumption."

"Something else I've been thinking. Moon said that Asa had him put the trackers in his cars about a month ago."

"Right."

"Before the first blackmail demands came in."

"Following you so far," he said.

"Now, the trackers were ostensibly installed to find out if someone was joyriding Asa's cars while he wasn't in them. Moon's records, though, would also tell him where Asa had been whenever he was driving the cars himself."

"Your point?"

"Moon knew that Asa was visiting bathhouses."

"Are you suggesting that Moon might have been blackmailing his own client?"

"Who knows? You have official standing. Get a warrant and find out from PayMaster who opened an account with the screen name *BathBoy*. Maybe this is just the way my head works, though. I have this active imagination. So here's one way it falls together. Moon knows that Asa is going bung-diving at WaterWorks, because the GPS records show long stretches when his car is parked there. He plants a guy in the club to check out the action."

"Anthony Luft?"

"Possibly. Luft and Cannon are buddies. We already know this from what Harold Stamey told me last night, that they had this business arrangement together. Luft used to take Cannon's head shots for auditions."

"Can't begin to tell you what kind of images that sentence brought to mind," Crymes said.

"So, Luft recruits Cannon, who's had just about everyone west of Sacramento up his butt at one time or another, to help out. Cannon approaches Asa at the bathhouse, they get it on, and Luft takes his secret pictures."

"With you so far."

"Okay," I said. "This is where it gets a little speculative. Luft and Cannon, they don't strike me as being young Einsteins. Someone had to figure out how to put together the computerized demands to Asa. Moon would have that kind of technology and would know how to open and close accounts with PayMaster, and how to establish untraceable screen names."

"I don't get it. You just don't like Moon, or what?"

"Still just speculation," I said. "Just tossing out ideas. What we have is Asa getting double-teamed. Luft and Cannon set him up, and Moon shoots him down. Moon can't afford to have the money transferred into any of his accounts, though, so he shows Luft or Cannon how to set it up. Asa pays off, and Moon sends this gun monkey Jack Delroy around to divvy up the take."

Crymes picked it up there.

"Only Delroy finds out that Cannon's disappeared."

"With all that cash."

"So, how does Luft get killed?"

"Two possibilities," I said. "First, Cannon kills him in order to keep all the money for himself."

"Or, maybe, Luft had the bad luck to show up the same time as Delroy, and Delroy killed him while trying to find out where Cannon had skipped to with the take," Crymes said.

"And then he set up shop outside Cannon's home, hoping Cannon would show back up."

"That's not the way Moon told it."

"No kidding."

"Moon told me who his client was. Apparently, his client was being blackmailed by someone using the same M.O. as Asa's extortionists."

"Who was his client?"

"Come on, Eamon. How far do you think I'm gonna go, sharing all this information with you?"

"The more I know, the more I can help you. Moon already knows I was working for Asa. Fair's fair."

Crymes kept his eye on the road. We were rolling down from Muir Woods toward the Golden Gate. The late afternoon sun was glinting off the whitecaps in the Bay, and the whole City had taken on this orange-yellow glow.

"Barrett Efird," he said.

I had seen the name before. I pulled out the list that Asa Corona had given me.

"That plays, damn it," I said. "Asa gave me a list of other people who had been seen with having sex with Ty Cannon at WaterWorks. Efird is on the list."

"Shoots the shit out of your theory, Gold. Efird approached Moon with more or less the same story as the one Asa Corona gave you, two months ago. He had a picture of himself trying to orally inflate Cannon at WaterWorks, sent to him by someone over the Internet. Moon was following up on Cannon almost step-by-step the same way you were. He says he set up Delroy's stakeout of Cannon's house to try and catch Cannon coming or going."

I sat for a moment and ran it back and forth in my head.

"Moon knew a lot of shit," I said.

"Doesn't make him the bad guy," Crymes said.

"What about this guy, Barrett Efird? What's his story?"

Crymes cracked the window, letting in a stream of salt-tinged, damp air.

"Now, there's one very nervous customer. Efird has a ton to lose."

"How's that?"

"You know that kiddie show on the ed channel? *Bloopie the Bloodhound?* The one where this big blue bloodhound dances around with kids and sings dumb songs?"

"Yeah?"

"Efird plays Bloopie."

NINETEEN

When I arrived at my office the next morning, there was already someone there. He was slightly taller than me, maybe six-three or four, but in nowhere near as good shape. He was half as wide as he was tall, and he bought his clothes off the rack, on sale, at discount stores.

He smelled like old cigarettes and cheap beer.

I instinctively checked my belt as I started up the stairs. The Browning clipped there was a comfort.

"You won't need the piece," he said, looking down at me from the landing. He already had a card wallet out, and he flipped it open, the way you learn to after a few years flashing a badge.

"Jack Delroy," he said, extending his free hand, when I got to the top of the stairs.

I grasped his hand. Wet and clammy. Just the way I love to start the day.

I rubbed my palm against my pants leg and turned to unlock my door.

"Come on in, Mr. Delroy."

He followed me into the office and was seated in one of my chairs before I even invited him to. Cheeky.

I pulled out my desk chair and took a seat myself.

"What can I do for you?" I asked.

"You know I work for Sheldon Moon."

He didn't phrase it as a question. It was, apparently, a given.

I nodded.

"Your name's come up," I said.

"Pretty neat trick the other day, having your girlfriend take down my license number. I almost didn't catch it."

"What gave it away?"

"Piece like that? Shit, how could I avoid checking her out? I looked in the rearview after passing her and saw her writing out the number. Boy, did I feel like a sap."

"Maybe you are a sap. Can I do something for you, Jack?"

He pulled an envelope from his jacket pocket and passed it across the desk to me. I opened it. Inside were some grainy video captures of a middle-aged guy bent over a reclining Ty Cannon.

"Barrett Efird," I said.

"You're fast."

"Forewarned is forearmed. I heard all about him yesterday. He asked Moon to look into a... delicate matter for him."

"That's right."

"That's why you were outside Ty Cannon's house the other day. Efird recognized Cannon in the picture and put you and Moon on to him."

"Right again."

"What does this have to do with me?"

"Mr. Moon figures we're all after the same guy, so maybe we can cooperate. Especially since your client is also our client."

"Meaning?"

"Meaning we can probably talk Asa Corona into using us for this investigation, since we're already working for him."

"Are you suggesting you might steal my client?" I asked. I tried to get this amazed, dumbfounded look on my face.

He shrugged.

"Take him," I said.

"Huh?"

"Take him. Cops have the case now. Detective Crymes knows all about the extortion racket, and now that there's a murder involved I'm probably benched anyway. Take him."

"Well," Delroy said, fumbling with his tie, "Actually, Mr. Corona, Daron that is, he wants to see you stay involved."

"What's in it for me?"

Delroy pulled another envelope from his jacket pocket.

"That's the GPS tracking records from Asa Corona's Boxster. Moon said you might want to look over them. The computer automatically put in street addresses for the coordinates wherever the car stopped for more than a minute."

He dropped the envelope on my desk. I let it lie there.

"I see a hitch," I said.

"Where?"

"Asa Corona's still missing. All those records can tell me is where the car went. For all we know, Asa wasn't in it at the time."

"And?"

"And, Daron Corona isn't Asa's keeper. If I throw in on this thing with you and Moon, I'll be working for Daron."

"I don't follow."

"It might be a conflict. While you and Moon work for the entire Corona clan, I only signed on to take care of Asa's problem—a problem, I might add, that is no longer mine to solve. Cops have that one now. I don't quite see where I fit in."

"Wherever Daron Corona wants you, that's where. I don't think you quite understand what this guy can do, Gold."

"Works both ways."

"Crossing Daron Corona can get you hurt."

"Aw, hell," I said, leaning my chair back. It might have seemed like a nonchalant move, but at that angle I could get to the Browning quicker if I needed to. "Here we were, having a nice conversation, and you had to go get all threatening with me. You don't get a cookie."

Delroy seemed to understand immediately that he had stepped out of bounds. Maybe he was afraid I'd call Moon and tattle on him. Maybe he was a relatively good guy with a short fuse. I didn't feel like testing him, at least not this early in the morning and on only one cup of coffee.

I sat back upright and picked up the envelope on the desk. I took it over to the copier in the corner and made dupes of the five pages inside, then stuffed the originals back into the envelope and handed it to Delroy.

"Tell Moon I'll think about it," I said.

TWENTY

The set of Bloopie the *Bloodhound* was painted about every color I could conjure. It hurt my eyes to look at it.

Anyone who tells you that kids' television doesn't contribute to attention deficit disorder needs to hang out at a taping for a few hours.

I had been around film sets before, so I knew enough to stay way back in the dark while the techies did their work. I watched as they set up shots, while a group of bored rugrats lounged around off to the side of the set, slurping down enough fruit juice to supply Sunkist for a year.

Finally, the constellations apparently aligned just to the director's preference, and the assistant director called for places.

The lights came up, raising the ambient temperature on the set to something slightly less than the melting point of lead. Barrett Efird jumped out from behind a teaser curtain off stage left, in a big blue bloodhound outfit, complete with huge floppy ears and drooping jowls.

What followed was about the closest thing I've ever seen to organized pederasty. He started hugging the children to him, and even picked up one little boy and danced around the set with him. This, as it happened, was just the warmup. Several seconds later the director called out that they were ready to shoot the scene.

Some sound tech started a recording, and the loudspeakers blared out a song about trees and birds and some other saccharine shit while Efird and the kids danced around the set and made cute faces.

Mercifully, it wasn't a complicated production number, and it was all over in a couple of minutes.

"That's a wrap for today," the director yelled.

From somewhere off to the side of the set, parents appeared from a separate room to collect their little darlings. The lights dimmed, and after my eyesight returned I saw the crew start to close up for the evening.

I walked casually behind the teaser curtain, and through a door leading to a clinically antiseptic hallway. Halfway down the hall, I saw the door labeled *Mr. Efird.*

I knocked on it.

"Come on in," someone called.

I opened it and walked in.

Barrett Efird was about forty. He wasn't bad-looking, I suppose, for someone who made a living inside a bloodhound suit. He wiped at his face with a wet cloth and stood in the middle of the room in a pair of tennis shorts and a tee shirt. I could tell he was in good shape, but that didn't bother me.

I was in better shape.

"Mr. Efird?"

"Yes?"

I handed him my card.

"I don't understand," he said.

I pulled the picture of Ty Cannon from my pocket and handed it to him.

"What is this?" he asked.

"A picture of Ty Cannon," I said.

"I know that. I mean, what is *this*. What do you want?"

"I'm trying to find Cannon."

"Well, join the fucking club, Mr. Gold. Join the fucking club."

He tossed the wet cloth on a sink in the corner of the dressing room and pulled the tee shirt off.

"Damn suit gets hotter every year," he said. "Look, Mr. Gold, I already have a detective working for me, and I want to find Ty Cannon as much as you do. Probably more."

"I know," I said. "There's a problem, though. It's not just about blackmail anymore. You should expect to receive a visit from a police detective named Crymes."

"I already did. This morning. I know about Little Tony. It's gruesome."

"I'm the guy who found him. He was in Cannon's house. What does that suggest to you?"

Efird sat on the couch.

"Probably the same as it does to Detective Crymes. Ty and Tony were working together, shaking down queens at the bathhouses."

"Somehow, I thought you'd be more nervous about discussing this," I said.

"Around here? Not at all. Most of the people here at the studio know about me. It's no big deal. You obviously know, or you wouldn't be here. What scares the crap out of me is having those pictures released to the tabloids or, even worse, distributed on the Internet. Probably everyone who knew a damn thing about the world knew for years that Richard Chamberlain was just this old fairy, but there were still some people who were shocked when he wrote a book about it and went public. I don't want that to happen to me."

"How did you and Ty Cannon get together?"

"By the mouth and cock," he said, chuckling.

I tried not to collapse with laughter.

"Okay," he said. "A little queer humor there. I know what you mean. I knew Ty from several years ago. One thing about playing a big old bloodhound on television, you sure don't have to worry about being typecast. I get to do guest shots on TV and in movies from time to time. Ty gets the occasional walk-on, sometimes even a speaking role. We did an episode of *The Blue Brigade* together a few years back. Played a couple of guys on a jury."

"Did he let you know then that he was gay?"

"Not right away. I mean, it wasn't like he carries these cards around. *Ty Cannon, Actor and Dick-Smoker.* Know what I mean?"

"But you suspected?"

"Of course. I'm no chicken-hawk, but Ty was in his early twenties, and I was in my mid-thirties, so we were pretty much on the same wavelength. There are signs. Tipoffs."

"He knew the secret handshake."

"And how. So, we went out a couple of times. Dinner, drinks, a little wham-bam, thank-you-Sam. It was nice. Then we drifted apart. He got a part in a movie shooting down in San Diego, and by the time he got back I was seeing some other guy. That was ten or twelve guys ago."

"The picture you received by email…" I said.

"It was pretty recent. I hang out at WaterWorks from time to time. I saw Ty there about three months ago, and he gave me the high sign. We caught up over a drink or two, and let nature take its course."

"Do you recall whether Anthony Luft was there that night?"

"Little Tony? No. Can't say whether he was or wasn't. Tony and I never really hit it off."

"When was the last time you saw Luft?"

"Like I told Crymes this morning, about two weeks ago."

"At WaterWorks?"

"No, at his place. I needed a new set of head shots. I made an appointment with him, but when I got there, he was in a big hurry. He told me we'd have to reschedule, because he had an emergency he had to handle."

"I suppose he didn't elaborate?"

"No. He just said he'd call me to reschedule when he'd finished."

I wasn't sure where to go from there.

"I don't suppose you know a guy named Asa Corona," I said.

"Sure I do. We've met from time to time at the Baths. We even had dinner together a couple of months back. I drink a lot of his wine. It's not bad, for a California varietal."

"Did he ever loan you his car?"

"Beg your pardon?"

"Just a thought. Have you ever driven any of his cars, especially when he wasn't in it?"

Efird sat back on the couch and spread his arms out on the top of the back cushion.

"Okay. Sure. I drove the Saleen once. But Asa knew I had it."

"How did that happen?"

"My car was broken down. I'd taken a cab to the baths, and I was short on fare to get back home. Asa offered to drive me home, if I didn't mind waiting around for a couple of hours, but I had an early call the next morning, so I wanted to get home. He let me take the Saleen to an ATM to get some money."

"That's the only time?"

"The only one I can recall. What is this? How is Asa Corona involved in me being blackmailed?"

"He probably isn't. I'm just filling in some holes. When was the last time you saw Corona?"

He rubbed his chin a little.

"About a week ago."

"At the baths?"

"No. At a restaurant in the Castro. *Three Sisters.*"

"Alone?"

"No. He had a date. Or, at least, he was with some guy."

"Did you know this guy?"

"I didn't recognize him."

"Could you describe him?"

"Sure. He was easy to remember, because I recall that he really stood out from the sprouts and krauts crowd you usually see in there. He was about your height, more or less, but really stout."

"Fat?"

"No, just very wide, like a weightlifter or maybe some kind of boxer. He looked like a real meat-eater. He was in a business suit, and I remember mentioning to my date that he really must have to pay a lot extra for the fittings."

"Did this guy and Asa Corona seem close?"

"No, not at all. They seemed more like business partners, or maybe like they were on a first date or something. They really didn't seem to be connecting."

I made a couple of notes, and thanked Efird for the information.

A thought occurred to me just as I was leaving.

"Mr. Efird, I need to talk with Asa Corona. If you happen to see him, could you ask him to give me a call?"

Efird had risen from the couch and was running a comb through his hair in front of the mirror.

"Sure thing," he said.

"And would you also call me when you see him? He's been a little hard to contact lately."

"You got it," Efird said, and went back to combing his hair.

TWENTY-ONE

I sat outside the studios and looked over the printout Jack Delroy had dropped on me that morning. I had seen similar formats on the output from my own GPS trackers, so it didn't take me long to figure out the progression.

Like the trackers I used, the ones attached to Asa Corona's cars didn't actually put out a continuous signal. Rather, they sampled his exact position every five to ten minutes and stored the information on a chip. Anytime the car was stopped for more than five minutes, it would register as multiple duplicate hits. The more dupes, the longer the car was stationary.

I checked the readout for the last several days. As I expected, my Jefferson Street office address showed up several times. So did the address for WaterWorks.

What was interesting, though, was some of the other data. According to the printout, Asa had not gone straight home after leaving my office a couple of days earlier. He had gone to WaterWorks, as he had told me he would do, but he'd made a couple more stops afterward.

I consulted the list of names he had given me and pulled out the metro area phone book.

Sure enough, one of the names on the list of guys whom Asa had seen have sex with Ty Cannon lived at the first address he'd gone to after leaving WaterWorks.

The name on the list was Greg Lyles. He lived in the Castro district.

I dialed his number. Got an answering machine.

I racked the receiver before it got to the beep, and hoped his machine didn't have a caller ID feature.

Now, I thought, what was this all about? Was Asa Corona doing a little investigating on his own, interviewing guys who had screwed Ty Cannon? Or was there some connection between Lyles and Corona?

I grabbed my jacket and headed down the stairs to my car.

———

Greg Lyles lived in a three-story townhouse on Albert Street. There was a one-car garage on the street level. It was closed. To the right of the garage door was a steep set of steps leading up to a Greene and Greene style arched front door.

I rang the doorbell, but nobody came.

There was a restaurant across the street and several doors down. I hadn't eaten lunch yet, so I decided it would be convenient place to set up a stakeout. I asked the hostess for a seat by the window, from which I could keep an eye on Lyles' front door.

While I waited for the server, I pulled out Delroy's printout and started highlighting dates and locations.

On the first day Asa Corona had come to see me, he had apparently been driving the Catera. He left my office and drove straight home. Later that day, though, the Z3 was driven back into the city, to an address in Haight-Ashbury. I didn't recognize the address, so I highlighted it.

He'd stayed at the Haight-Ashbury address for a little over an hour, and had then driven over to Russian Hill, where he stopped for about two hours, before driving back home. I highlighted the Russian Hill address.

The next day, he apparently drove the Catera again, this time across the bay to Berkeley, where he stayed for several hours.

I was going to pile up some serious mileage tracking down all his stops. At least he hadn't decided to take a joyride up to Canada.

I was enjoying a cobb salad when a new Beemer pulled up to Greg Lyles' house, and the garage door opened. The windows were tinted, but I thought I could make out two figures through the back glass. The Beemer pulled in, and I grabbed a good look at the license tag. I jotted it down and continued watching the house while I finished my lunch.

After paying my tab, I jogged back the street and hauled myself back up the front steps.

Greg Lyles answered the door on the first ring.

"Yes?" he said.

I handed him one of my cards.

"I'm sorry to barge in like this, Mr. Lyles, but I'm trying to find a fellow named Asa Corona. May I come in?"

Lyles stepped out onto the landing, and pulled the door shut.

"I'd rather you didn't," he said. "I have company. What's this about Asa?"

"You know him?"

"Of course."

"According to information I have, he came here a couple of nights ago, after leaving the WaterWorks baths. Were you here that evening?"

"Yes. He and I left the baths together."

"In the same car?"

"No. I drove my car, and he followed in his. What is this about?"

"Just filling in some blanks. Do you know Ty Cannon?"

"Is that what this is all about? Asa was asking about Ty, too."

"Ty Cannon is missing. I've been trying to find him for several days. Now Asa Corona is also missing."

Lyles may have been a terrific actor, but I would have wagered that his response was real. His eyes started to tear up, and he sat down on the top step. He stared across the street.

"May I ask you something?" I said.

"What?"

"Has anyone demanded any money from you lately?"

His head snapped around.

"How did you know?"

"Lucky guess. Someone sent you an email with a photo attachment. It showed you having sex with Ty Cannon, and the person who sent it demanded money or the picture would be distributed where it could hurt you the most, right?"

Lyles rubbed his brow with one palm.

"You'd better come inside," he said.

The second floor of the house consisted mostly of the living room and kitchen, with a small office/study off to one side and a breakfast nook at a bay window overlooking a courtyard garden.

Lyles led me into the living room, where a slim, nervous woman sat upright in one of the wing chairs situated at either side of the sofa.

"This is my wife, Lorna," Lyles said.

I introduced myself.

"We're separated," Lyles continued. "Lorna lives in San Jose, with our... our children."

"I see," I said.

Lyles sat down on the sofa, next to Lorna.

"Mr. Gold is a detective," he told her. "He's looking for a friend of mine. A couple of them, actually."

"Are they...?" she asked. Her face screwed up, as if she had bitten into an unripe lime. She couldn't bring herself to say *homosexuals.*

"Yes," Lyles said, and then he turned back to me. "Lorna and I are trying to work out our problems. She came here today to talk about some counseling."

"I'm sorry to interrupt," I said.

"It's all right," Lorna said. Her voice was strained, almost clipped. I suspected from the way she looked and her demeanor that—procreation aside—WaterWorks may have been Lyles' primary sexual outlet.

She turned her attention back to Lyles.

"I told you what would happen," she said. "I told you if you associated with those... *perverts,* they'd get you into trouble."

"I know. I know what you said," he said.

"It wasn't bad enough, the sneaking out at night, the 'working late.' Now you're in trouble with the police."

Lyles looked at me.

"I'm not a policeman," I said. "I'm a private investigator. I'm just trying to find a couple of guys who've gone missing."

"Probably off with each other," she said. Her voice dripped acid. "Probably indulging their *perverted* desires."

She seemed to enjoy dwelling on the concept of perversion.

"I don't think that's likely," I said. "I appreciate your time, Mr. Lyles."

I started to get up. I wanted out of that house about as much as I'd wanted anything over the last several days.

"No," Lyles said. "Just a moment, please. I want you here when I say this."

He turned back to Lorna and tried to take her hand. She made no effort to reciprocate. His hand gripped hers, which remained stock still on her thigh.

"Mr. Gold asked me a question out on the stoop," he said. "And I think you need to hear this, because it involves you. There is a man... or *someone*, out there, who has pictures of me."

"Pictures?" she asked.

"Of me. With another man."

She jerked her hand away from his.

"You let someone..."

"No. I didn't know the pictures were being taken. Someone wants me to pay them a lot of money, or they say they'll hand the pictures over to your attorney, to be used against me in the divorce proceedings."

She didn't say anything. She just shook her head, and her eyes darted around the room, looking at the fireplace, the pictures on the wall, anything to avoid looking at either her husband or me.

"Mr. Gold, I'd imagine, is trying to find the person who is threatening me, because he's also threatening other people. I wanted him to stay here, though, while I told you this. I didn't want you to find out when this sleaze sends you some pictures in the mail. I wanted to tell you myself."

She looked at me again, with something resembling revulsion.

"Where are these pictures?" she asked.

"I have copies in the study. They were sent to me by email."

"I want to see them," she said.

"Honey…"

"Don't *honey* me. I want to see what it is you find so much more appealing than me."

This was not going well for Greg. In his defense, though, I would probably have found most reptiles more appealing than Lorna Lyles.

Or at least warmer.

Lyles slowly rose and walked over to the office. He took a manila envelope from the desk drawer and handed it to Lorna as he sat back on the sofa.

She opened it slowly and extracted two sheets of paper. Her hands trembled slightly as she examined the pictures. I heard a tear plop against the paper.

"Sick," she said. "Perverted, sick, depraved. I can't find words bad enough for this, Greg."

"I'm sorry," he said.

"Excuse me," I said. "Would you mind if I took one of those pictures?"

Lorna looked like she was going to have a heart attack.

"It might help me find the people blackmailing your husband," I added.

Silently, Greg handed me a picture.

"Thank you," I said. "I really need to be going."

"Wait," Greg said. "Just a moment more."

If I didn't get out of the house soon, I was afraid I might wind up testifying in a murder trial.

Greg turned to Lorna and tried to take her hand. She pulled it away.

"Honey, I'm not going to pay this guy his extortion money," Greg said. "I know you hate what I do... what I *am*, but I don't think it could really have come as much of a surprise, after all. You knew what I was like in college."

"It was a phase..." she said.

"You wanted it to be a phase. You wanted me to change, and I tried. I really tried. I am what I am, though, and there's no way to change that. We made a mistake. Now we're paying for it. That doesn't mean our kids have to."

Lyles turned to me.

"Mr. Gold, you're trying to find this blackmailer, aren't you?"

I nodded.

"That's why I was hired."

"If you find him, then we don't have to worry about pictures being sent to my wife's attorney?"

"I don't know. Probably not."

He turned back to Lorna.

"See? He's going to make it all right, Lorna. The rest we were already working out. Nothing has to change."

Lorna was really crying now, and I was about to break down the door getting out.

TWENTY-TWO

The Haight-Ashbury address on the GPS printout was a men's clothing store. I marked through it with my pen and drove back home.

As it happened, the Russian Hill address was just a couple of blocks from my house. I parked my car in the garage and hoofed it two streets over.

The address was an apartment building. I cross-checked the mailboxes on the first floor against the list Asa Corona had given me. There was a match.

I walked up the steps to the third floor and rapped on Steve Csaba's front door.

It took a moment or two, but the door opened.

"Steve Csaba?" I asked.

He was about my height, but he almost had to walk through the door sideways. His shoulders must have been over a yard wide.

"Yeah?" he said.

I handed him my card.

"Your name was on a list provided to me by Asa Corona. According to information I have, he was here for a couple of hours several days ago."

"So?"

"Mr. Corona's missing. I'm trying to find him. Would you mind if I asked a few questions?"

"Yeah. I'd mind."

"Mr. Corona's disappearance is linked to at least one murder. The police are investigating. You're likely to be visited shortly by a Detective Crymes from Pacifica. I'd like to save him a lengthy conversation."

"A murder?"

"About two weeks ago, a man named Anthony Luft was killed in Pacifica."

Csaba was tall and built like a Caterpillar tractor, but at that moment I probably could have knocked him over with a hard look.

"What? Little Tony's dead?" he said. "Aw, jeez. Aw, hell. What in hell way is that to tell someone, dude?"

"I'm sorry. I didn't know you and Luft were... whatever."

He was visibly upset, almost teary.

"Come on in," he said. "You shoulda said something straight off."

His apartment was one of those four-hundred-square-foot wonders you find in some parts of San Francisco, that goes for about a half million and change. Usually described as a studio, it was little more than an efficiency, with a Murphy bed attached to one wall, a small kitchen and dining room combination, and a tiny bath set between them. The furniture looked like it had been mixed and matched from the local thrift store. Otherwise, it was neat and tidy, but it was my impression Csaba was sinking most of his income into the mortgage.

He swiped a paw at a recliner in the corner, which I took to mean he wanted me to sit there. I unzipped my jacket, so I could get to my Browning if I needed it. Of course, if I got into any real trouble with Steve Csaba, I had a feeling it would take an elephant gun to stop him.

He sat on a loveseat in front of the television set. It complained with a loud creak of tortured springs.

"How'd he die?" Csaba said.

"He was beaten to death in Ty Cannon's house over in Pacifica," I said.

"Damn. Fuckin' Ty Cannon."

"Don't tell me," I said. "You have a picture somewhere of you and Ty Cannon having sex."

"Came over the internet, by email," he said.

It had taken me a few minutes, but the pieces started to fall into place.

"I just realized. You're the football player."

"Raiders," he said.

"Yeah. Defensive tackle. I saw you play on television last season."

"You didn't come to the games?"

"Sorry. Forty-Niners fan."

"Yeah. That's me. Some asshole sent me an email, told me to pay him money or he'd send the pictures to the *Chronicle* sports desk."

"Did you have lunch with Asa Corona at Three Sisters in the Castro about a week ago?"

He looked up.

"Yeah. How'd you know?"

"A guy saw you with him. No big deal. Have you seen Asa Corona in the last twenty-four hours?"

"No. Little Tony. Damn. He was a sweet guy, you know?"

I didn't know, but I played along.

"How did you know him?"

"Met at a party. A friend of mine over in Berkeley had invited a bunch of us over for a cookout last June. It was the anniversary of the Stonewall Riots in New York. That's a big deal in the gay community."

"So I've heard."

"You're straight?"

"Like a Nebraska highway."

He grunted a little. I don't know whether that implied approval, so I didn't say anything.

"Anyway, Little Tony and I got to talking at this cookout, and I found out he was a football fan. You'd be surprised how many of us are. I mean, we like men and all, but we're still—you know—*men*. So we talked for a while, and I wound up bringing him home."

"How often did you see him?"

"Every couple of weeks or so. We weren't steady or nothing."

"So, how did you come to have lunch with Asa Corona in the Castro last week?"

He wiped a tear away from the bridge of his crooked nose and eyed me suspiciously.

"Is Asa Corona mixed up in this?"

"Why do you ask?"

"Because he was asking me about Ty Cannon at lunch."

"What did he ask?"

"Just stuff like where Cannon lived, how he might find him, that kind of thing."

"He didn't say why?"

"No. I figured he just wanted to hook up. I was kinda pissed off. Here, a guy asks me out to lunch, and then spends all his time talking about another dude. I felt a little used, you know? Then I got that photo in the email, and I kinda put two and two together."

"How did you and Asa Corona meet?"

"I was hangin' over at Little Tony's house one day, and Corona dropped by."

"Do you recall how long ago this was?"

He thought about it for a moment.

"Not more than a couple of months ago. Maybe ten weeks. He seemed like a nice enough guy, but a little distant. We didn't hit it off real well. I was surprised when he called and asked me to meet him at the restaurant."

"I hate to embarrass you," I said. "But would you mind if I were to take a look at the picture you received in the blackmail demand?"

He stood and lumbered into the kitchen area, where he had a desk inset into the wall underneath a cabinet. He pulled a sheet from the central drawer.

"May I keep this?" I asked, after he handed it to me. "I'll be very discreet, but it might help me find the person who's shaking you down."

"If it would help," he said. "You don't know when Little Tony's being buried or anything, do you?"

"I have a feeling the police will hold onto the body for a while. They still need to find his family and finish the investigation. You might want to keep an eye on the newspapers."

"Yeah," he said, nodding solemnly. "I'll do that."

TWENTY-THREE

The next address on the GPS printout was in Berkeley, and I really didn't feel like a trek across the Bay Bridge. It was already late in the afternoon, and I figured I could pick the chase up the next morning.

I returned to my office and tallied up the hours and expenses I'd pulled down that day and recorded them on the Excel file I keep on my computer. I printed out a copy and stuffed it into Asa's folder in my file cabinet.

I had just poured myself a congratulatory jigger of Glenlivet when I heard footsteps trudging up the stairs to my office. I instinctively checked my belt for the Browning, and then waited.

Crymes knocked and then pushed the door open.

"You got anybody?" he asked.

"No. Come on in. Want a drink?"

"Maybe later," he said, as he settled into one of the chairs in front of my desk. "Got anything for me?"

"Besides the fact that my client has been lying to me?"

He arched his eyebrows.

"Corona?"

"Yeah. Jack Delroy dropped off a copy of the GPS printouts this morning. Daron Corona wanted me to pal up with Full Moon and help find Asa. I've been visiting some of the addresses."

"Who've you talked with?"

"Three of the names on the list Asa gave me. Efird, Lyles, and Csaba."

"Steve Csaba? The football player?"

"Yeah."

"Man, that is disheartening. Gay guys in football? What's the world coming to?"

"Next thing you know, they'll let heterosexuals style hair."

"Disrupts the natural order. Don't know if I want to live in a world like that."

"Want to know how Corona lied?" I asked.

"Lay it on me."

I pulled the picture of Corona and Ty Cannon from my desk and slid it across to him.

He glanced at it and winced.

"Corona gave that picture to me near the end of last week," I said. "He told me he didn't know who the kid was he was humping. According to Steve Csaba, Corona had lunch with him about two weeks ago at a place in the Castro. Csaba says Corona was pumping him for information about Ty Cannon."

"Whom he didn't know at the time."

"Damn, you detectives don't miss a beat."

"What do you make of it?"

"Not a lot. All I know right now is Corona lied. I don't have a clue why. I also found out that Corona knew Tony Luft. Csaba says he was visiting Luft a couple of months ago, and Asa dropped by. I've shown you mine. You show me yours."

He walked over to the bar and grabbed a glass, and then poured himself a little bit of the Glenlivet.

"We were able to get the Fibbies to help obtain a federal warrant, and we got some information from PayMaster and a bank or two. BathBoy was registered with the Internet service provider as a guy from Pomona named Cleve Kohl. He paid for the account using a bank card issued about two months ago. So, I had a guy fly down there and talk with Cleve Kohl. Seems the address on the card was a vacant apartment."

"What about this Kohl guy's bank account, the one he had the money paid to?"

"Opened a month ago and drained a week ago. Same address. We checked around and found a guy with the same name at a different address."

"And?"

"He's about ninety years old, and hasn't left his apartment for almost two years, except to visit the doctor. His daughter takes care of him."

"Identity theft?"

"That's how it looks. The guy who opened the account had to give a social security number, and it was the same as the real Kohl's."

"How did he empty the account?"

"Waltzed in, wrote a check for cash, and waltzed back out."

"So, what did the camera in the bank show?"

"Nothing useful. Guy wore a big cowboy hat. You can't see his face on the camera."

"Didn't he need a driver's license to cash the check?"

"Sure he did. You know how easy it is to fake a California license?"

I took a sip of the Glenlivet. It floated down my throat and formed this amorphous cloud of warmth in my craw.

I nodded, sagely.

"This guy's good," I said.

"He's also smart. Remember how Asa Corona paid him again a couple of days ago? Well, we tracked down that screen name too, and found it was registered to a guy in Little Stinson Beach."

"Another identity theft?"

"Natch. We traced the PayMaster transfer back to the fake bank account, and it had also been emptied."

"Any pictures?"

"No such luck. This time, the owner went back into PayMaster and transferred the money to a third account, also registered to a stolen identity, and from there to a fourth."

"Just like that?"

"Very slick. PayMaster stepped on it every time, of course, but in the end the guy got about ninety-five percent of the payoff. The final destination was a numbered account in the Caymans."

"End of the line," I said.

"No way to check it, even with a federal warrant. Authorities in the Caymans don't have a lot of respect for Uncle Sugar's paper, unless it has pictures of dead presidents."

"Like I said, this guy's good."

He nodded and took a sip of the Glenlivet.

"So, what are you doing next?" he asked.

"Same as you. I'll keep following the GPS printout and see what jumps up. There're three names left."

I handed him the list, and he glanced at it. Then his eyes lit on the final name.

"You know who this is?" he asked.

"No."

"This guy, Russell Skeen. He's a special deputy to the mayor. It's his job to keep tabs on the anti-AIDS programs in town."

"Do tell."

We both thought about this for a moment while we took sips of our single malts.

"Fox watching the hen house," I said.

He nodded.

"I suppose you go with what you know."

"Think the mayor knows Skeen's been putting in a lot of overtime?"

"There's one way to find out."

TWENTY-FOUR

Crymes had left, and I sat around the office trying to decide whether I wanted to talk Heidi into dinner and a little bump-and-tussle, when Jack Delroy knocked on the door and walked in.

"Mr. Corona would like to talk with you," he said.

"Asa or Daron?"

"The old man. He was pretty insistent."

I twirled my glass and watched the light from my desk lamp bounce around in the film of single malt clinging to the sides.

"Tell him I'll think about it," I said.

"Think fast."

I set the glass down.

"I'm a little troubled by this," I said.

"Why?"

"Your relationship with Misters Corona, *pere et fils.*"

"Parrot feels?"

"Keep it up, Jack. I can't get enough of your razor-keen repartee."

"Huh?"

"Why do I get the impression your involvement with the Corona family exceeds the traditional role of the hired private investigator?"

"That's the way Full Moon works, Gold. You buy a total package. We're more than just rent-a-peepers. We provide a full range of security services."

"Does that include playing *Fetch*?"

"From time to time. C'mon, let's go. I don't want to keep Mr. Corona waiting."

I stared at him over the empty whiskey glass.

"Make me," I said.

I couldn't tell for certain whether he realized immediately that I was serious. He seemed to go into some sort of locked-up mode, where something I'd said just didn't make any sense at all.

"What?"

"You're issuing something like a summons. I want to know if you can back it up."

"I just told you. Mr. Corona wanted to talk with you."

"And you presumed I'd just drop everything and go. That was a mistake. You didn't ask me whether it was convenient for me to traipse all the way out to Sonoma County at this hour. That was also a mistake. So, now I suppose if you want me to come with you, you're going to have to make me."

"You think I can't?"

"I think you can try," I said.

I accented it by taking out my Browning and laying it next to my hand on the desk blotter.

"Mr. Corona won't like this," he said.

"I think you put entirely too much stock in what Mr. Corona does and doesn't like. I think you're losing objectivity when it comes to Mr. Corona. But I'll tell you what. You tell Mr. Corona I might drop by sometime in the morning. You tell him he should probably leave word with whatever ninth-grade dropout Full Moon has working at the front gate to let me through. Then you tell him the next time he feels like ordering a command performance, he'd better send fifteen of you, because this Browning only holds thirteen bullets. Savvy?"

He stared at me. He didn't look angry, or frustrated, or even particularly human. He just had this dumb gawp on his face, and for a second I almost felt sorry for him.

Almost.

"I don't get you," he said at last.

"I know," I said. "It's congenital."

God bless him, he actually glanced at his crotch.

"Maybe next time you'll see what I mean about Mr. Corona," he said.

"And maybe next time he'll see what I mean about me. Scoot along, now, Jack."

He stood and walked out the door.

I sat for a long time and thought about the conversation. Mostly I wondered what was so important that Corona had wanted me to drive halfway across California to meet with him.

Then I decided I wouldn't let it spoil the evening, and I locked up the office to go see if Heidi wanted to grab a bite or anything.

TWENTY-FIVE

I dropped Heidi off at her place the next morning, rosy-cheeked and satisfied, and I drove across the Golden Gate Bridge.

It took me a little more than an hour to reach Corona Farms. The guy at the gate had word to let me in. I drove up to the manor house.

There were two Full Moon Security guards on the front stoop again. I gave each of them one of my cards. One of them went inside the house to let Daron Corona know I was cooling my heels on his porch. The other looked at my card as if he were deciding whether to eat it.

After a few minutes, I didn't feel like standing anymore, so I walked down the porch to a set of rocking chairs and sat down.

I was about thirty seconds away from pulling out my gun and cleaning it, just to alleviate the boredom, when Daron Corona opened the door and walked out, followed by the guard.

"Hey, Daron," I said. "Jack give you my message?"

Corona said something to the guards, and the one who had fetched him nodded. Then Corona walked over to me.

"Feel like a walk?" he said.

"Sure."

"Come along then."

I followed him down to the walk and fell into step with him as he hiked up the hill. There was a stone path that wended this way and that, following natural breaks in the terrain, and broken occasionally by granite stairs at points where little hillocks made direct passage risky.

"Have you ever visited a winery?" he asked, huffing just a little from the exertion.

"Once or twice."

"What was your impression?"

"It's okay if you're a winemaker, or especially interested in drinking wine, but otherwise it's pretty much farming."

"Perhaps you're right. We're headed for the processing plant. Running a company like Corona Farms takes a lot of hands-on supervision. I like to think that every time someone uncorks a bottle of our wine, I'm responsible for the experience."

"The buck stops here," I said.

"Absolutely. Any yokel can make wine. People have been doing it for thousands of years. Making fine wine, though, requires experience and a personal touch."

He and I walked about a quarter mile, until we reached a single-story building with double glass doors and a faux stone exterior. It looked to be four or five thousand square feet, but I'm not an architect.

He held the door open for me. I walked in.

"Exterior appearances can be deceiving," he said. "From the outside, this looks like a small facility. Most of it is underground, though."

We passed through a reception area, where everyone said *Good morning, Mr. Corona*, and then down some stairs on the other side of another set of double doors. When we reached the bottom of the stairs, I found that we were on a square catwalk with linoleum floors, that ringed a recessed processing area filled with steel vats and a lot of electronic controls.

"Your secret evil lair?" I asked.

"Nothing so sinister, I'm afraid. This is where we do the crushing and juicing of the Corona Farms grapes."

"Geez," I said. "Now I'm disillusioned. I had this image of hundreds of barefoot women in peasant dresses, stomping around in huge wooden vats."

"Not even when we started. Back then we used actual wooden wine presses, though."

He pointed to one of the stainless-steel containers.

"This is merlot. We place the grapes in whole, and they're macerated to leave some of the skin in the mix. Promotes tannin. This vat over here is chardonnay. The grapes are also introduced into it whole, but the juice is filtered several times before reaching the drain."

"No skins."

"Skins would ruin the chardonnay," he said.

He pointed to the other vats.

"White zinfandel, pinot noir, and an interesting experiment we're doing with pinotage for Europe. That particular variety has never really caught on over here, you know."

"So tell me," I said. "Why did you want to see me last night?"

"All in good time, Mr. Gold. Come this way."

I followed him out a separate set of doors than the ones we entered. Beyond these doors, I realized we had entered a cave of some sort, with arched passages lined with natural stone.

"Clever," I said. "You built the processing plant next to your aging cellars."

"Yes," he said. "It seemed appropriate. This way we save time moving the new wine to the casking rooms and then storing it for aging."

"Is there another entrance to the cellars?" I asked.

"Claustrophobic?"

"Curious. It seems you'd have a difficult time taking the casks back out through the processing plant."

"Excellent! Very incisive."

I started to tell him it was actually inductive but decided not to worry about it.

"So there is another entrance?"

"Yes. We installed the bottling and shipping installation there."

"One big circle."

"It made sense. As you can see, we've divided the cellars into different areas based on the variety being aged there. Different grapes need different conditions to ferment correctly. Here we have the zinfandels and the pinots. Over here are the cabernets and merlots. Further on down the tunnel here are the chardonnays, the sauvignon blancs, and finally the pinot grigio."

"You depend on natural conditions in the tunnels?"

"At one time. We discovered a couple of decades ago that we could artificially manipulate climate in the tunnels to achieve a finer degree of control over the outcome. Most wineries do the same thing these days."

"You come here a lot?"

"You ask a lot of questions, Mr. Gold."

"Occupational hazard."

"Yes. I come here a lot. Every day, in fact. I start each morning with a walk through the entire processing installation, from the juicing department all the way to shipping. I find that the employees enjoy the personal attention."

"Does Asa go with you every day?"

"Not always. Here we are at the bottling plant. I won't bore you with the walk-through but suffice it to say that much of the final stages of bottling and corking has been handed over to automated processes."

"I had a couple of bottles of your chardonnay the other night. I noticed you still use real corks."

"For the time being. I'm afraid that, like most vintners, we will be switching to the newer fiber corks in a year or so. Economics, you know."

He continued the tour, until we passed through the shipping department. I realized we had made a large circle, and that once we traversed another hill we were back at the manor house. Huey and Louie, the two rent-a-cops, still guarded the front door. Someone had placed a pitcher of orange juice on a table between two of the rockers. Daron sat in the first seat. I walked in front of him and took the other.

"Juice?"

"Don't mind if I do," I said.

"You know," he said, as he poured the juice into glasses, "Not many people would have spoken to Jack Delroy the way you did last night."

"Not many people are me."

"What would you have done if he had become forceful?"

"I'd have applied greater force. You don't get far in my business letting yourself get pushed around, Mr. Corona."

"Did you feel that I was pushing you around?"

"Just a tad."

"I'm sorry. I'm an old man. I don't like waiting for things. For me, there isn't a lot of waiting left."

"I figure you do all right."

He nodded and took a swig of the juice. So did I. It was fresh-squeezed, from oranges picked just that morning. You can tell these things.

"I'm dying," he said, as he put the glass down.

There wasn't much I could say to that.

"Right now?" I asked.

He laughed. It was a deep, rattling laugh, kind of wet. It didn't take a detective to figure out what was killing him.

"Damn cigarettes," he said. "Oughta put a warning label on them. No, Mr. Gold, probably not today. Maybe not next week. But soon, you see."

"Tough deal."

"Not so tough. Did Asa ever tell you how I saved this vineyard?"

"We never got around to that."

"It was during the Depression. I was just a kid then. My dad was an immigrant, but he had brought enough money with him to buy some land, and in the thirties California farmland north of the bay was pretty easy to come by. Problem was, it was also Prohibition. You couldn't bottle wine for domestic use, and the French and Italians had most of Europe sewn up. So one day this guy drops in to visit my dad, and says he has this new wonder drug that will cure all kinds of stuff. Only problem is, the drug isn't water soluble. It would only dissolve in alcohol.

"Well, at that time, it was legal to distill grain alcohol for medicinal purposes, so for a couple of years my dad turned our operation into a corn-based business.

"Then, just before Prohibition ended, a few tough guys dropped by and said they were going to take part of whatever we produced, to sell in the speakeasies. They named a price, and my dad told 'em to ram it. So, they came back later, with some more tough guys, and we had ourselves the Battle of Corona Farms."

"I hear taking on the mob is risky business," I said.

"I don't recommend it. Times were tough, though. You did what you had'ta. I was about ten at the time, but Dad said I'd have to do my part. He stationed me up on that hill over there with a Springfield thirty-ought-six rifle he bought surplus after the war."

He refilled my glass, and his own, and set the pitcher back down.

"I killed two of them that day. Dad and some of his hands killed the rest. We buried them back on the edge of the fields, good and deep. Didn't bother with caskets or nothin', just dug a deep hole and pushed 'em in. Got a fine stand of merlot grapes there now."

I took a sip of the juice. It was excellent. I considered planting an orange tree at my Montara house, but I knew it would never grow in the San Francisco area climate.

"Guess I'll stick to the chardonnay from now on," I said.

He laughed again, but this time it took hold of him, and he started to cough. It sounded pretty bad.

"Excuse me," he said, as he wiped his mouth with a handkerchief he pulled from his back pocket. "Goddamn but I like you, Mr. Gold. I get tired of Sheldon Moon, always kissin' my ass, deferrin' to me like I was some kind of royalty. It's nice to talk with a man who's not intimidated by money."

"Money doesn't bother me. Don't care much for rifles, though. Here's the deal, Daron. I don't really give a rip what kind of bad-ass kid you were seventy years ago. I don't really care about the muscle you have backing you up today. Your grandson hired me to do a job. He's the one paying me the money, so I do what he asks. That's pretty much the way things work in my business, up until he asks me to do something I think is wrong."

"Well, where in hell do you think *his* money comes from?" Corona asked.

"I don't really care. Once it passes hands it's his. Once *his* money becomes *my* money, I like to think I can sleep at night over what I did for it. I don't work for you, though. I can't say that I'd care to. So, when Jack Delroy showed up at my office demanding that I come out to see you, I didn't feel terribly obligated to do it. If he'd tried to make me come, he'd have regretted it. Jack's smarter than I thought. He backed down."

Daron Corona rocked back and forth in the chair and stared out over his domain.

"I was hoping I could convince you to tell me what kind of trouble my grandson is in," he said at last.

"Sorry," I said. "You can't, at least until Asa tells me it's okay. Can we at least agree on that point?"

He rocked some more and thought it over.

"You'll find him?" he asked.

"I'll do my best."

"I suppose I'll have to trust you, then."

I set the glass down and stood to leave.

"You could do worse," I said.

TWENTY-SIX

I drove back to the city through Berkeley, so I could check out the address on the GPS printout there.

Before leaving Corona Farms, I'd asked Daron to give me a picture of Asa to flash around while I was looking for him. Somehow, I didn't think the kid would care for me sharing the photo of him humping away on Ty Cannon.

The Berkeley address was another bathhouse, called The Sauna. I parked my car and walked in.

The front desk was manned by a kid with about a dozen pieces of metal embedded in his face. He had rings or studs in his eyebrows, ears, nose, and that strip of skin between your lower lip and chin. There was a chain running from a stud over his left eye to the one in his left earlobe. His hair was about an eighth of an inch long, with lightning bolts shaved into the temples. He probably went a hundred pounds dripping wet and without the hardware.

"This a real bathhouse?" I asked.

"Real as it gets," he said. "Membership's six dollars. Towels and a tube of lube is eight extra."

I dropped my card and the picture of Asa Corona on the desk.

"Recognize this guy?" I asked.

"You can go in and ask around for fourteen dollars," he said.

I dropped a ten on top of my card.

"Sure, I seen him once or twice. Real straight looking. Not our usual trade here."

"How about a couple of days ago, say around mid-afternoon?"

"Can't say for sure," he said.

I dropped another five on top of the ten.

"Now that I think of it, he was here."

"Did he ask about anyone?"

"Not to me. He went in for a while, then he came back out. What's he done?"

"I'm still trying to find that out. Thanks."

I walked back out to the car and sat for a few moments, trying to fit it all together.

I couldn't, so I decided to go back to the city and find some more pieces.

Ray Klein was in his middle thirties, but his lined face had the rough-edged look of someone twice that age. He was almost emaciated, and he sniffed a lot while he talked. I couldn't tell whether he had a cold or a wicked coke habit, but the lost look in his eyes argued against any common virus.

I showed him my card and Asa Corona's picture.

"Yeah, so?" he asked.

"You know him?"

"Sure. I've known Asa for several years. What about it?"

"Seen him lately?"

"A few days ago. What's this about?"

"When was the last time you saw Anthony Luft?"

"Little Tony? About two weeks ago."

"At WaterWorks?"

"I don't know if I want to talk about this," he said, and he padded into his kitchen on bare feet. His toenails looked like they hadn't been clipped in months. From the smell, they'd at least been clipped since he'd last washed his feet.

Klein lived in a sty. When they coined the word *dump*, they were looking at his place. I had a hard time imagining anyone wanting to get near him at WaterWorks or anywhere else.

I sat down on a bentwood rocker in his living room. It seemed to be the most sanitary spot available.

Klein walked back in from the kitchen with an Anchor Steam in his paw.

"You still here?" he asked.

"Yeah. I wanted to give you another chance before I call the cops."

For the first time, he started to panic. I had a feeling I wouldn't have to shake the place down for long before coming across something illicit, even if it was just his breath.

"Ain't no call for that, dude," he said. "Just ask your questions. I got stuff to do."

I pulled my printout from the inside breast pocket of my jacket.

"According to this, Asa Corona came here about four days ago, and parked outside your apartment for about an hour. Want to tell me why?"

"Passin' the time of day," Klein said.

"Try again."

"He was just visiting. I mean it."

"What's your connection with Asa Corona?"

"We're friends."

"How about Ty Cannon?"

What little color there was left in his face drained immediately.

"What about Cannon?"

"That, if I recall, was my question."

"I don't want nothin' to do with that dude Cannon, mister. Understand? Cannon's bad news."

"I don't doubt it. By any chance, has someone been trying to shake you down, Ray?"

"What do you mean?"

"Do you have a picture somewhere of you doing the nasty with Ty Cannon?"

He wagged a finger at me. Then he sat down on his couch and took a long drag from the Anchor Steam.

"That's what this is about? On account of, Asa was asking about Cannon too."

"What did he want to know?"

"He asked whether I'd ever done it with Cannon at WaterWorks, said he wanted to track Cannon down, made out like he was interested in dating that piece of shit."

"He asked this four days ago?"

"No, man, a couple of weeks ago, when he was here with Little Tony."

Whoa.

"Back up for a second," I said. "Asa Corona and Anthony Luft were here together, looking for Ty Cannon?"

"No, man, they were here to score a little. But while they were here, they asked about Cannon, wanted to know if I'd seen him around."

"Score what?"

"Some *X*. Little Tony told me he was going to have a party at his place, and he wanted some Extasy to spread around. So, you see, man, I would really rather avoid any scene with the cops. If I can help you, I will, but I just don't know much."

"What about the picture with you and Cannon?"

"What picture? I ain't never done it with Ty."

"Asa Corona had your name on a list of people who had hooked up with Cannon."

"Only in a professional sense, you understand," Klein said. "Sometimes I'd help supply Cannon with some weed or something. We never made it, though. Water seeks its own level, man."

I thought things over for a moment. Something was way out of place.

"This day that Asa and Little Tony came to visit you – do you recall the date?"

"Jesus, Sherlock, I'm not even for real certain what *today* is. It was a couple of weeks ago, though. I'm pretty sure of that."

"Do you recall seeing Ty Cannon after that?"

"I ain't seen Cannon in weeks. Maybe a month. That ain't unusual, though. We don't travel on the same block. Once in a while he'd call me and ask if I could help him find some stuff. That was it."

I told him to call me if he saw Ty Cannon or Asa Corona, and headed back to my car.

I resisted the urge to go home and shower thoroughly, because I had a couple more stops to make, and the day was sliding quickly into late afternoon.

————

The next name on Corona's list coincided with another address on the GPS list. Miles Nickleby lived in North Beach, off Montgomery Street.

I started to turn up Montgomery, but it was blocked. Some film crew was shooting a hundred yards or so up the hill, so I swung around and parked on Greene Street.

There was a crowd gathered on some concrete steps near the shoot. I tried to blend in with them, which was kind of difficult since they were mostly female and seventeen years old.

"What are they filming?" I asked.

"It's an episode of *The Blue Brigade*," one of the girls closest to me said. "Danny Warnock is in the scene."

"Who's Danny Warnock?" I asked.

Three of girls looked at me with something like pity. They apparently thought I had just gotten out of some awful foreign prison somewhere.

"Okay," I said. "Let's try it this way. Which one is Danny Warnock?"

"The one in the leather jacket," the first girl said. "God, I could just jump his bones all day."

I looked down at her. She didn't seem very self-conscious. She did seem aroused. She also seemed very, very seventeen. I counted my blessings that I had foregone parenthood. I didn't know whether I could handle hearing my teenaged daughter cream her jeans over a television actor. I wasn't really comfortable hearing someone *else's* teenaged daughter do it.

We stood and watched Danny Warnock slap around some poor actor who was apparently supposed to be a snitch or something for three or four takes, until the romance was just plain sucked out of the experience. I continued my hike up Montgomery Street.

I reached the building listed on the printout and found a buzzer on the ground floor labeled *Nickleby*. I pressed it a couple of times.

Nothing happened.

I was about to head back down the hill when I heard a voice above me.

"What do you want?"

I looked up. A man was sitting in his third-floor window, leaning halfway out to talk with me.

"I'm looking for Miles Nickleby," I said.

"You selling something?"

"Nope. Just need some information."

"You a cop?"

"Private eye."

"No shit? Come on up."

The door buzzed open, and I walked up the three flights of steps to Nickleby's apartment. He was standing in the doorway when I got there.

"Miles Nickleby?" I asked.

"One and the same. My, you're a big one."

"They needed a big package for the giant heart. Name's Eamon Gold."

I handed him my card. He invited me inside.

"This about Ty Cannon?" he asked, after directing me to a chair near the window.

He sat in the sash again and leaned out to watch the filming.

"Sort of. I'm looking for him and..."

"Yeah, and Asa Corona. I know, man. I got a call from Stevie Csaba last night. Geez, Louise, is that guy Warnock a stud or what? I took the day off just to sit here and watch them shoot this scene. I am a fan, I gotta tell you."

"What do you do for a living, Mr. Nickleby?"

"Call me Miles. Promise you won't laugh?"

"Nope."

"Whatever. I'm a PR director for the local Republican Party."

"Do they know you're gay?"

"Who says I'm gay?"

"Asa Corona, for one. Declaring the hots for Danny Warnock kind of sealed the deal."

"Yeah, yeah. Okay, I'm gay. Big fat hairy deal. I don't know if the party knows I am or doesn't, and I don't really care. I came out years ago, and I am not going back in, baby. That is one dark and dreary closet."

"I'll just bet that someone doesn't know that, though."

"You mean that shit who sent me the picture in the email? Stevie told me you were asking him about blackmail."

"So you were threatened."

"Can't kill a man who's destined to hang, Mr. Gold. I sent them an email back, asking them if they had any more pictures. I'm keeping a scrapbook. Gotta have something to jerk off to when I'm old and ugly."

"What about your job?"

"Jobs come and jobs go. There are a lot of opportunities for a good publicist. Besides, I figure the Republicans would be more embarrassed to find out they hired a fag if it did come out. They'd probably give me a raise just to keep quiet." He leaned out the window again and sighed. "Good Holy Godalmightly, I could just climb all over Danny Warnock."

"You'd have to fight off a seventeen-year-old girl down there first," I said.

"No I wouldn't. I can tell. My gaydar is just pinging off right and left. That boy is a boy's boy, mark my words."

"Warnock?"

"Oh yeah. Hey, you want to see the picture they sent me?"

"Okay."

He climbed back in the window and walked into the next room. When he came back out he had a sheet of paper in his hand.

"Stevie told me you'd probably want a copy, so I printed one up for you. Want me to autograph it?"

"Uh, that won't be necessary. When was the last time you saw Ty Cannon?"

He pointed to the sheet.

"It was that night. I remember because I had just had my hair cut, and it was lying just right. Ty was about to go out of town to do some play or something, and he was hunting bear that night."

"And nobody's seen him since?"

"Can't speak for everyone. I know I haven't seen him. You think he's wrapped up in this blackmail thing?"

"I'm still putting the pieces together. What about Asa Corona? Seen him lately?"

"About a week ago."

"Did he ask you about Ty Cannon?"

"No. He was pretty quiet, though, like something was troubling him. I ran into him at this place over in Haight where I buy my suits. He didn't have a lot to say, but there was this wicked brown aura around him."

"A brown aura."

"You know, like he just didn't want to associate with anyone. We said a couple of words, you know, *hi, how ya doin'*, that kind of thing, but I could tell he wanted to be left alone, so I went about my business. And before you ask, I know you're going to want to know about Little Tony."

"You know about Anthony Luft."

"It's a tragedy. I cried when Stevie Csaba told me he was dead."

"When did you see Mr. Luft last?"

"The same night I saw Ty Cannon."

"At WaterWorks?"

"Yeah. They were hanging together at the bar a lot that night."

I thought about this a little.

"Did Anthony... Little Tony seem upset or worried or anything?"

"Not that I can recall."

"What color was his aura?"

Nickleby laughed out loud.

"Like everyone else in WaterWorks, Mr. Gold. Pure envy green. Oh, oh, hold on, Danny's about to slap around that poor boy again."

TWENTY-SEVEN

Heidi and I were sat in a new tapas restaurant in Union Square. She had convinced me it was the latest *chi-chi* joint in town, and as a representative of the arts community she was expected to make an appearance.

I was savoring a Scrimshaw pilsner and sampling various tapenades on grilled garlic pita points. Heidi was on her third Cosmopolitan. I noted that three Cosmos were a lot for most people, but I knew she was just getting started. I mentally calculated how many hours I'd have to bill Asa Corona just to pay her bar tab.

I had just filled Heidi in on the generalities of my investigation, carefully avoiding details that might violate confidentiality. I smeared some hummus on a pita point while I tried to get the waiter's attention to bring me another beer.

"So his aura was brown?" Heidi asked.

"That's what the guy said."

"Mmm. That's bad."

"How do you know?"

"I'm artsy. I know things. Brown auras are bad."

"Is this like mood rings?"

" *What* rings?"

I reminded myself that I was, for all intents and purposes, robbing the cradle with Heidi. Sometimes explanations just muddled up the conversation and made me sound *so* last week.

"How are you handling all this time hanging around gays?" she asked.

"What? You think I'm an insecure heterosexual?"

"Oh, I think the question of your butch security is nicely resolved, at least from my perspective. I was just wondering if you are encountering any culture shock."

"Heidi," I said, "I have lived in San Francisco for almost my entire life. I've known my share of gay guys."

"Another question well-evaded," she said.

"All that being said, since I started working for this client I could choke on all the fairy dust."

She drained her third Cosmo and held the glass up to get the waiter's attention. I wondered why this ploy had not occurred to me, and then figured I probably couldn't pull it off anyway.

The waiter materialized next to the table and took the order, and Heidi wolfed down five or six honey-lime-cilantro shrimp.

"What I can't figure," she said as she chased the shrimp with the dregs of my Scrimshaw, "is why you're still working for your client, knowing that he lied to you and all."

"It's what I do. He hasn't fired me yet. Since he's missing, I feel a sort of obligation to find him."

"What happens when you find him?"

"That depends on what his story is. If it turns out he's been screwing around with me all this time, I'll probably slap him around a little and resign from the case. If he has a good excuse for lying, then we'll take it from there."

"There are good excuses for lying?"

"You bet."

I didn't bother to mention that I couldn't imagine a good excuse for Asa Corona's lies.

"What if he's missing because something bad's happened to him?"

"I'd feel obligated to figure out what happened, and why, and who did it."

"Don't we have the police for that?" she asked.

"He didn't hire the police. He hired me."

The waiter brought me a new Scrimshaw, and Heidi a new Cosmopolitan.

She took a sip and her eyes took on this dreamy, faraway look.

"It's good?" I asked.

"Excellent. And very pretty. Tell me, Eamon, what would you do if you discovered that I had lied to you?"

"About what?"

"About anything."

"It would depend. If, for instance, you had some dread social disease and didn't bother telling me until I caught it, I would be very distressed. On the other hand, if you simply lied about your age, or your natural hair color, I would just suck it up and deal with it."

"It wouldn't bother you that I had misled you, even about something small?"

"Is there something you want to tell me?"

"No. I'm just trying to figure out this testosterone-laden code of yours."

"My client and I have a business arrangement," I said. "It implies that, in order to help him, I need to know exactly what the problem is. Once I take his money, I'm committed to do what I can to help him solve that problem. When he lies to me, I waste time heading off in directions that don't help him, and might hurt me. I don't like that. So, when I find out he's lied to me, I kind of feel like turning him into a pretzel."

"And if I were to lie to you?"

"About something trivial?"

"About anything."

"I'd decide whether it really impacts me, and I'd act accordingly. Is this going to turn into one of those *Where are we going* conversations?"

She didn't answer. We each drank some of our respective drinks, and I spooned some black olive tapenade on a pita point. She ate some more shrimp.

The carefree part of the evening, apparently, was over.

TWENTY-EIGHT

I dropped Heidi off at her place. She claimed she was tired, but I had a feeling she was upset with me for clumsily questioning her motives. Her mental distress aside, I was pretty sure I had accurately interpreted the direction of her conversation.

On the other hand, she is a woman, which means I don't really understand a damn thing about the way she thinks. That made dropping her off and giving her some time to stew the best of all possible strategies.

I dropped by my Russian Hill house. There were no messages on my machine, from Asa Corona or anyone else.

I packed a few things and drove down to my Montara house for the night. I had a lot to think through and working on the Maccaferri guitar seemed like a good way to think through them.

The Selmer Maccaferri was one of the more interesting guitars manufactured in the early years of the twentieth century, in that it was arched along the length of the soundboard, but not along the width. That meant literally bending the soundboard in the middle, sort of the way you would fold a sheet of paper. With paper this is easy. With stiff, close-grained Engelmann spruce, it's a royal pain in the ass.

But worth it.

I dumped my bag in the bedroom of the Montara house and, after tossing on a sleeveless sweatshirt and a pair of old jeans, set to work making a bending mold out of strips of Baltic birch plywood. The mold was about a foot and a half wide, and about two feet long, with nine strips of plywood between the frame.

The trick to making this guitar is that, while the soundboard is arched in the middle, toward the sides it has to be flat, to mate with the sides of the guitar. That meant graduating the degree of arch from the middle out.

It took me a couple of hours to make the mold, and this gave me a lot of time to review what I knew about the case.

First, I knew that Asa Corona had lied to me when he first came to my office. Not only did he already know Ty Cannon, but he also knew Anthony Luft. Since, at least so far, our primary suspects in the blackmail scheme were Cannon and Luft, I had to regard Corona's motives with suspicion.

What I couldn't figure out was why Corona had lied. If he knew that the other man in the blackmail photos was Ty Cannon, why did he make me go through the gyrations of visiting WaterWorks and getting him identified by Gary Chiklis? If he knew Anthony Luft, as Steve Csaba had said, and if Anthony Luft was as tight with Ty Cannon as Barrett Efird had implied, then why didn't Asa go straight to Luft in the first place after receiving the threats by email?

Or, perhaps he had.

Ray Klein had told me that Asa and Luft had come by his house about two weeks earlier, or at just about the time Anthony Luft was murdered at Ty Cannon's house. What if Asa had been doing a little detective work of his own, trying to track down Ty Cannon through Little Tony Luft?

As things do in my mind, the whole picture suddenly shifted a hundred and eighty degrees, and I started to see Asa Corona in a whole different light.

And I didn't like the way he looked.

Someone knocked on the front door. Before I could get to it, Crymes let himself in.

"You're going to get yourself shot someday," I said.

"Anything to drink?"

I nodded toward the refrigerator and crossed back into the shop. Crymes followed me a few seconds later, with a bottle of Irish Red.

"I was driving by on the PCH and saw your lights on," he said. "Place cleans up okay."

The last time Crymes had been in my Montara House, the walls and ceiling of the bedroom had been spattered with several pints of Taylor Chu's blood. I'd done some renovations since.

"I try to keep tidy," I said.

"Heard anything from your client?"

"Not a peep. I visited several of his friends today. Want to hear something funny?"

"Is this funny *ha-ha*, or funny strange?"

"Somewhere in between. It seems Asa Corona may have been doing a little sleuthing before he came to me for help. Specifically, he visited everyone on that list I gave you, and asked all of them about Ty Cannon."

"Whom, as you've already told me, he claimed not to know."

"The funny thing is, he made some of these visits with the late Little Tony Luft."

Crymes took a long drag from the beer.

"That *is* funny," he said.

"I note you are not laughing. The next thing you should know is he made these visits very near the time Luft died."

Crymes grunted a little and tended to his beer. I finished clamping up the mold for the Maccaferri soundboard.

"Seems we've both been busy," he said.

"Are we sharing tonight?"

"Why not? First things first, we have found out a few things about Ty Cannon."

"He's alive?"

"I wouldn't know. On the other hand, I do know that his real name isn't Ty Cannon. It's Byron Taggart."

I stopped working on the bending form and held up a finger for him to hold on.

"I think I want a beer before I hear this one," I said, as I retreated to the kitchen.

A moment later, I was back in the shop.

"Byron Taggart," Crymes continued. "Born March twelfth, twenty-nine years ago, in Billings, Montana. Father unknown, mother deceased. She was a prostitute, had her parental rights terminated when Byron was about five, after she left him in a car for a couple of hours so she could hand out a few sawbuck hummers in the back room of a pool hall. Some cop saw our boy in the back seat and took him into custody. Mom died of AIDS about five years later, but by that time Byron was living in a group home in Butte."

"One shudders," I said.

"It gets better. Byron, by this time, was a fixture at the local juvie court. Nothing big. Mostly shoplifting, and the occasional assault. His first serious bust came at thirteen, when he was caught in the men's room at the local park with a Presbyterian deacon. Seems the fruit don't fall far. They charged Byron with soliciting, and the deacon with sodomy. Byron got a couple of months in a treatment facility. The deacon might get out in time to see his grandchildren graduate from college."

"Didn't you say Ty Cannon was also arrested for soliciting?" I asked.

"Old habits die hard, I suppose. Shortly after he got out of the treatment facility, Byron Taggart took his act on the road. I don't think he's been back to Montana since, but he's logged plenty of time on the radar screens of various police departments all along the coast. He was arrested for running a male escort service in Portland when he was seventeen. He'd organized a group of other poor wastrels, and was peddling them out on street corners. Because he was still technically a juvie, he only got a little detention time for that, and shortly thereafter he disappeared."

"And Ty Cannon appeared, apparently out of nowhere."

"Precisely. We probably wouldn't have made the connection, except that Oregon recently changed their laws regarding disclosure of juvenile records. They showed a match between Cannon's prints and this Byron Taggart, and the rest was just good ol' footwork."

"Man," I said, shaking my head. "This kid never had a chance, did he?"

"Certainly not if you listen to him, I'd imagine. Most of these skells have some kind of hardluck story to peddle. I haven't met a crook yet that didn't want to blame someone else for being an asshole."

"Did you drop by to wax philosophic, or do you have anything else to share?" I asked.

"I just saw your lights on, and figured I could cadge a free beer," he said. "Just what in hell are you working on here, now?"

"A Selmer Maccaferri."

"You mean one of those Django guitars?"

I shook my head.

"Damn, Crymes, you are just one long series of surprising revelations, you know that?"

"I get around. Another thing I did find out, by the way. This gay boy fuck club where Luft apparently took all these pictures? It's owned by the mob."

"I'm not surprised. I read somewhere that those guys have been involved in homosexual bars all the way back to the Stonewall Riots in 1969. Like just about everything else they touch, they saw an opportunity to provide funding for some poor schnooks who couldn't get a business loan anywhere else. You think Gary Chiklis is mobbed up?"

"I haven't even talked with him," Crymes said. "Can't say one way or the other. He might just be an employee, hired to manage the place. We're still looking into it. According to the records, though, the building WaterWorks is housed in is owned by JuneBug."

"No shit," I said. "Well, that calls for another drink."

Junius Bugliosi was a very distant cousin of the district attorney who tried the Manson family. I was pretty sure JuneBug wasn't invited to the annual reunions, though. He was as dirty as his fourth cousin Vincent was squeaky clean.

"For the record," I said, after returning from the kitchen with two fresh bottles, "I'm getting a really hinky feeling about Asa Corona. Beyond the fact that he lied, his association with Anthony Luft is troubling. Two of the guys on that list saw Corona and Luft together, hunting for Ty Cannon, within a day or so of the day Luft supposedly died. I have to ask myself why. Maybe Corona was trying to find Cannon to stop the blackmail..."

"...Or maybe he wanted to put Cannon out of the picture," Crymes finished. "You think maybe Corona is in on the scam and became worried when a lot of people started getting emails demanding money. He tried to find Cannon, with Anthony Luft's help. Maybe Cannon got wind of this, and decided he'd take out part of the team himself, so he killed Luft at his Pacifica house and took his act on the road."

"You're fast," I said. "I have to give you that."

"I'm a cop. It's the way my head works."

"But that doesn't explain why Corona came to me for help."

"Maybe he was scared. He, Cannon, and Luft work out this elaborate scheme to extort money from WaterWorks customers. Corona, with his social connections, would probably know which ones were well-heeled. Cannon, everybody's fuck buddy, would provide the talent, and Luft would make the photos. When Luft was murdered, Corona panicked, figured maybe Cannon would come looking for him next, so he decided to hire some professional help to find Cannon first."

"And when I didn't do that, he disappeared."

"Works for me."

"You realize, of course," I added, "that this means Asa knew that the body in Cannon's house was Little Tony. He knew it the first day he came to visit me."

"And he didn't come to the cops. Makes him an accomplice."

"Or at least complicit."

We both chewed on this one for a moment while sipping our Killians.

"There's another possibility," Crymes said. "What if Corona knew the dead guy in Cannon's house was Luft, but he also knew Cannon didn't kill him?"

"We're still assuming Asa was in on the blackmail scam from the beginning?"

"Yeah."

"That would mean there's a fourth player here we don't know about."

"And if Corona also didn't know who this fourth player is, it might scare him enough to make him seek professional help."

I shook my head.

"That doesn't make sense. Why did he disappear? How could he know whether I run down this fourth player if he's out there hiding somewhere?"

"Who gave you the list of people we've both been interviewing?"

I thought about this one.

"Are you saying Corona suspects that one of the people on this list killed Anthony Luft, and he's hoping I'll figure it out and take them out of the picture?"

"It works," Crymes said. "He and Luft were running all over town in the week before Luft died, talking with those people on the list Corona gave you. He's bright enough to figure that one of them caught on to the scam, and went to Cannon's house to stop it, but killed Luft instead. So, he gives you this list, and takes a powder while you do his legwork for him."

"He couldn't know who I'm talking with, though. He's not tailing me, I know that. He's not good enough. Jack Delroy is pretty good at following, and I made him right away."

"Maybe he doesn't have to follow you," Crymes said.

It took me about five seconds to figure out what he meant.

"You don't think..." I said.

Before he could answer, I grabbed a flashlight from the kitchen and dashed into the carport. Crymes followed me out the door and watched as I dropped to the concrete floor and slid underneath my car.

The GPS unit was stuck to the front edge of the gas tank, where I wouldn't have seen it if I'd just taken a casual peek under the car.

"Son of a *bitch*!" I said. I grabbed the unit, which was attached with a couple of small rare earth magnets, and pulled it away. I slid back out from under the car and held it up to show Crymes.

"Tristar 3200," I said. "This is the same model Full Moon Security uses."

He nodded, and said, "The same model Asa Corona asked Full Moon to put under his own cars."

"The kid learns fast."

"Isn't that what we've said all along? Whoever is running this blackmail scheme is a smart cookie. What are you going to do?"

I thought about it.

"I guess I need to have a talk with Sheldon Moon, first thing tomorrow morning."

TWENTY-NINE

I pushed right past Moon's secretary and into his office.

"You can't…" she yelped.

Like that was going to stop me.

Moon was in his wheelchair, behind his desk, doing something with the computer. As I barged through his door, he seemed to jump a little, and his hand shot toward his desk drawer.

I already had my Browning out.

"Don't even think about it, Moon," I said.

His hand froze.

"What are you doing, Gold?"

"You and I have to talk."

Moon's secretary was standing at the office door, staring at me as I held her boss at gunpoint.

"It's okay," he told her.

"I'll call the police," she said.

"No," Moon said. "Just close the door, please. I'll buzz you if I need any help."

After she left, he rolled the wheelchair back from his desk.

"You can put that away," he said, nodding toward my Browning.

I stowed it at my belt and held up the Tristar 3200 I'd carried in my jacket pocket.

"You want to explain this?" I said.

"Explain what?"

"I found this under my car last night. It's the same model you use."

"It's a popular brand. A lot of firms use it."

"But you're the only detectives who've been tailing me lately. Did you have this put under my car?"

"No," he said.

"Easy enough to say."

"It's easy to prove, too. Would you have a seat, please? Your pacing back and forth is making me nervous."

I took a deep breath, and decided he was right. I probably looked like I was crazy.

I sat in one of the office chairs across from his desk.

Moon picked up the telephone and pressed a button.

"Could you bring in the Tristar inventory file?" he asked, and then racked the receiver.

"We do a lot of security work," he said. "Many of our clients have children they don't... well, they don't trust. You'd be amazed how many kids are driving around out there without a clue that their parents know every place they go. Of course, we need to know which trackers go with which cell phone numbers, so we can tell one from another. It would be, well, embarrassing to tell a parent that his son was hanging out at a strip club, only to find out it was a different person."

The office door opened, and Moon's secretary crossed to room to hand him a file. He thanked her, and she left.

"This is our current inventory of Tristar GPS tracking devices," he said. "It's arranged in a spreadsheet, with the serial numbers of the tracker linked to the cell number used to upload the data. Feel free to look over it."

I took the file from him and glanced at it.

"The serial number for each tracking device is stamped on the case, just underneath the battery."

I turned over the tracker and pried off the battery cover. When I pulled out the battery, I could see the number. I compared it to the list in Moon's file.

It wasn't there.

"I can understand your anger," Moon said. "But I can assure you that we had nothing to do with putting that tracker under your car."

I thought about it for a moment.

"You put trackers under all of Asa Corona's cars."

"That's correct."

"At his request."

"He had complained that he thought someone was driving his cars without his permission or knowledge."

"That was it? He just wanted to know whether his cars were going somewhere without him in them?"

"No, that's not it. He was very curious. He wanted to know all about the trackers. He wanted to know how they worked, and he even insisted on a demonstration."

"You showed him how to download the data, how to place the trackers in the cars, that sort of thing."

"Precisely."

I settled back in my chair.

"Damn," I said. "The kid set me up."

"Was there anything else I can do for you today?" Moon asked.

I stowed Corona's tracker in my pocket.

"I don't know. Could you answer a few questions?"

"As long as they don't violate my clients' privacy."

"When did Asa ask you to put the trackers underneath his car?

"About a month ago."

"More or less about the same time he claimed to start receiving blackmail demands."

"I wouldn't know. You'll recall that he chose not to confide in us regarding the blackmail."

"So, if Asa did place this tracker underneath my car, he had to order it within the last four weeks."

"More or less."

"I could check with Tristar, see if he ordered this tracker in the last month."

"They wouldn't tell you. At least, not without a warrant. I have a feeling, though, that it wouldn't matter. That's an expensive unit, but it's not the latest design. It wasn't manufactured in the last year or so. If it does belong to Asa, he probably bought it on the resale market."

"And who knows how many owners it's passed through."

"You could chase your tail for days, and still not find out that it's Asa's."

"Okay. Here's another question. Has Asa contacted you since he disappeared?"

"No."

"Would you tell me if he had?"

"Yes. I wouldn't tell you what he said, but since you know we work for the Coronas, it wouldn't hurt to tell you he'd called."

"I think you have a problem, Moon. If I'm right, Asa's in really big trouble with the law. He may have been at least complicit in the murder of Anthony Luft, and he may have also conspired to blackmail other customers at WaterWorks."

"We have considered that possibility."

"And?"

"We're still waiting for some proof."

"You don't have to give me names, but have any of your other clients, besides Barrett Efird, received emailed blackmail messages containing pictures of them with Ty Cannon?"

He seemed to think about the question for a moment.

"Yes," he said at last. "But that's all I can say about it."

I pulled Corona's list from my pocket.

"Steve Csaba?" I asked.

He stared at me stonily.

"Miles Nickelby?"

No response.

"Ray Klein?"

"Really, Mr. Gold. This is enough. I've already confirmed that some of our clients have been threatened. You already know about Barrett Efird. Do you think I'm going to open all my files for you? Would you do this for me?"

He was right. He was just protecting his clients. I'd do the same thing in his position.

"I'm sorry," I said. "You should know, though, that I'm convinced that Asa Corona lied to me, probably from the moment he walked into my office. He can be very convincing. If I were you, and if he were to call, I wouldn't believe anything he says unless he can prove it."

"Thank you. Now, if you'll excuse me, I'm very busy."

I stood and started to leave but stopped at his door.

"I'm sorry for barging in, and for alarming your secretary."

"All in a day's work, Mr. Gold," he said, without looking up from his computer screen.

THIRTY

I parked my car behind my Jefferson Street office and walked around to the gallery on the first floor. Heidi was sitting on the stool in front of her cash register, sipping something through a straw from a foam cup. She saw me through her front window just as I turned the corner.

I walked in, took the cup from her, placed it on the counter, and kissed her three or four seconds longer than I had intended. Her lips made a little popping sound as I disengaged.

"That was for me being an asshole last night," I said.

"Okay," she said. "It's a start."

"I suppose we should talk about this."

"Not if you don't want to."

"But it's the adult thing to do. Grownups talk about stuff that's bothering them."

"Am I bothering you?" she asked.

"Not you exactly. It's more what you represent."

She picked up the cup and sipped through the straw again. I could tell she was working really hard to make it look like more than drinking.

"I represent something?"

"You represent a lot. Most of it is stuff I've put a lot of effort into avoiding."

"Gawd. Sweep me off my feet again, cowboy."

"Not like that. How long have we been dating?"

"Damned if I know. Maybe a year. I'm not keeping count."

"Then why all the probing questions last night? What was all that about, asking what I'd do if I found out you'd lied?"

She put the cup down again and looked away from me, out the back window of her shop at the Golden Gate. It was one of those crisp, razor-keen days that was bound to end in fog, but for the moment the sun glinted off the whitecaps in the bay like hundreds of little firecrackers.

"This isn't the time, Eamon," she said.

"I have plenty of time."

"Not the kind we need. This could take hours, and I just opened for business."

"So close up again. We'll take the day, drive down the coast to Monterey, grab some lunch, walk on the pier."

She leaned over and put her elbows on the counter and cradled her chin in her palms.

"You are always in such a *hurry*," she said. "It'll wait."

I thought about it for a moment.

"What about this evening? I could grill out at the Montara house. We could talk there."

"I don't know," she said. "I mean, this isn't going to be one of those *Where are we going?* talks, is it?"

"How about one of those *Whatever you want* talks?"

She smiled. I liked her smile. I'd liked it ever since the first day we'd met.

"Yeah. I could get into a talk like that," she said.

———

I parked my car in the underground lot at the Civic Center and trotted up the steps to the lobby. It took a few moments to find Russell Skeen's office on the directory, and a few more to get to the actual place.

I had expected to run into a secretary or something, but Skeen's office was just this door opening out into the hallway, and it had his name on it.

The door was halfway open, and I could see Skeen sitting on a loveseat across from his desk, reading from a folder. I rapped on the door a couple of times.

"Come in," he said, without looking up.

I pushed through the door and walked over to him.

"Can I help you?" he said, standing.

"My name's Gold," I said, handing him my card.

He looked at it for a second, then pulled a leather cardholder from his pants pocket and filed it inside.

"Have a seat, Mr. Gold," he said, gesturing toward a chair set perpendicularly to the loveseat. "I hate to conduct business from behind a desk. It's just so informal, you know?"

Actually, I preferred to do business from behind my desk, but I didn't say so.

"I'll just take a few moments of your time," I said. "I'm looking for a guy who hangs out at WaterWorks a lot, and I could use some information."

"I don't understand," he said.

"You are the special assistant to Curtis Fleming, right?"

"That's right."

"And your purview has to do with the gay community?"

"Also right."

"I was just wondering about the political atmosphere surrounding the baths."

"Oh," he said, seeming to relax a little. I was swimming around in his end of the pool now. "When I saw your card..."

"It has that effect sometimes. I didn't mean to alarm you. Could you take a moment and tell a straight guy what all the fuss is over the baths?"

"It's pretty simple, actually," he said. "A strident portion of the gay community wants to reinstate licensing for baths with private rooms. The City Supervisors are opposed to it."

"Why is that, exactly?"

"Disease control, originally. When HIV first hit the public light in the early 1980's, it was seen as a gay plague. Some people ignored the fact that whole groups of heterosexual IV drug users were getting AIDS—or GRIDS, as it was called then—or that a large contingent of South Florida Haitian immigrants had it. They heard "gay" and went all batshit. A lot of public venues for the gay population became easy targets for politicians at the time, because the disease was so damned scary and nobody had any idea how it was transmitted. So, the city fathers decided to engage in a little vector control, and they closed down the baths and a number of gay nightclubs which permitted on-premises sex."

"They were allowed to reopen later, though?"

"Sure. After a few years the furor died down. People started to take a more rational look at AIDS, and realized that it wasn't quite as easy to catch as they had thought. When entrepreneurs South of Market requested permits to open a club or two, they were issued with just a couple of caveats."

"No private rooms."

"It had become a moral issue. The country had swung a little right of center, and the politicians didn't want to alienate a powerful voting bloc. They gave the gay voters part of what they wanted, and the Bible-thumpers got some of what they wanted."

"But the on-premises sex still takes place in the baths."

"The thinking is that the frequency of sex will drop if the guys know they're performing for an audience," he said. "And a couple of studies actually seem to support that."

"Oh, come on. How can they know?"

"Right across the bay, in Berkley, they allow baths with private rooms. Researchers have conducted studies of the frequency of sexual activity in both types of club. Believe it or not, clubs without private rooms tallied only about 79% of the nightly sexual acts compared to those with private rooms."

"So, some of the patrons of places like WaterWorks want the private rooms."

"Exactly."

"Are these malcontents organized?"

He grinned, showing two rows of perfectly aligned, ivory-white teeth.

"Aren't they always? That's part of my job, to provide liaison between Supervisor Fleming and that gay portion of his constituency, to assure that their voices are heard above the rabble when it comes time to write public policy."

"Is Supervisor Fleming listening?"

"With one ear. He keeps the other one to the tracks."

"If you don't mind me saying it," I noted, "You're pretty candid for a political hack."

He laughed this time.

"I'll guess I'll never get arrested for holding my tongue," he said.

"So, where do you stand personally on the private rooms?" I asked.

He started to speak, but stopped himself, and wagged a finger at me.

"Okay," I said, "Let's try this one. Who's heading up the contingent fighting for reinstatement of the private rooms?"

"I don't believe there's a single leader. Several people seem to have pooled their efforts."

"Are any of them on this list?" I asked, handing him the list Asa Corona had given me.

He looked over it but shook his head.

"I've met a couple of these guys, but none of them are in the forefront of the gay movement in SoMa. Miles, for instance, has to keep a low profile."

"Working for the Republican Party and all," I said.

"Exactly. You've already spoken with him?"

"Yes. What about Ty Cannon?"

"I know Ty. No, he's not particularly political."

"Anthony Luft?"

"Little Tony? You bet. He's one of the more active organizers."

"Do you know Asa Corona?"

Something like a dark cloud crossed Skeen's features.

"Why?"

"His name's come up here and there. In fact, I have a pretty good idea that he visited you a few days ago, looking for Ty Cannon."

"What's this about, Mr. Gold?"

"A lot of things. Have you received any strange or disturbing emails lately?"

"I don't follow."

"A lot of the guys on this list have been sent blackmail notes containing pictures of them having sex with Ty Cannon. You're on the list, so I figured…"

"You figured wrong. If you don't have any further questions, I'm very busy…"

"They won't stop," I said.

"What?"

"The blackmailers."

"I don't know what you're talking about."

"Little Tony's dead," I said.

He froze, halfway between sitting and standing, and stared at me.

"Say that again."

"Anthony Luft was murdered about two weeks ago, in Ty Cannon's house in Pacifica."

He sat down again.

"How?"

"He was bludgeoned. We don't know who did it. One train of thought has it the killer was actually after Cannon and got the wrong guy. Sure you haven't gotten any threatening emails, Mr. Skeen?"

"The police?"

"They're investigating. I'm just looking for Asa Corona. I don't suppose you might know where he's stashed himself, do you?"

"No, I don't. I think you'd better leave now, Mr. Gold. I… I'm going to be very busy for the next day or so."

"Covering your tracks?"

"Certainly not. Word's going to spread about Tony. They… some people are going to suspect he was killed for political reasons. I'm going to have to spread some oil on that water."

"Who are *they*, and why would they suspect that?"

"Because people are suspicious. Please go. I can't help you with Asa Corona."

"You have my card," I said. "Call me if you hear from him. It's very important."

"Yes," he said, his eyes focused someplace else, far away. "I'll do that. Now, please go."

THIRTY-ONE

As I drove back to Jefferson Street, I thought about what Skeen had told me.

Anthony Luft had been part of a cadre of gay activists working to change the City laws regarding private rooms in bathhouses. Suddenly, I saw more than one possible motive for his murder.

I pulled out my cell phone and thumbed Crymes' number on the speed dial.

"Crymes," he said.

"Tony Luft was more involved in the sex clubs than we thought," I told him. "He was trying to fight City Hall over the private fuck rooms."

"Is that a fact?"

"You don't sound surprised."

"I'm a cop, Eamon. I know a thing or two about solving murders. I stopped being surprised by the things dead people did years ago. You got any other names to go with his?"

"Not yet. Any news on Asa Corona?"

"Not a peep. Wherever he's gone, he's buried deep."

"Could we use another metaphor?"

"Sorry. Where are you?"

"On Powell, headed back to the office. I think I'm going to make a stop first, though."

"You'll keep me posted, right?"

"You'll be the first person I call."

I rang off and turned left at the next light to double back and head for SoMa.

It took me several minutes to get to WaterWorks. Chris Driscoll was working the front desk again when I walked in the front door.

"Mr. Astroturf," he said, extending his hand.

"Is the boss in?" I asked, as I took it.

"Just a minute."

He picked up the phone and hit an extension number to announce me. Several seconds later, I heard the door open upstairs, and Gary Chiklis lumbered down.

"Mr. Gold," he said, as we shook.

"I'm sorry to bother you again, but I have a few questions about the political climate around here."

"Like everything else, it's steamy. Come on up."

I followed him up to his office and sat in the same chair I'd used on my last visit. The curtains were drawn over the picture window looking out over the baths.

"So, what do you want to know?" Chiklis asked.

"Anthony Luft was part of a political action group working to change the licensing laws for places like WaterWorks."

"Yes. It's a shame about Tony. He was very well-liked around here."

"You know he's dead."

"Yes. Miles Nickelby called and told me yesterday. A terrible thing."

"Did you know I was the one who found him?"

"No. Tell me, did he suffer?"

"I can't say. Probably not. He was whacked over the head with something heavy. I'd guess he went out like a light bulb."

"I suppose that's a blessing. What would you like to know?"

"How involved was he with the drive to permit private rooms in the baths?"

Chiklis sat back and pinched nervously at his moustache.

"He was a heavy player, one of the first organizers. Tony was somewhat self-conscious. You've heard his nickname?"

"Little Tony?"

"Yeah. He didn't get that because of his height, dig? He was always a little shy out in the pool area, so he didn't get all the action he might have liked. Nobody really gave a damn, but he was bothered by it. So, when talk started about petitioning for reinstatement of private rooms, he was ready to get on board."

"Who were the other organizers?"

"Oh, hell, there were a bunch of them."

I handed him Asa Corona's list.

"Any of these guys?"

He looked over it.

"Not really. Some were involved on the outer fringes. Miles Nickelby gave some money to help pay for lawyers. I think he felt guilty about working for the Republican gay-bashers. He never marched or anything, though. These other guys I don't think were ever heavily involved."

"What are the chances Tony might have actually been killed over this movement?"

"What? Someone zipped him up because he just wanted a nice quiet place to screw? I don't see it."

"There are a lot of people out there who see homosexuality as a sin, and feel righteous enough to think that it's always Kill A Queer For Jesus Week."

Chiklis winced.

"Yeah," he said. "Don't I know it. You think I got all bulked up like this because I like to look at myself in the mirror? There aren't many fag-bashers who are going to fuck with me, not built like I am. I still have a hard time buying that angle with Tony, though."

He handed the list back to me.

"Could you put together a list of people who spearheaded the private room project? It doesn't have to be complete. I just need somewhere to start."

"Are you investigating Tony's killing? I thought the police were working on that."

"I'm looking for Asa Corona, but the two things may be related."

He thought about it for a moment, and then pulled a sheet of notepaper from a small lucite bin on his desk. He scribbled a few names.

"Give me a minute. I need to find the phone numbers."

He left the room. I sat for moment, staring at the walls, and then wandered over to the picture window. I pulled back the drape, and saw Chiklis standing next to the pool, talking with a young man sitting naked on a chaise. The discussion looked intense.

After a couple of moments, Chiklis nodded, and walked away. I closed the drape and sat back down in the chair.

Chiklis came back into the room and sat back behind his desk. He clicked the mouse on his computer a couple of times, and then started copying numbers down from his database.

"Did you need permission?" I asked.

"Come again?" he said, without looking up.

"The guy next to the pool. I took a peek through the curtain, and saw you talking with him."

Chiklis stopped writing.

"Okay," he said. "Sure. I needed permission. I don't own WaterWorks, Mr. Gold. I just manage it. The guy downstairs... works for the owner."

"JuneBug."

"He doesn't like being called that."

"Mr. Bugliosi keeps a close eye on this place?"

"I'm not at liberty to discuss Mr. Bugliosi's business. Do you want these numbers or not?"

"Sorry," I said. "Natural curiosity. Occupational hazard."

"Well, around here, you learn not to get too curious."

"It sounds dangerous."

"Let's not blow it out of proportion. You don't get too curious, because Mr. Bugliosi doesn't like people to get curious. It's a great way to lose your job."

He finished writing and handed me the list.

I didn't leave right away. Instead, I pulled my car across the street and parked in a grocery store lot. I listened to a Giants game on the radio and cleaned my nails with my pocketknife while I kept an eye on the front door of WaterWorks.

After about a half-hour, the man Chiklis had been talking with left the building and walked around to the rear. Seconds later, he drove out of the lot in a new Lexus. I gave him about ten seconds lead, and then pulled out in traffic behind him.

I didn't know exactly where I was going or what I was doing. I did know that Chiklis had lied to me about going downstairs to get some telephone numbers, and that he'd really gone to get permission to give me the numbers. That meant that, somehow, JuneBug was mixed up with the Free Bathhouses movement, and the guy I was following was mixed up with JuneBug.

Part of that didn't really mix well in my head, which was why I was following the Lexus. The mob tolerates a lot of stuff, but they tend to be a little rigid on alternative sexual orientation. On the other hand, I had brought up JuneBug, not Chiklis. Maybe when I mentioned Bugliosi, it gave Chiklis an opportunity to divert attention away from the guy on the lounge by the pool. That would mean that the guy I was following really wasn't mixed up with JuneBug, but still had the juice to make Chiklis touch base with him before giving me some phone numbers.

That made him someone worth following.

The Lexus headed down Douglass into the Castro, where he turned left on 20th toward the bay. He made a right on Noe and drove another block or two before pulling over in front of a mission-style bungalow. I pulled into another parking lot and watched from a couple of hundred yards away.

On the radio, Barry Bonds snapped a clean grand slam into the right field stands and cleared the bases to put the Giants up by six over the Braves.

I jotted down the address of the bungalow, and had just finished when two people I couldn't identify from the distance walked out the front door and down the steps to the Lexus. One got in the front, and the other in the back, and Juice Guy chirped the tires pulling away from the curb.

I fell into traffic seven or eight cars behind him after the next light. I tried to catch the license plate number as he cut back over to Church and started north toward downtown.

I was still trying to get his number when he pulled over to the curb next to Mission Dolores Park. I had no choice but to keep going. The two guys from the bungalow got out of the Lexus and stared at me as I drove past. I tried really hard not to stare back.

It didn't matter.

I was made.

THIRTY-TWO

The Lexus stayed next to the curb after I passed by.

I continued driving toward the business district while I recited the license number until I could stop and write it down. After a mile or so, I still couldn't see the Lexus in my rearview, so I pulled over, wrote down the number, and then continued. I was halfway back to Jefferson Street when my cell phone beeped.

"Gold," I said.

"This is Asa."

"Where are you?"

"I don't want to tell you."

"Fine," I said. I ended the call.

I wasn't going to let Asa screw around with me.

The phone beeped again.

"You want to tell me where you are?" I asked.

"I'm afraid."

"You should be."

"All I can say is, I think I'm in a safe place."

"You need to come in, kid. The cops are looking for you. They're figuring you for Little Tony's murder."

"I had nothing to do with that…"

"Don't tell me. Tell them. Where can I pick you up?"

"I don't know. If I go out, they might find me."

"Who?"

"How in hell should I know? Ty Cannon, the blackmailer. Whoever."

"I'll be honest, Asa. I don't know whether to believe you anymore. I know you lied about Cannon and Tony. I know you were investigating this blackmail thing for almost two weeks before you hired me. I know you already knew the other guy in the picture with you was Ty Cannon. I'm also thinking that you already knew Anthony Luft was dead before you came to me."

"How in hell can you know all that?"

"I'm a detective, kid. I know things. You think I've been sitting around staring at my navel while you've been missing? Now be a good boy and tell me where I can pick you up."

"I... I don't know if they'll let me..."

"Who won't let you?"

"I can't talk about that right now."

"You want me to hang up on you again?"

"No! Don't do that. I called you because I need your help."

"That's what I'm trying to give," I said. "You're not making it easy."

"Okay. Okay. Just wait a minute. Let me think."

I headed up the hill on Van Ness.

"All right," he said. "I know. The Zen Garden in the Japanese Tea Garden at Golden Gate Park, next to the museum. I can walk there from here."

"When?"

"Not this evening. Tomorrow, at noon."

"Just so you know, Asa, I'm going to have to take you to see Detective Crymes. It's obstruction if I don't."

"Oh, come on, Mr. Gold, not the cops."

"You are still laboring under the misconception that you can come out ahead in this thing. The cops are investigating Luft's murder, and they have you way up near the top of their list of suspects. First thing you have to do is clear your name. That is, if you didn't kill Little Tony."

"God! Of course I didn't kill him."

"Then we need to go to the cops. I'll see you at noon. You'd better be there."

"I will."

I ended the call and cruised down the hill on Van Ness toward Fisherman's Wharf.

I had just pulled in behind my office when the cell phone chirped again.

"What is it now?" I asked.

"What are you up to?"

I didn't recognize the voice.

"Can I help you?"

"You were following me. I don't like that."

Uh-oh.

It took me about a second to figure out what had happened. The guy in the Lexus had called Chiklis, whom I'd given a copy of my business card, which had my work cell phone number on it.

"I wanted a closer look at your car."

"Why?"

"Thinking of buying one."

"That's a laugh. Not on your richest day. Did you get an eye full?"

"I saw enough. I have a couple of questions."

"Fuck off. Here's the way you want to play this, Gold. Forgetting you ever saw me at WaterWorks is just about the smartest thing you can do right now."

"I'm just trying to find my missing client."

"I don't give a flying fuck what you want. You don't want to cross paths with me again, and the best way I know for you to do that is to drop this bullshit case right now and back away."

"Maybe you could sort of fax me your itinerary for the next day or two, so I'll know where I shouldn't go. How would that work?"

"You're playing with fire, Gold. You heard me. Drop it now."

He shut off his phone, just a half second before giving me the satisfaction of beating him to it.

It was still mid-afternoon, so I called Shirley Jones at the Clerk of Courts office as soon as I got up to my own office.

"Got a number I need you to run," I said.

"Can you hold?" she said.

She put me on hold before I could answer. So far, I was making myself very popular. Maybe dinner with Heidi that evening wasn't such a good idea.

I heard a click, and she was back on the line.

"Christ, Gold, my supervisor was standing right next to me. You trying to get me fired?"

"Sorry. I was just threatened by some rump ranger in a Lexus, and I'd like to threaten him back a little."

"Homophobe. Give me the number."

I recited the number I'd written down.

"You at your office?" she asked.

"Yeah."

"Call you back."

I crossed my office and grabbed a shot glass and the bottle of Glenlivet I keep in the rolltop secretary.

It had been a long day.

I was staring out my back window at some windsurfers in the Golden Gate when the phone rang.

"Gold," I said.

"Eamon, what are you up to?" Shirley asked.

"That's the second time someone's asked me that in the last half hour. I'll get back to you when I have an answer."

"That license number belongs to a corporation."

"It's a corporate car?"

"Well, *duh*. It has about fifty outstanding parking tickets. What is it with you and vagrant cars this week?"

"Any moving violations?"

"Just one. About six months ago. Some patrol cop saw your Lexus blow through a red light off Embarcadero and pulled him over. The driver was some guy named Enfante. Tobias Enfante."

"What's the corporation name?"

"San Mateo Concrete. Ring a bell?"

"Yeah. It's one of JuneBug's legitimate fronts."

"So your guy is somehow hooked up with Bugliosi. Good thing he didn't make you."

"Yeah," I said. "Isn't it? You got any more history on this guy Enfante?"

"Hold on a second."

I heard her tap away on the keyboard for a moment. Then I heard her whistle, and not in the good way.

"Remember that bulletproof vest you have hanging in your closet?" she asked.

"Yeah."

"Start wearing it. This guy Enfante likes to hurt people. There are about twelve outstanding Assaults with Intent to Kill listed here, over the last five years. Not one of them was disposed."

"Meaning?"

"They may have gotten to court, but they all stopped there. Who knows? Witnesses don't show, or they recant on the stand. Whatever the reason, Enfante hasn't served a day without getting bailed out. He's dangerous."

"So am I."

"How are you mixed up with Enfante?"

I took a sip of the Glenlivet.

"Damned if I know," I said.

THIRTY-THREE

Just in case Enfante was a lot better at tracking me than I had been at tracking him, I packed my shotgun in the trunk before picking Heidi up to head for Montara. I had my Browning stowed on my belt, and there was an extra Python under my driver's seat.

I wasn't wearing my vest, because I didn't have one that would fit Heidi, and it seemed a little selfish to bogart the body armor. Just in case, though, I stuffed it in the trunk along with the heavy artillery.

I helped Heidi close the gallery, and then drove her to the bank to make her deposit. We stopped at a Safeway in Pacifica, where I picked up a couple of filets and some silver queen corn, along with a bag salad. Heidi started to put a couple of bottles of Corona Farms merlot in the buggy, but I politely switched it out for another label.

I didn't tell her why.

We drove on to the Montara house. I seasoned the steaks while Heidi stowed her gear in the bedroom and took a shower.

I finished preparing the steaks and wrapped the corn in aluminum foil, and then strolled out to the car to bring in the hardware.

The shotgun was a serious business piece, a pistol-gripped Mossberg Persuader twelve-gauge pumper. It was only about two feet long, which made it easy to conceal if needed. I had outfitted it with a spreader choke and double-ought stainless buckshot. I know you aren't supposed to use the stainless because it damages the bore. On the other hand, I didn't plan to do a lot of hunting with this piece. If it came down to me or the other guy, I wanted to be able to inflict the maximum possible damage with the fewest possible shots.

The Python was a standard issue piece in .357 Magnum, but I had settled for the four-inch barrel over the six-inch Elite series, partly because using the longer piece made me look like Dirty Harry, and partly because I wasn't compensating for anything. I had a couple of speed loaders in my jacket pocket.

I had just stowed the weapons in my closet in the bedroom, where I could grab them quickly if needed, when Heidi opened the bathroom door and steam flooded out into the hallway. It smelled like green apples and hyacinth. She walked out wearing a towel wrapped around her head in a turban, and nothing else.

I think my heart skipped a couple of beats.

"I'm starving," she said. "When's dinner?"

"The steaks have to marinate. Maybe an hour. I have some chips in the pantry, and some clam dip in the fridge. Did you use all the hot water?"

"God, what a weenie," she said, as she waltzed into the kitchen.

I hoped the neighbors weren't watching.

Then, on second thought, I decided it was okay if they were.

I grabbed a quick shower to knock off the day's dust and changed into a pair of jeans and a pullover shirt. When I came out of the bedroom, Heidi had tossed on a long, oversized tee shirt, and was munching on some corn chips and salsa. She had tuned the radio in the living room/shop to the local public station, and Jim Hall's guitar jazz filled the room.

"I'm going to start the fire," I said.

I gave up on gas grills years ago. I know it's politically incorrect to eat stuff cooked over hardwood charcoal, because of all the chemicals that that get burned into the meat, but I just like the taste.

Hell, something's going to get you. Nobody gets out of life alive.

It took the charcoal about a half-hour to ash over, and I put the corn on first, since it would take longer to cook. While I waited, I tossed the salad and ate some of Heidi's corn chips.

By the time the filets had grilled for about seven minutes per side, the sun was dipping behind the Chart House restaurant across the PCH, and it was getting chilly outside. I suggested that we eat at the table in the kitchen.

"Are you expecting trouble?" Heidi asked as I uncorked the wine.

"No more than normal. Why?"

"Because you still have your pistol clipped to your belt, and there's a shotgun in the closet that hasn't been there before."

"You missed the Colt Python on the overhead shelf."

"Is there something you want to tell me?"

I slid her plate in front of her and filled her wineglass.

"Yes. I'm afraid I didn't have time to make béarnaise."

"Do you at least have steak sauce?"

I gave her an offended look but retreated to the kitchen to grab a bottle of A-1.

By the time I got back, she had sliced a sliver of the filet, and was chewing contentedly. I placed the sauce in front of her. She waved it off.

"I was fucking with you, Gold. Sit down and eat."

I sat and unwrapped my corn.

"I'm serious about the other thing, though. Are you worried about something?" she asked.

"I can handle it," I said.

"Because you know you can talk to me. I'm not afraid of dangerous stuff. I mean, I know you can take care of yourself. I'd just like to know if there's a problem."

I took a moment to savor my first bite of the filet and to figure out what I was going to say next.

"Okay," I said, after swallowing and trying the merlot. "I'm looking for my client, who's gone missing. In the process, I've pissed off a guy who works for the local Mafia boss. I don't know whether he plans to do anything about that, so I just decided I'd be ready if he does."

"Oh," she said, looking a little perplexed. Then she took a sip of the wine and went back to work cutting her steak. "Well, if that's all it is…"

"It's not like that," I said. "The Mafia in San Francisco isn't what it used to be. The tongs and the Russians have carved out a lot of their business. Nowadays, the Sicilian dudes have to content themselves with a lot of small-time action."

"Which makes them hungrier."

"But not as dangerous. In the old days, when Jimmy Lanza and Jimmy the Weasel Frattiano were in control, they had their fingers in just about everything. Lanza's been dead for almost fifteen years. These days, what's left of the old organization just skims off a little union action, runs some bars and clubs, and does some nickel and dime gambling and prostitution business. It's not like they can snap their fingers and make you disappear like they used to."

"Good thing you aren't worried," she said. "I think you'd have a hard time fitting a howitzer in the house."

There was nothing to say to that, so I just ate. I had done a good job on the steak and the corn. The salad tasted like a bag salad, but what can you do?

"You're not going to say anything?" she asked.

"Let's enjoy the meal," I said.

We ate quietly. It was a fine dinner, but I wound up ruining it with self-doubt.

Heidi volunteered to do the dishes, which pretty much amounted to rinsing off the plates and sticking them in the dishwasher. I opened the second bottle of wine.

Heidi came back into the room, refilled her glass, and sat next to me on the sofa.

"Okay," she said. "Let's talk."

"I don't know what to say," I said.

"We can discuss anything other than work—-yours *or* mine."

I drank some wine and stared at the glass. Off in the distance, I could hear the waves beating a syncopated rhythm on the sands of Montara Beach.

"All right," she said. "I'll start. I lied."

I looked up at her.

"That's what last night was about. I lied to you."

I nodded.

"It doesn't matter," I said.

"I think it does. I told you about my bitch mother, and how she married my father just to get citizenship. Well, it wasn't entirely like that."

"She didn't marry him?"

"No, they were married. And she *was* a bitch. What I didn't tell you was that when my father came back to the states, she didn't come with him."

"That's why you grew up in Germany."

"Right. This is where I get to the part about how I lied. I told you that I left Germany when I turned eighteen so that I could come to the States and find my father."

"Right."

"That's not why I came."

"Look, Heidi, I…"

"And the reason I came is also the reason I can't go back."

I sat back and took a sip of the wine.

And waited.

"I was a wild kid," she continued. "My mother couldn't control me. Hell, she couldn't even control herself. I started screwing around when I was just fourteen, and then I started hanging out with a real goth crowd in Hamburg. My senior year at the American High School, I was following this band around, a group whose German name roughly translates into *Fire In The Blood.* The bass guitarist and I swung pretty good. When we weren't drinking or smoking pot or skin-popping heroin, or just fucking, he would spend a lot of time spouting off this crazy ultra-nihilist rant. I didn't even know what *nihilist* meant back then, but I knew his take on it was way out in the boonies.

"What I didn't know, *couldn't* know, because he'd have killed me if I'd found it out, was that he was hooked in with *Brigate Rosse.*"

"The Red Brigades," I said.

"Yeah. And what a fun bunch of knuckleheads *they* were."

"I thought they were in Italy."

"They had cells all over Europe, but I didn't find out about that until after I came to the US. There was a huge crackdown in 1989. The police and Interpol arrested hundreds of Brigades members, including this bassist for *Fire*

In The Blood. He got a message out to me, telling me that the police were going to come after me next. So, I called my father, he pulled some strings, and I got out of the country."

"You can't go back because there's no statute of limitations on terror crimes," I said.

"That's right."

"Your mother?"

"I haven't seen her since I left. No big loss there, I suppose. My father was afraid that I'd be tracked down by some of the Brigade dregs, though, so he arranged to change my name."

"What's your real name?"

"I can't tell you. My father made me promise not to ever tell anyone. Fluhr was my grandmother's maiden name. Heidi is just something we... well, we made it up. Eamon, I know how curious you are, and I know it would be a walk in the park for you to find out who I really am, but I would genuinely appreciate it if you didn't. I'm Heidi Fluhr, now, and I will be for the rest of my life."

I drained my glass and poured some more merlot into it.

"So," I said, as I freshened her glass, "why are you telling me this now?"

"Because of the way you talked about your client last night. You were furious that he had lied to you. I was worried that, if we kept seeing each other, you might do something really stupid at some point and run some kind of detective check on me. If you did, you'd find that I materialized several years ago, with no background at all. I didn't want you to find out that way."

"You thought I'd be angry."

"Wouldn't you?"

"I don't know. I think I'd probably be more curious than upset."

"Well, how in hell could I know that?"

I looked at her for the first time since she had revealed her past. Her eyes were glossy wet. She was just seconds from a major dam break.

"Come here," I said.

She fell into my arms. She didn't bawl, as I had thought she might. That was probably something she'd never do, at least with me around. She had invested most of her life in becoming independent. She wasn't about to risk that over a guy like me by falling apart. It would have given me way too much power over her.

"You are so hard to talk to," she said. "You have all these walls thrown up. Every time I try to get close to you, to understand how you feel, what you think, I hit this barrier. You either toss off some one-liner and change the subject, or you get all quiet, and that's the end of the conversation."

"I..."

"No, don't say anything. I have to get this out, because if I don't I never will. I never told you about my past because—damn it, Eamon—I didn't know if I could *trust* you. Fact is, I don't know anything about you at all. We go out, we stay in, we have a good time together, but it's all *surface* with you. It's like that bulletproof vest you keep in your closet at the Russian Hill house. Nothing gets through. Looking at you is like looking at a reflection. There's no depth."

"Maybe there's just not that much there," I said.

"I don't think so. I want to know things. I'm a woman, you know. Sometimes I need more than just company."

She disentangled herself from my arms and walked over to my workbench on the other side of the living room.

"I've sat on the couch and watched you work on your instruments for months," she said, as she reached out and ran one finger across the dreadnaught lying on a workpad. "Yet,

I don't have a clue what it feels like to you. I don't know what you find in the wood that excites you, or raises your spirits, or simply inspires you. You work, and the work is beautiful, and I think you're proud of it, but I don't know for sure because you never show me any of that feeling.

"When I visit one of my artist clients, I see their passion in action. They rant, they rave, they throw paint and clay around the room. They cry when the work doesn't meet their expectation. Last year, someone broke into your house here and bludgeoned Taylor Chu to death with the neck of an instrument you were building. You never seemed to grieve, either over the lost work or over Chu. I just don't get that."

"I don't know whether it's possible for you to compare me with one of your artists."

"Why not? You create beauty and utility from dead trees, Eamon. Isn't that art? Doesn't it take the soul of an artist?"

"Maybe it's just a craft."

"And you're just a craftsman."

I sipped the wine.

"Something like that."

"So it's about achieving some kind of soulless perfection? Because I just don't understand that."

"It's not like that. I don't know if I can explain it in a way that will satisfy you."

"Try me."

I thought about it for a second. I took a sip of the wine and made a stab at it.

"I never intended to be a private eye," I said. "Up until I blew out my knee, I was going to be a football player. There's nothing poetic or particularly artful in playing a kids' game for a living. When that disappeared, I finished school and screwed around for a while, until it struck me one day that I might be a decent cop.

"I was wrong. I never really liked the force. Too many rules. Too much politics. All the bullshit you can eat. I found nothing noble or enriching in it. It was just one long string of lowlifes trying to fuck each other over, and that was just the station house. So, when the opportunity to hang out a shingle came along, I jumped on it. I never planned on my partner dying over dinner in the Mark Hopkins, so I had to learn it all on the job. That was over a decade ago, around the time you were fleeing Europe.

"The instrument building clears my head. That's just about it. I don't spend a lot of time musing over the esthetics. Fact is, I don't spend a lot of time thinking about my life at all. I do what I have to, I enjoy the good times, I try to forget the bad times, and that's just about all there is. There isn't this constant stream of consciousness monologue running through my head. I just don't work that way."

She stared at me for a tick, and then walked over to the wall where I had my instruments hanging from padded bifurcated hooks. She pulled down the Martin D-28 copy I had made two years earlier and handed it to me.

"Play it," she said.

I held the instrument in my hands and felt the twelve layers of nitrocellulose lacquer squirt around under my palm like baby oil. The rosewood glowed warmly underneath the shellac sealer. I had used tung oil on the neck to make it faster. I remembered the day I had buffed it out.

"I can't," I said. "I never could. You might not believe it, dear, but I have absolutely no musical ability. I can strum a couple of chords, and I can play a couple of pentatonic scales, but I don't know the first song on this thing by heart."

"You're joking," she said.

"Not at all. Sometimes people ask me if I can play every instrument in here, and I'll just tell them that each one takes a different learning curve. I never bother to tell them that I never learned to play any of them, at least not competently."

"Then why…"

"It's an intellectual exercise. No, wait. That's almost completely—but not entirely—incorrect. It's an *anti-*intellectual exercise. This is something I lose myself in. I come here, to this shop, to take my mind off everything else. When my work starts to close in on me, or when I feel like I can't take one more cuckolded husband without cutting loose in Ghirardelli Square with the shotgun in the closet, then I come here and challenge myself to block it all out."

"This is therapy," she said.

"If you want it that way."

She finished her glass of wine.

"Give me that," she said.

I handed her the guitar. She cradled it in her lap, and immediately started fingerpicking a rendition of Rodrigo's *Concierto de Aranjuez*. I knew the piece by heart, if only to hum it, from a copy I had on CD by Pepe Romero.

I refilled my wineglass and listened as she played almost the entire *adagio*. It wasn't flawless, but it was delightful.

She finished and hung the guitar back on the wall.

"Shit hot," I said, not much more than a whisper.

"I could have done it better on that Hauser classical copy on the other wall," she said.

"I had no idea."

"You never asked. And I never volunteered. Kind of mirrors our relationship, doesn't it?"

"Well, live and learn."

"Die and forget it all," she said. "Here you thought I sell art because I can't create it."

"It's not that," I said. "I guess—please don't take this the wrong way—but I guess I just thought of you…"

"As the girl you've been fucking for the past year?"

"Wait."

"No. It's okay, Eamon. I don't mind being the girl you've been fucking for the past year. As it happens, I kind of like that. It's uncomplicated. After the shit I've put up with in my life, *uncomplicated* kind of suits me. I just don't want you to take me for granted."

"I don't think I could," I said. "Not anymore."

"There's a lot more where that came from. Someday, when you're really vulnerable, I'll torture you with my poetry. Here's the deal, okay? I'll try really hard not to lie to you again, and you try really hard not to make assumptions about me. Can we start there?"

I looked at her again and tried this time to actually see her.

I had made a mistake in underestimating this girl. I had presumed our dalliance was nothing more than that, and it would run as long as it was good, and would end when it turned bad, and that was all there was to it.

I hadn't lied to Heidi, or whatever her real name was. I have never been an introspective person. I don't question my actions very often, perhaps because I don't deliberate them in advance. I spend a lot of time reacting to the twists my cases toss at me and waiting to ask the right question of the wrong person, so that they try to stop me from asking any more. That's when I know I'm on the right track.

I heard somewhere that individuals who volunteer to pursue dangerous occupations must avoid imagination, because if they really stopped for a moment to consider what could happen to them in the course of their pursuits, they would never get out of bed in the morning.

Had I approached my relationships with others the same way? Was I only capable of superficial physical closeness, because I denied myself actual intimacy?

Now, as I looked beyond that surface, I saw Heidi's real face, the Zen face that I tried to find in myself during my meditative wrestling with the exotic hardwoods in my shop. It was as if someone had been holding a gauzy sheet before her that was suddenly stripped away, and I saw that she was neither exotic nor alluring, but simply *there*. I, the most unromantic person I know, had romanticized her into some kind of sexual icon. Her real face, the one I had allowed my hormones to mask, began to shine through, the way you can look at a picture a dozen times, and only on the thirteenth do you see what it really depicts.

She was still beautiful, but it was not the overtly sexual, lascivious kind of beauty that had first attracted me to her. When I stopped looking at her through lustful eyes, I saw, for perhaps the first time, the person behind the face.

"What are you thinking?" she asked.

"I'm not sure. I think I'm seeing you differently."

"Uh-oh. This could be dangerous."

"I can handle dangerous," I said. "What I'm not certain I can handle is permanence."

"Well, thank God for that!" she said, as she emptied the last of the merlot into her glass. "I don't care for permanence, Gold. I don't even know if I care for love. I do care— deeply—about respect. I think I'm lucky to have whatever it is we have. I also think you should feel lucky to have me around. I respect myself that much."

"I never gave it that much thought, I suppose."

"Now's a good time."

I stared at my empty glass, trying to come up with something to say.

"Okay, let's try it this way," she said. "Just a simple exercise. I'll tell you the truth, and you don't shut me out. You tell me how you feel, as closely as you can approximate it. You tell me when I'm pissing you off, or what would piss you off, so I don't have to go around guessing all the time. You're a stoic old goat, you know that?"

I smiled and tried again to see her real face.

It was easier this time.

"Thank goodness your other attributes make up for it," she said. "And if I don't get some air, the wine is going to give me a headache, so let's go for a walk on the beach."

"Yes ma'am," I said.

THIRTY-FOUR

It was a long, busy night. Sometime during the blue-black hours, it started to rain. My Montara house is notable for a lack of insulation, outside what is called for by code, and when it rains the drops can make a racket on the asphalt roof. We awoke to gray, dreary skies and rain that varied from moment to moment from drizzle to downpour, as only rain near the ocean can manage.

I dropped Heidi off at her house, and then headed for my place on Russian Hill. According to the Weather Channel, it was going to rain for several days, so I grabbed my black oilskin duster from the living room closet and headed over to Jefferson Street to check my office. I got there around nine.

There was a message on my machine.

"Mr. Gold, this is Russell Skeen. I need to see you right away. Could you come to my office this morning?"

I had apparently just missed the call, as the machine said it had come in at eight-forty-nine.

I picked up the phone and dialed the Civic Center.

"Mr. Skeen, this is Eamon Gold. I just got your message."

"Thank you for calling back so soon. I need to talk with you."

"I have a meeting at noon. Maybe this afternoon?"

"No. I need to see you right away. It's rather… delicate."

"Have you received a blackmail note?"

"I can't talk about it over the phone. Please come this morning. I can make it worth your while."

I agreed to see him on the way to Golden Gate Park and racked the receiver.

It was a fifteen-minute drive from my office to the Civic Center. I parked in the deck and made my way up to Skeen's office.

He was waiting for me.

He was sitting behind his desk this time, staring at a sheet of paper lying on the blotter in front of him, when I tapped on his door. He quickly pulled another sheet of paper over the one he had been reading but seemed to relax a bit when he saw it was me.

"Please, come in, Mr. Gold," he said. He was nervous and twitchy, not at all the relaxed, in-command bureaucrat I'd met the previous day.

"What's the paper?" I asked.

He handed it to me.

It was a picture. It was a little grainy, and poorly composed, and it featured a well-framed Russell Skeen lying back on a chaise, naked, his hands clasped behind his head, and his eyes closed in an ecstatic reverie. Crouched next to him, facing the camera, his lips locked firmly around Skeen's phallus, was Asa Corona.

"Whoa," I said.

"What is it?"

"I expected Ty Cannon, not Corona."

"I received this via my fax this morning, just as I was walking into the office."

I checked the top of the page. It listed a phone number, but I was already certain that if I traced it I'd find a booth somewhere.

"There was a demand?"

He handed me the second sheet of the fax. It read: *This is one of several very nice pictures we have at our disposal. We could be convinced to destroy them if Supervisor Fleming votes to restore the private rooms in bathhouses at the next Board meeting.*

"They want you to put some pressure on Fleming," I said.

"There is a proposition set to come before the Board of Supervisors at tomorrow evening's meeting."

"How does Fleming plan to vote?"

"He's in a tight spot. His district is split almost three equal ways between middle-class Hispanic Catholics, blue-collar workers, and latecomers overflowing from the Castro. He's constantly juggling their priorities. It's two-to-one on this issue, though, so he was planning to vote against it."

"Any idea which way the rest of the Board is leaning?"

"Fleming would be a swing vote."

"And he's vulnerable."

"No," Skeen said.

I looked up at him.

"*I* am," he finished.

"Have you told him about this picture?"

"Not yet. I wanted to talk with you first."

I looked at the picture again. Something about it looked very familiar, but I couldn't put my finger on it.

"Do you know when this was taken?"

He nodded.

"Sure. I've only made it with Asa once. It was about three weeks ago."

Before Asa had come to me asking for help.

"It was a slow night," he added. "There were only five or six people there. Some weeknights are like that. I knew most of them. Hell, I'd had most of them, at one time or another. Asa and I started talking, and one thing led to another, and…"

He covered his mouth.

"What am I going to do, Mr. Gold?"

I thought it over for a second.

"Nothing for right now," I said. "I'm hoping to run Asa Corona to ground later today. If I do, maybe I can interdict this extortion attempt. If not... well, you may have to show this to Mr. Fleming."

Skeen shook his head.

"I'd really rather avoid that."

"He does know you're gay."

"Of course. He even knows that I sometimes visit the baths. He counts on it. I'm his source of information regarding what happens there. Sometimes I ferry information back and forth."

"Information? From whom?"

"The people who own the baths are constituents too, Mr. Gold."

"You take messages from JuneBug to your boss?"

Skeen winced.

"Mr. *Bugliosi* was a heavy contributor to Mr. Fleming's last campaign. At the time, we didn't know he owned WaterWorks. After the election, he dropped by to talk with Mr. Fleming about several issues, including the bathhouses problem."

"Where did he stand?"

"Mr. Bugliosi is a businessman. He knows that reinstating the private rooms will increase his profits. Where do you think he falls?"

"Tell me about Tobias Enfante," I said.

"What about him?"

"Anything you've got."

Skeen leaned back in his chair.

"Will this help you get these people off my back?"

"It could."

"You don't think Mr. Bugliosi is sending these extortion demands?"

"I think blackmail is a crime, and JuneBug is a criminal. You do the math. What about Enfante?"

Skeen chewed his thumbnail while he thought that one over.

"He goes by Tobe at the baths. He's one of those guys you read about in the hetero relationships, where he's all smooth and ingratiating at first meeting, and then he turns out to be a malicious spouse-beater."

"He's violent?"

"He's one mean faggot, that boy. Mostly, he likes to use verbal intimidation. If that doesn't work, he shames you."

"Shames?"

"You know, calls you names like Limpdick, or Tinyballs. Nothing outright threatening, but he does it in a crowd, and not just once. That boy has too damn much testosterone."

"How do the other customers at WaterWorks take him?"

"At a distance, mostly. He's not very popular. That might be why he's so rude. He's probably compensating for feelings of rejection."

"Sounds kind of deep to me. You sound like a psychiatrist."

"Psychologist. I was in practice for almost a decade before I got sick of it and went down another road."

"So, in your professional opinion, is Enfante dangerous?"

"Probably. I did see him lose it one night, but not at WaterWorks. We were at this bar in the Castro, place called Whizzers. He tried to cut in on a couple of guys who were dancing, but they didn't want to let him. First he started trading words with the larger guy, and when that didn't work he went ballistic and started shoving him across the floor.

When the kid went down, Enfante kicked him three or four times, once on the side of the face."

"Life of the party," I said. "Yesterday I asked you about the principles in the movement to reinstate the bathhouse private rooms. What role does Enfante play there?"

"He helps to fund the effort."

"With JuneBug's money."

"I don't know, but I suppose you could presume that."

I pointed to the fax on his desk. "May I keep this picture?"

All the color drained from his face.

"What will you do with it?" he asked.

"I'd like to compare it to others I've collected over the last week or so. There's something familiar about it, but I can't figure out what it is."

"You won't...show it around?"

"I could take a retainer and make you a client, if you'd like. That would guarantee you confidentiality."

"You wouldn't show it around if I were your client?"

"I won't show it around in any case. Paying me a retainer is for *your* peace of mind, Mr. Skeen."

He slid the picture across the desk.

"I suppose I have to trust *someone*, don't I?"

I folded the fax and slipped it into the inside pocket of my duster.

"I'd be a good place to start," I said.

THIRTY-FIVE

The rain intensified as I drove west on Geary toward the Great Highway. By the time I reached the intersection at the beach, I could only barely make out the ocean just a couple of hundred yards away.

I turned left, and then made another quick left into Golden Gate Park on Martin Luther King. I cruised by the Tea Garden a couple of minutes later. It was ten-twenty. I wasn't scheduled to meet Asa for another hour and a half. Being very early was fine with me. It was part of my plan.

I pulled my car into a lot on the far side of the deYoung Museum. The museum had been closed for almost a year, while it underwent reconstruction and installation of an underground parking garage. When the downpour started, I'd figured that there wouldn't be any work done on the site for the day, and it made a perfect vantage point to scope out the Tea Garden.

The Zen Garden was at the very back of the Tea Garden. There was no way to access it except through the Main Entrance, which was right across the street from where I was hiding.

There were several possibilities. One was that Asa was sincere about meeting me. If so, he'd show up around noon, alone, and make his way through the Tea Garden to our meeting site.

Another possibility was that Asa was setting me up. After my visit with Russell Skeen that morning, I was more inclined to believe the second option. Somehow, Asa Corona was involved in the blackmail scheme. There were a number of things I couldn't figure out yet, though.

For one, why did he come to me in the first place? If he was part of the extortion conspiracy, why did he want me snooping around? My first impression was that it endowed him with the appearance of innocence. Nobody in his right mind would ask a private cop to investigate a crime in which he was a knowing participant.

He might have come to me to set up his buddies Ty Cannon and Anthony Luft. Maybe he got scared when Luft was killed and figured he could put some distance between himself and Ty Cannon by pretending to be a victim.

That still didn't explain where Tobe Enfante fit into the picture. Maybe I was just running down a blind alley with him. On the other hand, he was actively involved in the movement to reinstate the private sex rooms in the baths, and the most recent extortion note had demanded help in doing that from Supervisor Fleming.

I was still trying to make it all fit together when the Lexus I'd followed the day before pulled up and parked across Hagiwara Tea Garden Drive from the Main Gate.

I pulled a pair of miniature 3x binoculars from my jacket pocket and checked out the license number. It was the same car, all right.

Two men got out and strolled across Hagiwara to the entrance. Like the rest of the park, the Tea Garden was empty because of the torrent. It was possible that the two thugs and I were the only people within a mile.

I didn't see Asa Corona anywhere.

Through my binoculars, I could make out the bulges under the two guys' jackets. They were strapped with some high-caliber hardware.

The taller of the two wore his hair very long and braided in the back. The braid was blond, but the rest of his hair was dirty brown, or at least it looked that way wet.

The other man was about half a foot shorter, maybe five-nine, and built like a fullback. I couldn't tell for certain, but I thought they were the same two joes who had gotten into Tobe Enfante's Lexus the day before. I kind of hoped they were. That would indicate that JuneBug didn't provide him with much of a posse, which was to my advantage.

I watched as the pair lumbered up to the main gate and into the Tea Garden. Most people hang a right at the first intersection inside the garden to make the big scenic circle. These guys made a beeline past the Tea House to the Hagiwara Gate. They were heading straight for the Zen Garden.

I lost them after the Hagiwara Gate, so I stowed my binoculars and made certain I couldn't be seen from the Tea Garden.

It was only eleven-thirty by my watch. I was scheduled to meet with Asa Corona at noon. There was only one way to interpret this new set of events. Braids and the Halfback were positioning themselves to ambush the stupid detective when he showed up to make the meet with Corona.

The real question was, would Asa show up to meet the stupid detective?

It was a certainty that I wouldn't see the two thugs again until at least noon, so I decided to wait and see if Asa kept our appointment. If he did, I was in a good position to grab him and get him away before the gun monkeys could stop me, and then I'd throttle some answers out of him.

It started to rain harder as I moved from my position in the museum construction debris to a more advantageous spot near the Music Concourse across Hagiwara. From this new spot, I could dash out, stick the Browning under Asa's chin, and spirit him away as quietly as possible.

If he resisted, maybe I'd just shoot him and be done with it.

The best part was that now I had a sort of roof over my head, and I wasn't getting drenched by the deluge.

I became so comfortable, in fact, that I almost missed the green Ford cruise up King and turn left onto Hagiwara. I recognized it immediately, and all my cards were reshuffled.

Jack Delroy parked about a hundred feet from the South Gate of the Tea Garden, about a hundred yards to my left. I pulled out my binoculars again and scanned the car. He appeared to be alone.

What in hell, I thought.

The questions were obvious. How did Delroy know I was supposed to meet Asa here, and what connection, if any, did he have with Big and Bigger who were waiting for me in the Zen Garden?

I continued to watch him from the shadows of the Music Concourse, until my watch read ten after twelve. Through the windshield, I saw Delroy hold a cell phone up to his ear. He talked for a couple of moments, and then slowly eased his car back onto Hagiwara to turn back onto King in the direction from which he had come.

I took this opportunity to walk the long way around back to the deYoung. From my previous hiding spot, I saw Enfante's two thugs walk back out of the Garden and take off in the Lexus.

I hung out at the deYoung for another ten minutes, just to assure myself that they weren't trying to draw me out, and then I grabbed my car and left the Park via John F. Kennedy Drive, heading west.

I had a feeling I knew where the Lexus was heading, but I wanted to avoid being caught tailing them. I grabbed some lunch at Historic John's – Sam Spade's Chops with sliced tomatoes seemed somehow appropriate after the last couple of days – and then headed back into the Castro for a quick drive-by.

I slowed up after turning off 20th onto Noe, just enough so I could get a good look. Sure enough, the Lexus was parked in front of the same house where Enfante had picked up the Doublemint Twins the day before.

I was willing to bet that Asa Corona was in there with them, but I didn't want to take the chance that they might answer the bell with a load of deer shot through the mahogany Greene and Greene door. Discretion, in this case, appeared to be the better part of valor, so I drove back through the City to my office at Jefferson.

I parked behind the building and grabbed the shotgun from under the front seat. I left the Python. If the Mossberg didn't get the job done, I sure wasn't going to need a revolver.

My phone rang just as I walked up the stairs to the office. I hung my oilskin duster on the rack to dry, and waited for the message machine to kick in.

The machine beeped, and a familiar voice came over the tinny speaker.

"*This is Asa. I'm sorry I couldn't make it. I really need to talk with someone I can trust. I can't leave a number, but I'll call you back later.*"

The machine beeped again and clicked off.

I picked up the receiver and star-sixty-nined him.

The phone rang twice on the other end, before someone answered.

"Yeah?"

I didn't recognize the voice.

"Put Asa on," I said.

"Who da fuck is this?"

"Who da fuck is *this*?" I asked back. I tried to sound as dumb as the guy I was talking to, but I don't think I was naturally equipped for the job.

"Fuck off," he said, and slammed down the receiver.

I let it go.

Hell, I can tell when I'm not wanted.

I poured myself a shot of Glenlivet from the bottle in my secretary and turned on the radio. I wasn't particular about the station. I just needed a little noise to help me think.

After ten minutes of futile attempts to make all the stray pieces I'd run across fit together into a coherent picture, I decided to try something else. I grabbed my collection of blackmail photos and laid them across the top of my desk.

It was a depressing sight, all these guys humping and blowing away, desperately trying to steal a moment of intimacy on the crowded floor of the WaterWorks pool room. In all except one of them, Ty Cannon squatted, knelt, bent over, or reclined on the chaise, always with the same Botox-inspired, indolent expression on his face. In the last one, the one I'd acquired from Russell Skeen that morning, Cannon was replaced by Asa Corona, but the scenery was still the same.

The scenery was still the same.

"Holy shit," I whispered.

The telephone rang.

I picked it up.

"Mr. Gold?"

"What the fuck are you up to, Asa?"

"I'm sorry. I couldn't get away."

"So you sent some replacements?"

"What?"

"Where are you, Asa?"

"I can't tell you."

I already had a pretty good idea where he was, so I hung up the phone.

I barely had time to take another sip of the Glenlivet before it rang again.

"Quit doing that!" he said. I could almost hear the tears in his voice.

"Quit fucking around with me," I said.

"I couldn't make it today because they were watching."

"Which one? The fireplug, or the one with the blond pigtail?"

There was a long silence.

"I think I'm in big trouble," he said, quietly.

"Tell me something I don't know."

"I don't know who to trust."

"I'm probably not your best choice. If I were you, I'd call the cops."

"I…I can't do that."

"You're dealing with a lot of *can'ts* right now, Asa. Must be tough being you."

"What do you want me to do?"

"I already told you. If they won't let you go, it's kidnapping. Call the cops."

"They won't let me."

"Then call your grandfather. At least let him know you're alive. I think he'd like that."

"You're making fun of me."

"Asa, that's the one thing I'm not doing, because the shit you're into right now is anything but funny. The way I see it, though, you have to grow up someday, and this seems like a good one to start. I suspect that you're deeper into this thing than you've let on, and that means you need to reevaluate the way you're handling your life. You call the cops. We'll take it from there."

He didn't say anything, but I could hear him breathing.

Then he hung up the phone.

I cradled the receiver and pulled a magnifying glass out of my desk drawer to examine the pictures a little more closely.

Hot damn.

I'd found the piece of the puzzle that tied everything together.

I was working on my account books, tallying up Asa's bill, when the phone rang again.

"Did you call here an hour ago?"

It took me a second.

"Oh, Tobe, nice to hear from you."

"Okay, so you know my name. What in hell are you doing calling this number? I thought I told you to lay off."

"Now how would it look if I laid off every time some two-bit hood threatened me? I wouldn't be able to look at myself when I shave in the morning."

"Why did you call here?"

"Wrong number."

"It could be real wrong."

"Is this the part where you tell me you're going to send around a couple of your boys to rough me up a little?"

"Maybe I will."

"Now I know why none of the other boys at WaterWorks will play with you."

"Don't call here again."

"You know, I'd be frightened if at this exact moment I wasn't looking at a picture of you taking it up the chute from some nancy boy."

"What?"

"Thanks for calling, Tobe."

"Wait a min…" he yelled.

I hung up the phone.

Enfante wasn't in any of the pictures spread out in front of me. I figured it wouldn't hurt, though, to sow a little disinformation in the system. If I could keep him off balance, he might think twice about sending over his flying monkeys to squib me.

Sometimes, I am just too clever for my own good.

This would turn out to be one of those times.

THIRTY-SIX

A couple of years ago, I bought a used minivan that I kept in a lot off Jones Street just for occasions like this. Enfante had made my car, so I couldn't use it to stake him out. Besides, I had modified the minivan for comfort, for just those times when I expected to be watching something—or someone—for an extended period. The minivan was dirty and beaten up, and just inconspicuous enough to blend in with just about any background. I had installed a partition between the driver's seat the back seats made of quarter-inch plywood, behind which I could essentially camp out for days if I had to. The rear windows were heavily tinted for privacy.

After rounding up some equipment from my office, I stashed it and my weapons in the back of the van, hidden under the bench seat.

If I was right about what I had seen in the blackmail photos, I needed to get into WaterWorks without being seen. That meant creeping the place after it closed.

I knew from my discussions with Asa that WaterWorks stayed open until at least two in the morning, sometimes later.

By the time I completed all my preparations, Heidi was ready to close the gallery. I left the van parked behind my office and drove her over to the bank to make her deposit. Then we went to Alioto's for dinner on Fisherman's Wharf. It was kind of touristy, but it was also convenient, and I didn't feel much like driving around openly in the City with a mobster gunning for me.

Heidi was still tired from the night before, and I figured I could use a few winks myself, so I drove her home after dinner and dropped by my house on Russian Hill for a nap.

The alarm woke me at two in the morning. I jumped into the shower to wake up, and then girded myself for a little midnight skulkery.

It was still raining off and on when I drove into my space behind the office. I had been walking around with just my Browning for most of the night – practically naked – because I still had the heavy firepower hidden in the back of the van. Now I moved the shotgun to the front and secured it under a towel on the floor between the front seats.

It only took ten or fifteen minutes to make it to WaterWorks. I parked in the same lot down the street where I had staked out the place two days before, and waited.

Around three, I saw the lights go out in Gary Chiklis' office on the second floor. He walked out the front door several minutes later and locked it behind him. I watched him drive off and waited another fifteen minutes before making my move.

Security is my business, sort of. I tend to note what kind of alarm system most people have in their homes when I visit, mostly because I know what they are and how they work. WaterWorks had been notable primarily for its lack of a burglar system, which was going to make my job a whole lot easier.

It took me a couple of minutes to pick the lock on the back door, and then I was inside. I waited for a few minutes for my eyes to adjust to the near-darkness. I had a flashlight, but I wanted to avoid using it if I could, because I was afraid of raising any suspicions outside should the local cops drive by.

Within ten minutes, I could see pretty well, so it was time to start hunting.

I pulled the pictures from my jacket pocket and a miniature Maglite from my belt. I had painted the lens red, a trick I had learned from a friend who is an astronomer. Dark adaptation is very important if you're stargazing, and the red light doesn't cause you to lose that adaptation. It's pretty much the same theory as the red light in a photography darkroom. It's also hard to see from outside a building should anyone be looking.

In the pinkish beam from the Maglite, I examined the pictures again. I circled the pool until I found the right angle, and then I turned and started to scrutinize the wall.

There was a bench secured to the wall with lag bolts. Using the scarlet-tinted light, I angled the beam and ran it along between the slats until I found exactly what I had expected.

There was a minute glint of a reflection from the light. I pulled out a jeweler's loupe, and leaned in closely, still shining the red light on that area of the wall behind the bench.

Through the lens, I saw another lens winking back at me.

Reasoning that anyone who had gone to the trouble to install a hidden camera would probably want a backup, I continued the search. Sure enough, I found the second camera secreted about a foot to the right, and between the next set of slats up from the first.

I switched off the light and pulled out a small toolkit from one of the deep pockets of my jacket. Inside, I had a three-eighths inch ratchet and one of those universal sockets with the spring-loaded needles, designed to fit any bolt.

I loosened and removed the lag bolts securing the bench to the wall and pulled it out of the way.

As I had expected, the cameras were installed behind a portion of the wallboard that had been sawed away and then placed back. The saw marks had been hidden by the slats and uprights on the bench, so that nobody could tell that someone had monkeyed with the drywall.

Using my pocketknife, I wedged the blade into the tiny gap between the wallboard and the patch and wiggled it until it began to come loose. Then I grabbed both sides of the patch and pulled it away from the rest of the wall.

It was a clever installation. The cameras were high-resolution pinhole jobs, the lenses no more than a millimeter in width. They were secured to the back of the wall patch with tiny screws. Wire nuts connected them to a small wire leading to a transformer that was also attached to the patch, which in turn was grafted into a piece of the electrical wiring running through the wall with scotch clips. Once installed, they could be operated indefinitely without a need to replace batteries.

The transformer was also wired to a 2.4 gigahertz wireless transmitter, which presumably sent a signal to a receiver somewhere in the building, or at least nearby.

I reached into another pocket of my jacket and pulled out an almost identical pinhole camera and transmitter. Most of these jobs were made in Japan by a well-known television manufacturer, so no matter whom the ultimate distributor was, they all looked more or less alike.

It took about ten minutes to disconnect the second camera and transmitter, install my replacements, and graft them into the system. The last part was a little tricky, because I had to install the transmitter further back in the wall, where it couldn't be seen, and I had a hard time getting my large hand between the wallboard and the insulation.

When I had completed the switch, I carefully replaced the cutout panel, then slid the bench back into place, and retightened the lag bolts.

After checking around with the Maglite to assure that I hadn't left any tools or debris lying about to testify to my visit, I snuck back out the back door and walked at a leisurely pace across the street to the van.

I didn't leave immediately, though. Instead, I crawled to the back of the van, over the partition I had installed, and opened a plastic storage chest I'd secured there earlier in the day. Inside was a battery-powered camcorder, fully charged, and the receiver for the transmitter I had installed behind the drywall in the pool area. The receiver was designed to operate on either battery or transformer power, and I had just installed new metal hydride batteries that afternoon.

I powered up the camcorder and the receiver and tuned the receiver to the frequency of the transmitter I'd installed inside WaterWorks.

The image on the screen of the camcorder was grainy and indistinct, but I had expected that since it was practically pitch-black in the pool area. The camera was capable of registering images at only a tenth of a lux, which didn't mean a damn thing to me except that the salesman had said you could take some damn fine pornos in a completely dark room. I knew that once the lights were turned on in the pool area the next day, the picture would be as crisp as if I were watching it in my own living room.

I was counting on that.

I had one more stop to make that evening.

I drove further into the Castro and parked about a block from the house on Noe where I had seen Enfante's Lexus pick up the Beastie Boys a couple of days earlier. I was still convinced that Asa was holed up inside, but it was too dangerous to check that theory out.

I went back to the plastic storage bin I'd placed in the rear of the van, and pulled out a GPS tracking unit, similar to the one I'd found underneath my car. This was one of mine, though, and of a slightly more sophisticated design. This model could track a car in real time and display its progress on my computer screen back at the office, or on a cellular PDA I also had packed in the box.

I stashed the unit in my jacket pocket, and hiked nonchalantly around the block, until I was in sight of the house. As I had expected, the Lexus was parked there, in a drive right off the street.

It was four-thirty in the morning, so I wasn't terribly afraid of being detected, unless some pre-dawn jogger ran across me.

I walked across the front lawns of the two houses next to Enfante's, and then up to the Lexus. I had to be careful. I didn't know whether the car had an alarm on it, set to go off if it was disturbed, and I sure didn't want either Enfante or his boogie men to come out looking for whomever was tinkering with their ride.

I lay on the ground behind to the car, and slowly scooted myself under the rear end. When I was in deep enough, I pulled my red-coated Maglite out, flicked it on, and stuck it in my mouth so I'd have both hands free.

Then I mumbled something like *I'll be damned.*

There was already a tracking unit there.

Someone else was already keeping tabs on Enfante's movements.

They had done a pretty neat job of wiring their tracker into the car's electrical system, too, which saved me a lot of effort. I simply attached my tracker next to their tracker using the rare-earth magnetic base, and grafted my power wires into theirs using scotch clips.

The whole operation took about three minutes. I shinnied my way out from under the car and was back in my van in a couple of minutes.

The hot wire the GPS transmitters were grafted into was always hot, which was a bonus. Now I'd be able to tell where the car was even when it was parked. The only thing I had to worry about was whether the owner of the first unit might return to retrieve it, and take mine with him.

My guess, though, was whoever else was tracking Enfante wasn't in any hurry to get their equipment back.

THIRTY-SEVEN

Since I'd pissed Enfante off, I figured it would be a good idea to stay away from my home and office for a while. I decided to set up shop in the van.

I dropped by my house to pick up some clothes and toiletries and drove back over to the parking lot near WaterWorks. The rain had returned after a brief lull, and it was cool enough to sleep in the back of the van, where I had set up a sleeping bag.

I woke around nine. Even through the darkly tinted van windows, I could tell that the sky was leaden and roiling. The rain bounced off the top of the van, creating an incessant dull roar. I avoided it by listening to CDs through headphones.

WaterWorks opened around noon. I watched as Gary Chiklis drove up and parked at eleven-thirty, and Chris Driscoll followed him about ten minutes later.

I reached over and switched on my camcorder and the 2.4-gigahertz receiver. The LCD screen on the recorder stabilized in only a few seconds and, as I had predicted, the picture from inside WaterWorks was vivid and defined, if somewhat static. I watched for a few moments while Driscoll cleaned the pool and checked the water, and then switched off the equipment until something interesting happened.

I pulled out my PDA, dialed up the GPS unit through the cellular connection, and checked Enfante's Lexus. It was still parked on Noe.

I was already a little stiff from lying around in back of the van. The parking lot was attached to a small strip mall, which included a chain sub shop. I crawled out the back of the van and walked to the shop, where I used the bathroom and grabbed an Italian sandwich and a drink to go.

After eating, I checked the PDA again. The Lexus was on the move, but it was heading south, not north. I watched as it hit the PCH and followed it all the way to San Mateo.

JuneBug's offices were in San Mateo. Visiting the boss. The question was, did Enfante have the thugs with him? There was only one dependable way to find out.

I dialed Enfante's number. It rang a couple of times before someone picked up.

"Yeah?"

It was the same guy I'd spoken with the first time I called.

"Is Mr. Enfante available?" I asked.

"Who is this?"

"Fred. I work at WaterWorks. Mr. Chiklis asked me to call."

"Chiklis? What's he want?"

"He had to run an errand, but said he needed to talk with Mr. Enfante today. He was wondering whether Mr. Enfante planned to come by the baths."

"How in hell would I know?"

"Do you know when Mr. Enfante will be back? I'd really hate to tell Mr. Chiklis I couldn't get up with him. I'm new, and I really need this job."

"Hold on."

The phone was muffled for a moment. I could hear Thug One talking things over with Thug Two, which answered my question. If Asa was still at the Noe house, he was being well-guarded.

Thug One returned to the phone.

"Tobe should be back around two-thirty. He just had to make a run to deposit some money. I'll have him call Gary. All right?"

"That would be fine. Can I tell Mr. Chiklis who I spoke with? He'll want to know."

"Tell him you talked with Greg."

"Thanks, Mr...."

"Greg."

I hit the *END* button on the cell phone and wrote *Greg* down on my notepad. Of course, I had no idea which one was Greg, but at least I could stop calling him Thug One.

I pulled out a book by Tom Clancy that I had been trying to read for several months and made another stab at it to pass the time. The rain just kept rolling down.

Enfante's Lexus was back at the Noe house the next time I checked, around two-thirty. I had been keeping an eye on the front door at WaterWorks, but nobody I recognized had entered or left since Driscoll had arrived. I made a note to check the PDA every fifteen minutes and went back to reading.

When I fired up the PDA at three-forty-five, the GPS showed the Lexus just a couple of blocks away. I stowed the book and took a look through the window I had sawn in the plywood partition between the front and back of the van.

Enfante pulled up beside WaterWorks a couple of minutes later. He had the short thug—*Greg*, maybe?—in the car with him. Enfante walked into WaterWorks alone, leaving his thug in the car.

I switched on the receiver and the camcorder. When Enfante didn't appear within a couple of minutes, I figured he had gone up to Chiklis' office, so I shut down the devices to save battery power.

Fifteen minutes later, when Enfante hadn't left WaterWorks yet, I turned the camcorder and receiver back on. As the image cleared, I saw Enfante on a chaise. He was naked, lying on his back with his hands behind his head. He was wearing sunglasses, so I couldn't tell whether he was awake or asleep. He might have been taking a nap, which at that moment seemed like a pretty good idea. Skulking around town all night had left me a little logy.

A couple of minutes after I started watching, a young man walked over to Enfante and sat on the chaise next to him. He was slim and hairless from the neck down, with this skinny little Boston Blackie moustache and a Caesar haircut. Other than a watch, he was naked also.

He spoke with Enfante for a moment, almost as if asking whether Tobe was awake. Tobe nodded, and said something back to him. I could tell that he was smiling, but I couldn't read his lips.

I reached down and hit the *RECORD* button on the camcorder.

Enfante and the new guy talked about something for a minute or so, and then Enfante opened his legs and placed one foot on the floor on either side of the chaise. The kid sat on the end of the chaise and leaned over.

I won't describe in detail what happened next. Let's just say I captured it in crystal clear digital color on the camcorder, and it took less than three minutes.

When he was finished, the kid wiped his mouth with his index and middle finger and said something to Enfante. Enfante nodded and said something back. Whatever he said didn't sit well with the kid, who frowned a little. He said something with the slight toss of his head, and Enfante pushed himself up on one elbow. He made a brief comment, and I could almost see the kid blanch on the miniature camcorder screen. He stood up, walked away quickly, and headed straight for the dressing room.

A couple of moments later, I saw him walk out the WaterWorks front door and hurry to his car.

I wondered whether he would ever return.

―――――

I left the camcorder running just in case anything interesting happened and dialed the Noe house on my cell phone. It was answered after two rings.

"Yeah?"

"Is this Greg?"

"No this is Barney."

"Thanks," I said, and ended the call.

Now I knew something else. The guy with the long blond braid was Barney. The short stubby square guy was Greg.

My guess was that Greg was the smart one, since they let him answer the phone when both were at the house.

When I looked at the camcorder, Enfante was still lying on the chaise. He had the sunglasses back on, and he was breathing deeply. It looked like he was asleep.

He wasn't the only one. I trained my binoculars on the Lexus and saw Greg's head leaning backward against the headrest. His mouth was open. He appeared to be snoring.

Nothing like a slow rainy day to bring on the sandman.

I thought about it for a second and decided to stir up the pot a little.

I rummaged around in the plastic storage bin until I found what I wanted, and stowed it in my jacket pocket. Then I crawled out the back of the van and jogged across the street to the WaterWorks lot.

I didn't make it very artful. I just jerked open the driver side door of the Lexus.

"Hi, Greg!" I said.

He snorted and opened his eyes.

I shot pepper spray into them.

He was stunned for just a half-second, and then the burn started. He screamed and raised his hands toward his face.

Before he got there, I swung up from the rocker panel as hard as I could. I connected with his chin. His head snapped back. In a few seconds, he was snoring peacefully again, his breaths making little bubbles in the stream of blood coagulating around his nostrils.

I was back in the van in less than a minute. On the screen of the camcorder, Tobe Enfante lounged serenely, completely unaware that I had just coldcocked his driver.

————

Greg was still out cold when Enfante walked out of WaterWorks. The rain was coming down in sheets again, and he covered his head with his jacket as he ran to the Lexus. He beat on the passenger side window a couple of times, and I thought I saw his lips move in a silent curse through the binoculars.

Then he stopped, peered more closely through the cascade of water on the window, and I saw him run around to the driver's side. He pulled open the door, and grabbed Greg by the lapels, trying to wake him. Greg's head seemed to bobble a little, but I couldn't tell whether that was voluntary or simply a reaction to being jerked around.

Enfante flicked the automatic lock lever on the door and dashed back around to the passenger's side. I didn't blame him. I wouldn't have wanted to try to lug Greg's dead weight out of the car either.

A couple of moments later, my cell phone rang.

"Hello," I said.

"What the fuck are you up to?" he said.

"Tobe? Is that you?"

"You know damn well who it is. What did you do to my driver?"

"Come again?"

"My driver! He's unconscious and bleeding all over the damn place. You know how hard it is to get blood out of leather?"

"Tobe, I really don't have a clue what you're talking about. Maybe you should call the cops."

"I don't need the cops to deal with a pissant shit like you. You don't know who you're dealing with."

"If I had a clue what you were talking about, I'd probably tell you to bite me. Didn't you just tell me to lay off the Corona case? So, I'm doing what you said. Hell, Corona has Full Moon Security on a retainer. What's he need me for?"

There was a long silence on his end.

"What the fuck?" he said, finally. "You saying you really don't know what I'm telling you?"

"I've been lying around for most of the day, reading a book. All of a sudden, you call yelling about your driver.

How am I supposed to know what you've gotten yourself into? Where are you, anyway?"

"Never mind. I got stuff to do. You better not be fuckin' around with me, Gold, you understand?"

"Hey, you don't have to hit me over the head with a hammer. Tell you what, though. If you happen to run across Asa Corona, you might want to ask him to give me a call. I need to know where to send his bill."

He didn't say anything back. There was a crisp *beep*, and he was off the line.

I watched through the binoculars as he opened the passenger door and tugged Greg across the front seat. Then he dashed around in the driving rain to the driver's side, slid in behind the wheel, and threw up a rooster tail of mud as he peeled out of the parking lot toward the Castro.

I decided it was time to head back to the barn. My work here was done.

THIRTY-EIGHT

I sat in my office, reading the *Chronicle*, when Crymes called.

"We found Cannon," he said. He didn't sound happy about it.

"What's he say?"

"Not a damn thing. City utility got called because of a flooding situation near a small drainage ditch in Daly City. Seems the water couldn't flow through the culvert because of the dead bloating dick smoker stuffed into it."

"You're sure it's Cannon?"

"He still had his ID in the back pocket. The crime lab boys are running his prints and dentals."

"How was he killed?"

"Standard guinea goodbye. Took a coupla .22 longs behind the ear, and one up through the chin."

"I take it the bullets are still inside."

"In splinters. The M.E. will dig them all out, and we'll see if there's any way to piece them back together to get a ballistics pattern. Won't matter though. The piece they used is probably at the bottom of the bay."

"Sounds professional."

"So, you think maybe I ought to consider looking up JuneBug?"

"Do you have any reason to believe he was behind it?"

"No. I just like to yank his chain once in a while."

I folded the paper and put it aside.

"I have a better idea," I said. "How would you like to find the camera they used to shoot the blackmail pictures?"

"You know where it is?"

"I think I can locate it. Why don't you meet me over at WaterWorks in a couple of hours? I'll explain when we get there."

I needed the time to put together part of my plan against Enfante.

I had a pretty high-quality video of Enfante on the receiving end of a hummer from Hairless Harry at WaterWorks. Now I needed to do some work on it.

I fired up the desktop computer and plugged the digital output from my camcorder into the USB slot. My video card did the rest. In about five minutes, I had a sharp, high-fidelity color video grab of Enfante getting his ashes hauled. The best part was, it had the exact same background as the blackmail pictures.

I printed the picture out on some glossy photo paper and made three or four more copies for good measure. I figured I might need them later. Better to have them and not need them than need them and not have them.

I pulled together all my equipment and put together a folder. Then I packed some tools. The last thing I did was move my weapons from the van to my car. I didn't want to take the chance that anyone might recognize the white rental van that sat in the parking lot across from WaterWorks all day.

Crymes was waiting for me in the parking lot when I got to the baths.

"Nice coat," he said, when he saw my duster. "You auditioning for a wild west show?"

"Yippee ki yay," I said, trying really hard to sound like Bruce Willis. "Why didn't you wait for me inside?"

"You know," he said.

We walked in, and Chris Driscoll greeted us from the front desk.

"Mr. Gold! Finally got seduced by the Dark Side, I see. This your date?"

Crymes growled something and flashed his shield.

"Sorry officer," Driscoll said.

"That's *Detective*," Crymes said back. "With a capital '*D*'. We need to see Mr. Chiklis."

Driscoll picked up the telephone and buzzed the upstairs office. Seconds later, Chiklis hit the bottom the stairs.

"Mr. Gold," he said, as he shook my hand. "Nice coat."

"Thanks. This is Detective Crymes," I said.

"Pacifica Police," Crymes finished.

"You're out of your jurisdiction," Chiklis said. "Social call?"

"Hardly," Crymes said. "You're aware of the blackmail pictures that have been taken in your... uh, club?"

"Mr. Gold told me about them."

"And the murder of Anthony Luft?"

"Yes. Terrible tragedy. What can I do for you?"

Crymes looked over at me.

"Maybe we should take this upstairs," I said.

We followed Chiklis up to the second story office. Unlike my previous visits, the blinds over the picture window opening to the pool area were raised. Crymes strolled over to the window and looked down. He shook his head.

"Jesus," he said.

I pulled the folder with all the pictures I had collected during my interviews and placed it on the coffee table in front of the couch.

"I've been interviewing a number of your patrons," I told Chiklis. "Asa Corona gave me a list of people to talk with, people who might know what happened to Anthony Luft. I'm afraid we have some more bad news, Mr. Chiklis."

I looked over at Crymes. He was still gazing down on the scene around the pool.

I cleared my throat.

He looked up at us.

"Oh, yeah. Bad news, Mr. Chiklis. It seems that Ty Cannon's been killed also."

"Oh, my god," Chiklis said, sitting heavily on the couch. "When? Where?"

"*When* we don't know yet," Crymes said. "*Where* we're not sure about. He was found stuffed into a storm drain in Daly City. Someone shot him in the head."

Crymes seemed to draw the description out for maximum effect.

"Christ," Chiklis said, his hand covering his mouth.

"That's two murders *in my jurisdiction* that are connected with this blackmail case. Gold here thinks he knows something about the camera used to take the pictures."

"Take a look," I said, pointing to the pictures I had spread out on the coffee table. "Each of these pictures were given to me by people being blackmailed by the same person or persons. Here's the first one I received, of Asa Corona with Ty Cannon. Here's Barrett Efird with Ty Cannon. Greg Lyles, Steve Csaba, Miles Nickelby, all with Ty Cannon. All blackmailed."

I pointed to the picture of Russell Skeen.

"Russell Skeen, the assistant to Supervisor Fleming. A liaison between the Board of Supervisors and the gay community in SoMa and the Castro. Only, here he isn't with Ty Cannon. Instead, he's with Asa Corona."

"Why, do you suppose?" Chiklis asked.

"Perhaps because by the time this picture was taken, Ty Cannon wasn't around anymore. He was either on the run, or already stuffed in the sewer pipe," Crymes said.

Chiklis winced.

"Notice anything about these pictures?" I asked.

They both looked from one photo to the other.

"They're obviously all taken at WaterWorks," Chiklis said. "I recognize the background. I don't understand, though. We don't allow cameras in the pool area. No cameras at all past Chris Driscoll's desk downstairs. We try to protect our customers' privacy."

"Take a closer look," I said. "At the background, not the people."

Crymes caught it first.

"Damn, Gold. They're all identical."

"Meaning the camera that took these pictures was in the same place every time."

"How in hell could anyone do that?" Chiklis asked.

I gathered my pictures and placed them back in the folder.

"Mr. Chiklis," Crymes said, "Gold and I will have to take a look down in the pool area."

Chiklis looked back and forth at us for a moment.

"Come with me," he said.

We followed him down the stairs, past Chris Driscoll, and through the door to the locker room.

Crymes tried to keep his eyes straight ahead as we made our way through the group of a dozen or so naked men congregated in the area. They had been laughing about something when we opened the door. Now they stood silently watching as the obvious cop cruised by them.

There was a swinging door at the other end of the locker room. Chiklis held it open for us.

Even though I had been in this room the night before, I was unprepared for the solid wave of humidity that slammed into me as I entered the pool area. Apparently Chiklis cranked up the heat when customers were on the premises.

Probably to avoid shrinkage.

There were, maybe, twenty or thirty young men arranged casually around the pool. To our right, as we walked into the area, one muscular youth had another pushed up against the wall as he rammed him from behind. They were oblivious to us for about ten seconds, before the kid squeezed against the wallpaper opened his eyes and almost panicked.

On the other side of the pool, a couple that had been enjoying an oral interlude disengaged and rolled over on their backs to inspect us.

"It's okay," Chiklis announced. "This isn't a bust. These men are trying to find the people who killed Little Tony. They'll only be here for a few minutes. Meanwhile, please enjoy a drink on the house."

The crowd around the pool relaxed, but only a little. Within moments, half of them had wrapped their lower torsos in towels and were lounging on chairs pretending to ignore us. The other half congregated around the bar.

I knew exactly where I was going, but I made a show of walking around the pool, examining a picture I held in my hand, and looking for just the right perspective.

When I was right in front of the camera I'd discovered the night before, I checked the picture again, and then turned to look over the wall. I pulled a magnifying glass from my pocket and began to look at the drywall between the slats of the bench.

"What's in the other pocket?" Crymes asked. "A deerstalker?"

"No," I said. "It's either a salami, or I'm happy to see you. Wait a minute."

The minute hole leading to the first camera lens fell into line with the glass. I pulled a pen from my shirt pocket and drew a circle around it.

Then I pulled Swiss Army knife from my pants pocket, opened the long blade, and poked it through the drywall.

"Hey!" Chiklis yelped.

"It's okay," Crymes said. "If there's nothing there, we'll see to it you're reimbursed for repairs."

I quickly cut out a four-inch square from the drywall, then wedged my blade into the crack and levered the patch from the rest of the wall. When it cleared, I grabbed the sides with both hands, pulled the patch through the slats of the bench, and turned it over.

"CMOS video camera," I said. "About the size of a dime."

"I'll be damned," Chiklis said.

I reached into the hole and pulled the transmitter loose, being very careful not to cut the connections I'd made to the camera I'd installed over the first one. I wanted it to continue functioning.

"This is a wireless video setup," I said, holding the entire assembly out to Crymes. "I use them in my surveillance work sometimes. The transmitter sends out a 2.4 gigahertz signal, undetectable with standard radio equipment. You can pick up the picture anywhere within, say, five hundred feet of the transmitter."

"On a television?" Crymes asked.

"Yes, on a television that has the receiver attached. Without the receiver, you'd never see the signal. A lot of people use some kind of digital camera attached to the receiver, so that they get a nice crisp picture."

"This nice crisp picture," Crymes said. "Would it look like a photograph?"

"There are hardware peripherals around that can freeze the video image and produce a still picture, sure. The end result would be a very high definition image. It would look like something taken with a film camera."

"How did it get there?" Chiklis asked.

"Funny you should ask that," Crymes said. "Mr. Chiklis, as the manager of this club, I think you have a lot of questions to answer."

"Me! You think I put it there?"

"The way I see it," Crymes said, "it had to be someone who had access to the baths, probably after hours."

By now, the crowd that had been eyeing us suspiciously had begun to find its way around the hole in the wall. I could hear whispers between them.

A camera?

They've been photographing us?

Is that legal?

I think it's time to go.

The nerve!

Chiklis turned to them.

"I'm sorry, gentlemen. Perhaps I should have said something earlier. Someone—I have no idea who—has been extorting money from a very small group of WaterWorks members. I can assure you that neither I nor the owners had any idea that a camera had been hidden in the wall. I only found out about it just now. I can understand if you should wish to leave, but I would like to assure you that we value your privacy very highly here, and I'd hate to lose your business. I can't speak for the owner, but as manager I would like to offer each of you a free month's membership. I can assure you that, from this point on, you should have no fear of being photographed at WaterWorks."

It was a pretty speech. For a second, I almost believed him. I also felt just a little sorry for the camera I'd left hidden in the wall.

I got over it, though.

Chiklis turned to Crymes and me.

"Gentlemen, I need to pour a little oil on the water, here. Would you like to wait for me in my office?"

"Just a minute," Crymes said. "I'm not sure yet that I don't want to arrest you."

"Oh, for Christ's sake," Chiklis said. "This is my business. I'm not going to run away. Here, take my driver's license. Take my whole wallet, if you like. I haven't done anything wrong, and I'll be upstairs in just a few minutes, as soon as I can calm things down out here."

Chiklis handed me his wallet. I offered it to Crymes, but he held up his hands. Probably afraid of being accused of skimming if anything in the wallet came up missing. I shrugged and placed the wallet in my pocket.

"We'll wait upstairs," I said. "I think I speak for Detective Crymes, though, when I say I'd rather you don't take a lot of time."

"Of course."

He turned back to the irritable crowd of young men and started to address their concerns. Crymes and I walked back through the locker room, where the other crowd of men were already talking in low tones about the camera. Apparently the word was spreading fast. Chiklis would be lucky to have any customers at all the next day.

Back up in the office, Crymes again walked over to the picture window and watched the scene below.

"Afraid he's going to bolt?" I asked.

"Of course. What do you make of all this?"

"Hard to say. Now we know how the blackmail photos were taken, which is more than we knew before. Makes me wonder about Anthony Luft, now."

"How's that?"

"I always figured, as a photographer, he was involved in the scheme somehow. I had him pegged as the guy who took the blackmail pictures. Now I'm not so sure."

"Why? Just because whoever took the pictures used a remote video camera rather than film?"

"Partly."

"I don't know," Crymes said. "Seems to me that a photographer would know about all kinds of ways to get a shot of someone, including digital means. Luft isn't cleared yet."

"What do you think about Chiklis?" I asked.

"He had access to the club after hours."

"He's also been completely cooperative to this point."

"You want a list of all the perps I've busted over the years that went out of their way to cooperate with me? Some guys figure they're not gonna get popped, no matter what. Maybe Chiklis is one of them."

I still couldn't tell him what I was up to, or that I would probably know before the night was over who had actually placed the cameras in the wall.

Hell, I couldn't even tell him there was more than one camera.

"That wasn't what I was talking about, though," Crymes said, after a few seconds. He was still looking out the picture window at the pool.

"Say again?"

"When I asked what you make of all this. I meant *this,*" he said, pointing out the window. "All this faggot shit."

"Feeling a little threatened?" I asked.

"Me? Naw. I just don't get it. I've been a cop over twenty years. I've seen everything, even that kind of stuff down there. I don't shock easy. I gotta tell you, though, if I'm bangin' the missus, and someone walks in the door, I'm not going to just keep layin' pipe. Understand?"

"I think. You're a decent guy, though. You have values that you don't compromise."

"And these queer boys? They aren't decent?"

"Sure they are. But a major part of their lives is made of compromise. They spend the first decade telling themselves they're not gay. The second decade they face up to not being straight, but still make sure everybody else thinks they are. From then on, they're compensating for discrimination."

"Discrimination?"

"Beat up some guy because he's black or Asian these days, and see if the feds don't come down on you like a sack of bricks for hate crimes. Beat up a homosexual, though, and it's just another fag-bashing. Most times, the cops won't even take it seriously."

"Yeah. I've seen that happen…"

"It's all about compromise. These guys, some of them at least, guys like Asa Corona, feel like they can't express their real feelings for other guys in public. So, they do it wherever they can. The baths are a safe territory. Maybe the first time you come in, you just talk with a couple of guys, have a drink, maybe watch some of the action. The second or third time you come in, you're a little more relaxed, maybe you sneak off to a corner somewhere and let some guy suck you off. By the fifth time, you've rationalized the whole thing as a necessary evil. From there on, it doesn't seem to matter much who's watching."

"Maybe," he said. "I guess I just don't understand it."

"You're looking at it through a straight cop's eyes."

"And you? How are you looking at it?"

I thought about that one for a second.

"Good question. I thought I was all jake with the gay thing. Live and let live, that sort of approach. Some of the people I've met the last week or so, man, they are *suffering.* This guy Greg Lyles got married just to prove he wasn't some kind of freak. Steve Csaba. A fuckin' *football* player. I mean, is there any greater icon for manhood out there than a defensive tackle? He's scared to death his teammates will find out he's a butt pirate, and the whole game will be ruined for him. Miles Nickelby makes out like being blackmailed is no big deal, but he knows he'd embarrass his Republican bosses if word got out. So, he sits in his window and fantasizes about schtupping a television actor who's filming a show outside his apartment, and then comes to a place like this to get some real action. It all kind of puts a human face on the whole gay-straight thing."

"Yeah. I can see that. I knew a cop once, was gay. He tried to hide it, but you know cops. Sooner or later, everyone's in on the secret. Once they found out, he was in hell. The other guys, a bunch of testosterone cases, they'd put panties and dildoes and shit in his locker. He just trashed it all and went on with the job, like nothin' had happened."

"Tough deal," I said.

"More than tough. You have any idea how hard it was for me to walk into a sex store and buy that damn dildo?"

We both chuckled.

"Some weird shit to sort out," I said.

"Damn near put me in therapy. You think maybe this guy Chiklis is on the up and up?"

"I don't know," I said. "I just don't know."

Several moments later, Chiklis tromped back up the stairs, and walked into his office.

"Thanks for killing my business, guys," he said, as he crossed to his desk and sat down. "Half those fellows will drive to Berkeley to hang out at The Sauna before they drive six blocks to come here again."

"I think you should worry about more than this bathhouse," Crymes said.

"Like I said downstairs, I don't have any idea how that camera got into the wall. I just manage this place, keep the books, keep the place running."

"This building is owned by JuneBug?" Crymes asked.

"Mr. Bugliosi," he said. "Yeah. We don't dare call him JuneBug around here. He has a temper."

"What about Tobe Enfante?" I asked. "What's his role?"

"He's just a bagman," Chiklis said. "He drops by several times a week, takes Mr. Bugliosi's cut. Sometimes he hangs around, carves off a little tail."

I thought about the picture I hadn't shown them, of Enfante getting blown by the guy with the cheesy moustache.

"When I visited the other day, you had to go to him to get permission to give me some telephone numbers. Sounds like he's more than just a bagman."

"He's Mr. Bugliosi's primary contact with the club," Chiklis said. "I talk to him, it's like I'm talking to Mr. Bugliosi."

"So you don't really have that much contact with JuneBug?" Crymes asked.

"Maybe once a month. Once in a while twice a month, but that's mainly when we're having work done to the place. June... Mr. Bugliosi likes to keep close tabs on his property."

"He wants to be certain that he isn't being cheated," Crymes said.

"Okay. Yeah. He's afraid of getting ripped off. Who isn't, these days?"

"Beside you and JuneBug, who has access to the building?" Crymes asked.

"Tobe Enfante has a set of keys. I also gave a set to Chris Driscoll, so he can open up on days when I'm not around. The janitorial crew comes in afterhours three times a week, and they have keys. That's about it."

Crymes and I looked at each other, and then back at Chiklis.

"What do you think?" I asked Crymes.

"Run him in? Sweat him a little?"

"Oh, come on!" Chiklis protested. "Why in hell would I want to plant a concealed camera in the wall downstairs? Look. Look at this."

He stood and walked across the room to the picture window. He pointed out at the pool area.

"I want to take pictures of my customers, it's no big deal. I can just turn off the lights here in the office and shoot to my heart's content. No one would ever see me. They're all too busy grabbing off a little down by the pool."

"Wait a minute," I said. "Chiklis, I want to take a look at your computer."

"Why?" he asked.

"Yeah, why?" Crymes asked.

"Because most people don't know shit about computers," I said.

Chiklis pointed at the machine on his desk.

"Be my guest," he said.

I sat at his computer and was gratified to find that the operating system was a recent release. That would help things a bit. I clicked on the *Search* function and asked the machine to look for all pictures modified in the last four weeks.

It took about four minutes for the computer to locate all the files. There was a lot of gay porn saved in the various directories, but none of it was apparently shot at WaterWorks. None of the pictures matched the blackmail pictures I'd received.

"Maybe it doesn't mean anything," I said, after showing Crymes the pictures. "Most people, though, don't understand you might not get rid of a picture if you delete it, because it might be saved in several places. Maybe Chiklis is a computer whiz. Maybe he knows how to get rid of something for good. Best guess, though, is that he didn't know we were coming here today, and he hasn't had the opportunity to wipe his computer of incriminating pictures since we got here. So, either he's saving the blackmail photos somewhere else, or he's not involved."

"What do you suggest?" Crymes said.

"Keep him on a short leash."

Crymes thought it over.

"Okay," he said to Chiklis. "Here's the way it is. I can arrest and detain you any time I want on suspicion of blackmail and murder. You understand that?"

"Of course," Chiklis said.

"That means you don't plan any out-of-town trips. If I want to talk with you, I'd better be able to find you in five minutes. As far as I'm concerned, you're not off the hook until I know exactly who put that camera in the wall, and who killed Anthony Luft and Ty Cannon."

Chiklis nodded.

"I understand."

"And you might want to pass the word along to JuneBug that I'll be paying him a visit tomorrow. Enfante, too. I'll need the name and address of your janitorial service."

"Do you want to talk with Chris Driscoll this evening?" he asked.

"Yeah. You go on downstairs and tend the shop. I'll talk with him now."

THIRTY-NINE

Driscoll was a short interview. He didn't have a clue who had put the camera in the wall, and he didn't know that Ty Cannon was dead. I was pretty sure of the latter, because he broke down and cried when he heard the news.

We had run out of people to grill for the evening.

"I'm heading back to the barn," Crymes said. "Gotta write all this up."

"The job's not finished until the paperwork's done," I observed.

"Damn skippy," he said. "You know anything else you're holding back on, here?"

"No. Asa Corona's still missing. I have a feeling that once I catch up with him, a lot of the pieces are going to fall together."

"You'll bring him in to visit me when you do find him, right?"

"You'll be the first person I think of."

Crymes left a few moments later. I drove my car back to the office, switched weapons back to the van, and drove back to my handy parking lot across the street from WaterWorks.

It was still raining in the bay area, sometimes torrentially, and the drumming of the drops on the roof of the van reminded me of camping out in Yosemite. It was fine sleeping weather, but I didn't expect to grab any shuteye until at least the next day.

I didn't expect any real action until after the club closed, but I didn't want to miss any opportunities. I climbed over my rigged plywood partition to the back of the van and switched on my camcorder and video receiver. The picture from the camera I'd installed in the wall was still crisp and crystal clear.

I wasn't interested in recording any of the club sex parties, so I shut down the equipment and focused on reading my book by the clip-on light I had brought for that purpose.

After about twenty minutes, I had an idea. It was still just eleven-thirty. The club wouldn't be closing for at least another two hours.

I pulled out my PDA and fired up the cell program linking me to the GPS tracker I'd installed under Enfante's car. The image showed the car parked at the Noe Street house.

I climbed back into the front seat and drove down into the Castro, to Noe Street. The Lexus was parked exactly where it had been the night before. I parked one street over and walked around the block. As I passed Enfante's house, I dodged quickly up his front steps and dropped a manila envelope on his front porch. It sailed across the floor and landed well inside the dry area protected by the porch roof. I did it almost without breaking stride, and then resumed my trek around the block.

On the way back to the parking lot, I stopped at a drugstore and dialed the telephone number for the Noe Street house on the payphone.

Barney answered. I partially covered the mouthpiece with my hand, and affected a high, feminine voice.

"Is Tobe there?" I asked.

"Who is this?" Barney said.

"Tell Tobe to check the front porch."

"What?"

"The front porch. There's something there for him," I said.

Then I hung up the phone.

I drove back to the parking lot and resumed my watch from the back of the van.

I hoped that Tobe Enfante was somehow involved with the blackmail scheme and the murders. For one reason, I really didn't like him much. For another, he was capable--through JuneBug--of putting some serious hurt on me, and I would really have liked to knock him out of action.

My reasoning was that if Enfante was part of the scheme, and he realized that his camera was being used against him, he'd hustle on over to WaterWorks and make certain the camera was removed.

Correction: Make certain *my* camera was removed.

My cell phone rang.

"Eamon Gold," I said.

"Are you fucking with me?" Enfante demanded.

"This is getting old, Tobe. You sound paranoid."

"Don't get cute. You dropped an envelope by my house tonight."

"Tobe, I don't know what you're up to, but I think you have a lot bigger problems than me fucking with you. I've been with Detective Crymes of the Pacifica PD all night. You don't believe me, you can ask Gary Chiklis."

"What the fuck?"

"We found the camera," I said. I emphasized the word *the*.

"What camera?"

"The one somebody planted in the wall at WaterWorks. Don't you know about it?"

"Let me talk to this Detective," he said.

"I'm not with him now. I'm on the way home. It's time to hit the sack. You'll see Crymes soon enough. He specifically said he planned to talk with you tomorrow."

"You're not shittin' me?"

"Why? What's this envelope you're talking about?"

There was a long silence. For a second, I thought he'd hung up on me.

"Never mind. I'll take care of it. You remember what I said, Gold. You keep your nose out of my business."

Then he did hang up.

I settled back to read my book again. This time, though, I could tell I had a very self-satisfied smile on my face.

————

WaterWorks closed at two in the morning. I watched as the last of the customers slogged through the sodden parking lot to their cars, some alone, some in pairs, and at least one giddy threesome. Several minutes later, Chris Driscoll dashed from the door around back to his car. He was followed shortly by Gary Chiklis, who locked the front door and puddle-jumped his way to his car.

It was time to put my book away and keep an eye on the building. I turned on the receiver and the camcorder. The inside of the pool area glowed eerily in the low light. There was no movement inside the building. To save the batteries, I switched off the equipment, until I saw something interesting outside.

By three-thirty, I was beginning to get drowsy. I turned on the radio, but there wasn't much interesting to catch there. I almost dozed off and missed the show.

About ten minutes after I started listening to the radio, a car drove up and circled WaterWorks before parking in the rear. I didn't get a clear look at it, but since there was no other business in the WaterWorks building, it was pretty certain where the driver was headed.

I hoped it wasn't just the janitorial service arriving to mop down the place.

I powered up the camera receiver and the camcorder, and watched the small screen intently. There was a brief sliver of light as the back door to the pool area swung open and the shut again. A shadowy figure made its way around the pool toward the position where I had hidden my camera.

Within seconds, the camera picture was blocked as someone leaned across the bench. I could see a rhythmic oscillation, like an arm moving up and down. It took me a second to realize that the person inside WaterWorks was unbolting the bench from the wall.

"Bingo," I whispered, as I watched the picture.

After a couple of minutes, the figure pulled the bench away from the wall and leaned in close to examine the hole I had cut to remove the first camera. As he did, I got a direct shot of his face.

It was Chris Driscoll.

I flashed back briefly on the interview with him earlier in the evening, and how he had wept when he heard that Ty Cannon was dead. Then, almost as an afterthought, I recalled that he had not been able to identify Cannon in the picture with Asa Corona when I first visited WaterWorks, and I realized he had been lying to me.

I don't like it when people lie to me.

I grabbed the shotgun from the back of the van and walked across the street and around to the back door of the bathhouse, where I waited next to the door. The overhang of the roof kept the rain off me, but it fell in a sheet just two feet from the door.

Seconds later, the door opened, and Driscoll walked out. I swung the shotgun and caught him right behind the knees. If I had been playing football, they'd have called me for clipping.

He collapsed and rolled over onto his back, just under the sheet of water roiling off the roof.

"What?" he cried. "Take whatever you want!"

"I'll start with my camera," I said.

"Huh? Gold?" he blubbered.

"Get up."

He rolled over to his knees and started to stand. I recognized the three-point stance by instinct, and I knew what football players could do from that stance. I whacked him behind the right ear with the shotgun.

He made an *oof* sound, and his arm collapsed under him.

"Let's try that again," I said. "This time, try not to make it look like you're about to blitz."

He was more careful gaining his feet this time. He stood to face me. I had the shotgun pointed right at his chin.

"Your car," I said. "Give me the keys."

He dug in his pocket, and then handed me a key ring.

"Let's go," I said.

I followed him to his car. He got in the front. I climbed in the back, and kept the Mossberg aimed at his head.

"What do you want?" he asked.

"Cooperation. Who sent you back to the club tonight to get that camera?"

"Oh, man, don't make me do this…"

I poked him in the back of the head with the Mossberg. I have discovered this to be a very persuasive maneuver.

"Okay! I got a call from Tobe Enfante. He told me to go back and get it."

"You already knew it was there?"

"Sure I knew. I was a little surprised when you took the first camera out of the wall last night, but you didn't check to see if there was a backup. So I called Tobe and told him what you'd found. He called back an hour ago and told me to go get the other one before the police came back."

"What about Chiklis? Did he know?"

"Naw. Gary wasn't in on it."

"Who was?"

"Tobe, me, Ty Cannon. That's about it."

"What about Little Tony?"

"No. Tony was never part of it."

"Why?"

"Why wasn't Tony part of it?"

"No. Why did you do it?"

"Jesus, Gold. What do you think? For the money."

"What about Russell Skeen? You didn't try to get money from him."

"I didn't have anything to do with Skeen. We were going to blackmail some of the richer members of the club, guys like Stevie Csaba and Asa Corona. Barrett Efird. Guys like that."

I thought it over.

"Who set up the fake bank accounts?"

"That was Tobe. He has connections."

"Did he also set up the false email addresses?"

"His connections again. He was paying a bunch for all that, but he figured it was, like, an investment. It worked, too. So far we've pulled in over a hundred grand."

"Why was Little Tony Luft killed?"

Driscoll shook his head.

"I don't know nothin' about that. I heard about it the same time everyone else did."

"What about Jack Delroy?"

"Who?"

That stopped me. I had seen Delroy at the Tea Garden in Golden Gate Park. He'd arrived just after Barney and Greg, and I thought I'd seen him call them just before he left.

Or maybe that was what I had wanted to see. I saw him make a call on the phone, and then he drove off. Several seconds later, Barney and Greg left the Tea Garden. I had just presumed he was calling them off. Maybe it had just been a coincidence.

"Why did they kill Ty Cannon?"

"I didn't know about that either. I found out about it when that detective told me last night."

"What was your relationship with Cannon?" I asked.

"We were on again, off again. Ty was like that with everyone. I had a crush on him, though. He was the one that brought me in on the scheme."

"He and Enfante planned it together?"

"Sure. They knew each other from when they were kids. They were in the same foster home, something like that. I heard them talk about it one night in the club."

I paused for a second to put the whole picture together in my head. I had thought for certain that Asa Corona was involved in the blackmail scheme, after he disappeared so suddenly. I'd also figured that Anthony Luft was involved, since he was found in Ty Cannon's house.

I'd never considered Driscoll at all.

Some detective I was.

"Uh, what are you gonna do?" Driscoll asked.

"What?"

"You gonna kill me, or what?"

"Lie down on the front seat," I said.

"What?"

"I don't want to put a hole in the windshield."

I could hear him start to cry.

"Oh, shit, man, don't do this. You don't have to do this. I can give you Enfante. I can give you whatever you want. Understand?"

"Lie down," I said.

"Oh, Jesus, God, don't do this," he said, as he went prostrate on the bench seat.

"Put your hands behind you," I ordered.

He wiggled a little, and then his hands were crossed at the small of his back. He was sobbing, blowing gobs of mucus across the passenger side upholstery.

I pulled several heavy nylon tie-wraps from the pocket of my duster and used them like handcuffs to tie his wrists together.

"I'm getting out," I said. "You stay put. I'm coming around to the passenger side, and I'm going to open the door. You climb out when I do."

Seconds later, I had him out of the car. He stood in the rain, crying and blubbering like a baby. I walked him around to the back of the car and opened the trunk with his keys. I checked to make sure it didn't have the new release cable installed, and then I told him to get inside.

"What are you gonna do? You gonna shoot me in the trunk of my own car?"

"Just get inside," I commanded. "Do it quick, or I'll shoot you and leave you to die out here in the rain."

He slowly sat in the trunk and rolled over to get his entire body inside. It was a tight fit. I slammed the lid. He was still yelling for help as I walked away.

FORTY

I parked the van half a block from the Noe Street house and waited. It was almost four-thirty. I didn't expect to see any action for several hours, so I set my alarm watch for seven-thirty and tried to catch a little sleep.

It seemed as if I had just nodded off when the watch chimed insistently, wakening me. The sun was supposedly up, but the thick scudding clouds overhead didn't let a lot of light through. The rain still came down steadily, drenching the sidewalks and making the ground a soggy mess.

I could see the house out the side window of the van. The Lexus was in the driveway. I couldn't see many lights on in the house. Everyone was probably still asleep.

I waited. After about fifteen minutes, my eyelids started to hang like barbells. I had put off serious sleep for far too long, and I was paying for it in alertness. I had to be very careful. If I lost my concentration at this point, I'd be easy pickings for Enfante and his gun monkeys.

I didn't realize it at the time, but I dozed off for maybe a half hour. When I woke, I cursed at myself for not being vigilant.

The Lexus was gone.

Experience told me that Enfante always went somewhere with Greg or Barney. To the best of my knowledge, he didn't have anyone else in the house, except--I hoped--Asa Corona.

I checked to make certain my Browning was loaded, and I stowed it on my belt inside the duster. Then I climbed from the van and hiked up the street to the house.

I rang the bell. It sounded a pleasant Westminster chimes tune inside. In seconds, I saw a shadow cross the leaded glass insert. I pulled the Browning from inside my coat and held it at my side as soon as the shadow passed.

Barney opened the door.

"What the fuck d'you want?" he demanded.

I stuck the Browning up under his nose.

"Inside," I said.

He slowly backed up. I was careful to watch his shoulders for any sign he was about to uncoil and turn me into a human pretzel.

"What is this?" he said.

"I want Asa Corona."

Barney nodded his head backward.

"In the back bedroom."

He turned and started down the hall.

"Not so fast," I said. "Keep it nice and slow. If you break for it, I'll shoot you dead before you take three steps."

"No you won't. But tha's okay. You're the boss."

I followed him down the hall. He came to the door at the end and reached for the knob.

I felt something hard slam down on the back of my head.

The next thing I knew, I was lying curled up on the floor, as Barney rifled through my coat pockets.

"He ain't got any more weapons," Barney said.

"Good," Enfante said. "Stand him up."

Barney grabbed me underneath my armpits and pulled me up off the floor. I had never been completely unconscious. It would take more than a whack on the back of the head to take me all the way out. Even so, I was woozy, and I could feel a trickle of blood wending its way through my hair and down the back of my neck.

"What are you doing here, Gold?" Enfante said.

"Came to get Asa Corona," I said. I think it came out a little slurred.

"Why?"

"He's my client. I told him I'd take care of him."

"So you think you can just walk in here and take him away? That's some balls, man."

"I didn't think you were here. Your car was gone."

"We sent Greg out to get some breakfast."

"My bad. I should have paid better attention. Tell you what. You just let Asa come with me, and I'll go light on you."

Enfante laughed then. It didn't come out evil or anything, not a bad guy kind of laugh. He actually seemed amused.

"That's very kind of you. Now *I'll* tell *you* what. You can go in there with him while I decide what to do with you."

"Okay. While you're thinking it over, though, you might want to get up with Chris Driscoll."

The smile on Enfante's face disappeared and was replaced by puzzlement.

"What about Driscoll?"

"He gave you up. I know where he is. You let me have Asa, and I'll give you Driscoll."

Enfante reached across me and opened the door to the bedroom. Barney tossed me inside. The door slammed, and I could hear the lock turned from the outside. They had reversed the doorknob, just to keep Asa in the room. Now it kept me in as well.

I looked around. Asa was sitting in a chair over in one corner. His knees were drawn up under him. His face was drawn, his hair greasy. He looked like shit.

"You shouldn't have come," he said.

"I thought you were skipping out on your bill. How long have you been here, anyway?"

"About a week. Since the last time I saw you."

"Well, it's time to go. Let's get you back to your grandfather."

I walked over to the windows.

"They're barred," he said. "Burglar protection. Only thing is, with burglar bars you're supposed to be able to open them from the inside. Even I know that."

Just to be certain, I checked them. Sure enough, there were ornate cast-iron bars bolted to the outside of the window frames.

"Okay. So if we go, we have to go through Barney and Tobe. That's just peachy. How in hell did you get mixed up with this crew, Asa?"

"It's kind of complicated."

"I appear to have time. When did you first hook up with Enfante?"

"It was at WaterWorks, months ago. He seemed all right at first. Maybe a little edgy, but after a couple of drinks... well, you're a bright fellow. You get the picture."

"I owe you a first-class ass-kicking."

"Why?"

"You knew a lot more than you told me when you first came to my office asking for help. I think I'm beginning to put all the pieces together. You tell me where I go south."

He didn't say anything, so I continued.

"When you received the first blackmail demand, you resisted paying. You didn't know where to turn, so you drove around until you just happened to be in Anthony Luft's neighborhood. You dropped by, had a few drinks, and told him what was happening."

"It was a couple of joints, but otherwise you're right."

"The joints were provided by Ray Klein?"

"He was Little Tony's connection."

"Little Tony knew him from the movement to open up the private rooms in the bathhouses."

"That's right."

"You showed Luft the pictures you'd received, and he recognized Ty Cannon. As it happened, he also knew where Cannon lived."

"Right."

"So you and Luft started looking for Cannon."

"Right again."

"You went to Ray Klein's place, on the pretext of buying some Extasy, but you were really looking for Cannon. Klein told you he hadn't seen Cannon in weeks."

"Jesus. You've been making the rounds, haven't you?"

"Just doing my job. You and Luft were all over the place, talking to a lot of people. Then, Luft called you and told you he had run into Ty Cannon at WaterWorks."

"Yeah. I'll bet Miles Nickelby told you about that."

"That's why you put him on the list? Because you knew he and Ty Cannon had done the nasty the night before Cannon disappeared?"

"Sure."

"So when did you go to Cannon's house and find Little Tony dead?"

He seemed to curl up even tighter in the chair.

"A couple of days before I came to you. Tony had called me the week before, and he told me that he had seen Ty at WaterWorks getting it on with Ray Klein. He said he had talked with Ty, but that Ty hadn't been very interested in the conversation. He said that Ty had told him to come by the house the next day. Then he didn't call again."

"After a few days, you went looking for Tony."

"I met with Steve Csaba for lunch down in the Castro. He and Tony were friends. I thought maybe he had seen Tony around, but he hadn't."

"Barrett Efird saw you there."

"I saw him too, but I didn't talk with him."

"It doesn't matter. Finally, you decided to check out Cannon's house, and when you went around to the back you saw Tony dead on the floor through the French doors."

A tear coursed down Corona's cheek.

"It was awful," he said. "I could tell he was dead. He looked deflated, and I could see the bugs on him. I knew I was in really big trouble. I could tell it wasn't Ty, so I was pretty sure it was Tony. I got scared, and I ran away."

"Why didn't you call the cops, Asa?"

"I told you. I was scared. I told you the truth that first day in your office. I really couldn't stand for my grandfather to find out that I'm gay. It would kill him."

"Probably not before he wrote you out of the will."

"Don't be crass. The money's important, but that man raised me, Mr. Gold. The way my dad behaved, Grandpa was more of a father to me than anyone else. I know he doesn't have much time left. Anyone can see it. I don't want him to die... *disappointed* with me."

"I'll let that one ride. After you found Tony, you decided to play detective yourself for a few days. That's when you talked with Greg Lyles, Miles Nickelby, and Ray Klein. You even dropped by The Sauna in Berkeley, maybe thinking Cannon was going in for the rough trade."

"I did a lot of things. I was desperate. Finally, I realized I was out of my league. I needed professional help, but I couldn't go to Mr. Moon."

"Because he works for your grandfather."

"Right. I was afraid that if he found out why I was in trouble, he'd tell Grandpa, and that would be that."

"But you were afraid that something might happen to you, too, so you had Moon put GPS trackers under your car."

"You've figured it all out, haven't you?"

"The larger parts of it. What I can't figure out is how you wound up here."

"The night I was in WaterWorks, asking around about people who'd shagged Ty Cannon, Tobe Enfante came up to me and asked if I was in any trouble. I guess I started crying a little, because he took me aside and bought me a drink. I... I told him everything. He was very comforting. We didn't hook up or anything. He just told me that if I needed anything, I could call him.

"Then, when they found Little Tony's body, and you said you were going to bring that police detective to the house, I called him. I asked him if there was anything he could do. He told me to take one of the cars and meet him about a mile from Corona Farms. When I drove up, he was in the Lexus, and there was another car, some kind of Japanese econobox. I don't recall for sure what make. Barney and Greg were in it. Tobe told me to get into the Lexus, and that the other two would take care of the Boxster."

"They took care of it, all right. They put it at the bottom of a pond."

"I didn't know they were going to do that. Tobe told me that it was in my best interests to disappear for a while, wait until this whole Luft thing blew over. So he brought me here."

"How did you call me?"

"It wasn't hard. When Tobe and Barney and Greg weren't around, I pretty much had the run of the house."

I recalled that the first time Asa had called me, I had just passed all three of them on Dolores Street.

"So you called and asked to meet me at the Tea Garden?"

"Yeah, I thought I could sneak out. Tobe and the other two were usually gone around midday. The problem was, after the first day I called you, they suddenly stopped leaving me alone here. Then they put me back in this room and locked me in. I figured they were up to something."

"Barney and Greg went to the Tea Garden. How'd they know I'd be there?"

"I... I told them. I still believed that Tobe wanted to help me, Mr. Gold. I didn't know... I just didn't know."

He started crying again.

"What? What didn't you know?" I asked.

He looked up, his eyes reddened and swollen.

"I didn't know that they killed Little Tony and Ty Cannon."

FORTY-ONE

"Wait," I said. "You can prove this?"

"I heard Tobe talking about it, through the door the other night. These guys, I've figured out they're not all that bright. They stuffed me back in this room and after a while they forgot I was here. I heard Tobe talking with Barney about Little Tony. Apparently, Tony thought Tobe had a line on Ty Cannon. He told Tony to meet him at Ty's house. When they got there, Tobe opened the door with a key he said Ty had given him.

"Tobe told Barney that Tony started questioning him, wondering why Ty might have given him a key. Tobe said he realized Tony was getting too close to figuring out that Tobe was involved in the blackmail scheme, so he pulled a baseball bat out from behind the drapes and beat him to death with it."

"And Ty Cannon?"

"Tobe killed Ty weeks ago, around the time he disappeared. From what I could figure out, based on what I overheard, Ty and Driscoll were more interested in shaking down the blackmail victims for money. Tobe wanted to expand the scheme to try to extort votes from the City Supervisors to reinstate the private rooms in the baths. He told Barney that Ty and Driscoll were too short-sighted, that in the long run he'd make more money from baths with private rooms than he could from extortion.

"Anyway, Ty and Tobe got into an argument about this one night. Tobe wanted to shut down the blackmail-for-money operation, because it was becoming way too difficult to keep establishing blind alley internet names and bank accounts. Ty got greedy, and threatened to turn Tobe in. Tobe had Greg take Ty home, only they didn't get there. Greg shot Ty and stuffed him into a drainage culvert."

"Enfante said that?"

"No, Greg did. I heard him tell Barney about it in detail. He said he took Ty out of the car and made him kneel on the ground. Greg bragged about how Ty begged him not to shoot, how he wet his pants when Greg put the gun behind his ear. He sounded pretty proud of it."

"Probably made his bones."

"What?"

"It's a gang term. It means he gets to be a full-fledged gangster now. Didn't you know Enfante was all mobbed up, Asa?"

"No. Seriously. I never suspected. Like I said, he seemed okay at the baths. He really seemed interested in helping me."

"He was interested, all right. He had to cover his ass."

I heard the key in the doorlock and turned as Enfante opened the door.

"What did you do?" Enfante asked me.

"Couldn't locate Driscoll?"

"Where is he?"

As he said it, Enfante pulled my Browning from his belt and pointed at me.

"Where I left him. He's in the trunk of his car," I said.

"Where's his car?"

"Behind WaterWorks."

"Did you kill him?"

"I'm not like you, Tobe. He's scared, but he's breathing."

"Maybe you should've gone ahead and killed him. Might have been better for him in the long run. He's trying to shake me down."

"Come again?"

"That envelope I told you about. I think Driscoll's trying to play me for a sap. Behind WaterWorks, you said?"

"Last time I saw him."

Enfante kept the gun on me, as he rubbed his chin.

"You better not be shittin' me," he said.

Then he turned to Barney and handed him my Browning.

"Here," he said. "Greg and I are going to collect Driscoll. If this asshole tries to come through the door, shoot him with his own gun. Got it?"

"Sure," Barney said.

Enfante pulled the door closed with a slam, and I heard the key rasp in the lock again.

"Turn on the television," I said to Asa.

"What?"

"We need some cover noise. Turn on the television and crank up the volume a little."

Asa got up from the chair and pushed the power switch on the television set mounted on the dresser in front of the bed.

"What are you doing?" he asked.

I looked around the room, and then out the window.

"How old would you say this house is?" I asked.

"This is a fairly new neighborhood. Maybe ten years old?"

"That's what I was thinking. The exterior is stucco. About fifteen years ago, builders stopped using wire lath on exterior stucco, and switched to a polyurethane foamboard backer."

"How in hell do you know that?"

"Habitat for Humanity, kid. You learn a lot building one or two of those houses."

"So, what about it?"

"Just this. The way they build these synthetic stucco houses, they're really pretty flimsy. They put up a two-by-four frame, cover the outside with some thin fiberboard, then the poly foam, and then a very thin layer of concrete-based stucco. The inside wall is just gypsum board."

"And?"

"And if we have the right tool, we could cut a door right through the wall in just a few minutes."

I looked around the room, but it had been nicely stripped. There was the bed, the chair Asa had been sitting in, the television, and that was about it.

I checked out the attached bathroom. There wasn't much there, either. Maybe I could have pulled one of the bathtub faucet handles off, but it didn't look sharp enough to cut through the drywall, let alone the outside fiberboard.

There was the mirror on the medicine cabinet, and another mirror on a scissors arm hinged to the side of the wall, presumably so Enfante could look at his profile. It looked like the ticket. I twisted the scissors arm, and the mirror came loose.

Back in the bedroom, I noted the ring on Asa's finger.

"Is that diamond?" I asked.

He looked down.

"It has a diamond in it," he said.

"Give it to me."

He twisted the ring from his finger and handed it over.

I carefully etched a blade shape in the mirror and ran the diamond over it several times to make sure the glass was properly shaped.

"Now the pillowcase," I said, as I handed the ring back to him.

He pulled the pillowcase off the pillow and passed it to me.

"Turn the television up a little louder."

He increased the volume. I wrapped the mirror in the pillowcase and brought it down sharply across my kneecap. When I unwrapped the mirror, I found that it had snapped neatly along the etched lines. I applied pressure to the sides of the mirror, and the etched glass knife blade fell out onto the bed.

"Cool," Asa said.

"Only if it works."

I wrapped the pillowcase around the blunt end of the broken glass.

"Now," I said. "Where do you reckon Tobe would like his new back door?"

It took a moment or two, but we decided that it would be best to cut the hole as far from the bedroom door as we could, to keep Barney from hearing me at work. I found the most likely spot, and carefully sawed at the drywall with the sharp edge of the glass.

"It's working!" Asa said. "It's cutting the wall."

"Don't get too excited yet," I said. "If we hit wire lath behind this wall, we're screwed. I didn't bring any clippers with me."

I quickly cut a section two feet wide by three feet high in the wall. I dug out a small section with our makeshift knife, and pulled it away, then stuck my hand in the hole and pulled the entire section away from the two-by-four studs. The heads of the drywall screws easily pulled through the gypsum board, and in a few seconds I had the entire piece on the floor.

We were in luck. The house had been constructed with synthetic stucco. After pulling away the cotton-candy insulation, I could see the fiberboard backer in front of me. It took another three or four minutes to saw through it, and then I was down to the polyurethane foam.

"We don't have much time," I said. "Tobe and Greg will be back with Driscoll soon."

I sat on the floor and kicked at the foam with my good foot. It broke right through, with almost no sound. When I pulled my foot back, I could see dim light and rain through the hole. I started kicking the hole bigger.

Two minutes later, I climbed through the crude opening in the side of the house and dropped three feet to the sodden dirt at the foundation.

"Come on," I said.

Asa climbed out behind me. I steadied him as he came through the hole.

"Where are we going?" he asked.

"My van's parked half a block away. I have something to do, first, and then you and I are going to the Pacifica Police Department, and you're going to tell Detective Crymes everything you just told me. Then, if we're lucky, I'll take you home. Let's go."

We ran through a couple of backyards in the rain until we reached the point where I had parked the van. I pulled open the back door and grabbed my Mossberg shotgun and the Python from the box in the back. I handed the Python to Asa.

"You know how to use this?" I asked.

"Grandpa taught me how to shoot when I was just five. I can handle it."

"Okay."

I slammed the door and started up the street, the Mossberg concealed under my duster.

"Where are we going?" Asa said.

"Back to Enfante's place."

"Why?"

"Unfinished business."

I didn't break stride as I walked up the steps to Enfante's front porch, pulled the Mossberg out from under my duster, jacked a shell into the chamber, and blew the living shit out of the door lock.

I kicked in the door and dashed into the front parlor of the house. Barney was sitting there, watching a European football game on the television. His jaw dropped as the door exploded open. He started to reach for my Browning, which was sitting on the table next to his chair, but I was already all over him.

"Don't," I said. "You wouldn't like what this hogleg can do to you."

Barney froze.

"How'd you get out?" he asked.

"Does it matter? Asa, get my Browning off the table."

Corona picked up the pistol and stowed it in his belt.

"Barney, I'd like you to close your eyes," I said.

"Why?"

"Because this is really going to hurt."

I swung the Mossberg and caught him in the left temple. He rolled out of the chair, cradling his head. I kicked him in the back of the head a couple of times, and he stopped fighting. He rolled over, twitched spastically a couple of times, and then laid still, his breath coming in long, steady drafts.

"Why didn't you kill him?" Asa asked.

"Because I'm not Enfante. I just needed to make sure Barney didn't let Tobe know we were gone until we had a decent head start. Now, let's go see Detective Crymes."

FORTY-TWO

Three hours later, I sat in the waiting room outside Crymes' office in Pacifica, nursing a cup of lousy cop house coffee, and reading a year-old issue of *Guns and Gardens.*

Asa had been inside with Crymes for a couple of hours. Ten minutes after he went inside, Crymes called for a court stenographer to take down Asa's statement. Apparently, she'd been busy.

Crymes door opened, and he walked out with Asa.

"You got a safe place to stow this guy?" Crymes asked.

"Sure. His home. The place is crawling with Full Moon Security guards."

"Good. I'm going to need him later. We're going after Tobe Enfante in an hour or so, soon as the chief can pull together a strike force team. I made a few calls. Seems these two guys Greg and Barney are a real piece of work. Greg's last name is Freund. He's been a major pain in the ass for police all up and down the California coast for the last decade, but he never seems to stay in one place long enough to get nabbed. Barney Navvo has been mobbed up with JuneBug for about five years. He's mostly muscle, does a lot of debt collecting, but we don't have any previous suspicions of murder on him."

"I got the idea that Greg was the really dangerous one," I said.

"You were right. We're going in on the presumption that these guys aren't coming out without a fight. Now, you want to tell me how you figured out Corona was in Enfante's house?"

"It was easy. Asa called me on the telephone, and when I star-sixty-nined him, Greg answered the phone. I had already tailed Enfante to the Noe Street house, and I put two and two together."

"And how long ago did you do this math trick? No, wait. I don't want to know. It would break my heart to discover you've been withholding evidence."

"What about Driscoll?" I asked.

"Bubbletop cops checked out his car at WaterWorks about an hour ago. The trunk was popped. He was gone."

"He's with Enfante," I said.

"Or maybe he's clogging a drain pipe somewhere. From what Junior told me, Enfante was really pissed at Driscoll when he stormed out of the house."

"That's another possibility."

Crymes reached out and poked me in the chest.

"You're wearing the vest," he said.

"A Boy Scout is always prepared."

"You might want to keep that on for awhile. Even if we grab Enfante, you still might have to deal with JuneBug."

He turned and walked back to his office door, but stopped, as if he wanted to say something. He stood there for a second, then walked back over to me.

"I don't say this often. Good job, Eamon."

He extended his hand.

I took it. It was about the nicest thing Crymes had ever said to me.

———

I drove Asa to Jefferson Street and walked him up the stairs to my office.

"You hungry, kid?" I asked.

"I could eat."

"You stay put. I'm going to lock the door. I'll be back in fifteen minutes." I pulled the Browning from my belt. "That door being locked, if anyone but me comes through, you shoot him. I'm not expecting company, and if they get through the door they aren't coming to chat. Got it?"

"Sure. I'm cool."

"Sure you are, kid."

I locked the door and walked back down the stairs.

I really didn't need fifteen minutes to grab some food from Fisherman's Wharf. It was only a hundred yards away. I wanted a few minutes to talk with Heidi.

She was in her gallery, reading a new copy of *ArtNews*, when I walked in the door.

"Was that your client?" she asked.

"Nosey. What are you doing later?"

"I don't have any specific plans. Thought I might wash my hair."

I came around the counter and pulled her to me.

We did the liplock thing for a few moments. I liked it. She was a dynamite kisser.

"You're wearing the vest," she said.

"Everyone seems to notice that."

"Are you in danger?"

"With any luck, no. I think the dangerous part is over."

"You will tell me all about it, right?"

"It's a long story."

"We have all night."

"I thought you were going to wash your hair."

She smiled and kissed me again.

"Got to do something while it dries, lover."

We agreed to get together later that evening, after I took Asa home. She didn't want anything to eat, which I considered a truly rare event, so I trotted down to the Wharf and picked up a couple of sourdough bowls of clam chowder and some shrimp cocktail for Asa and me.

When I got back to my office, I knocked on the door.

"It's me, Asa. I'm going to unlock the door. Don't shoot me, okay?"

There was no answer.

"Asa?"

Still no answer.

I set the food down and grabbed for my keys. It took me three seconds to unlock the door and swing it open.

Asa was sitting in my chair. He didn't look happy.

"Call Crymes," he said.

FORTY-THREE

Asa had written a cell number on my desk blotter. I handed him the food and picked up the telephone.

Crymes picked up on the second ring.

"What is it?" I asked.

"Eamon, the house is empty. Nobody's here. I found the hole you broke in the back wall, but when we got here the front door was hanging open, and the place was deserted."

"Enfante's bugged out?"

"It looks that way. You might want to call Sheldon Moon and make sure he has people up at Corona Farms. By now, Enfante's figured out that Asa probably ratted him out. I have an APB issued for that Lexus you described, but he could have changed the plates or even switched cars."

"You don't really think he'd make a run at Asa, do you?"

"I don't know. We want to take every precaution, though. Asa Corona can put Enfante away."

"I'll take him home right away, and call Moon. I'll stay at Corona Farms until the Full Moon reinforcements arrive."

Then I thought of something.

"Crymes, I didn't mention this earlier. Sheldon Moon's operative Jack Delroy might be wrapped up in this deal somewhere."

"How so?"

"I was supposed to meet Asa at the Japanese Tea Garden in Golden Gate Park a couple of days ago. Greg Freund and Barney Navvo showed up instead, so I kept myself hidden. A few minutes after they arrived, Delroy drove up and parked in front of the second gate."

"You think he tipped Greg and Barney off?"

"No. Asa told them about the meeting. I don't know where Delroy fits in, though."

"Okay. Keep an eye out for Delroy too. Maybe if he shows his face, it will mean that Enfante and the other two aren't far behind."

"Gotcha. I'm leaving with Asa in a few minutes."

"You be careful, Eamon. Check in with me before you leave Corona Farms."

I rang off and looked at Asa.

"We can eat on the road," I said. "I need to get you home."

The rain fell harder as we crossed the Golden Gate Bridge and made the turn toward Richmond and Napa Valley. I had moved all my hardware from the van to my car, because I didn't want to try slogging the van around on the highways with all the standing water.

It took about an hour to make our way to the front gate at Corona farms. We drove right past the empty guardhouse and took the right turn to head for the manor house. We pulled up in the circular drive, where two men in Full Moon Security uniforms were waiting on the front porch.

"Have either of you seen Jack Delroy?" I called as I climbed from behind the wheel.

They looked at each other. Then one shook his head.

"He hasn't been here tonight," he said. "Why?"

"I'd appreciate it if you'd let me know if he shows up."

"Sure thing," the guard said.

"Where's my grandfather?" Asa called, after running up the steps to the gallery.

"Last I saw him, he was heading up to the processing plant," the same guard said. "You want me to call up there?"

"No, that's okay. I'll go myself."

"I'm going with you," I said.

We drove as far as we could, to the point where the driveway ended and the sidewalk started, and from there we trekked up the hill toward the plant. I could see the lights on in the main office. We had forgotten to get umbrellas, and the driving rain slicked our hair down against our foreheads. I could feel water running down my neck inside my oilskin duster.

It took us about five minutes to get to the front door of the plant. Asa yanked it open and walked inside. I stayed by the door, to keep an eye on the house.

Daron Corona must have heard the door open and close, because he came out of his office.

"Asa?" he said.

"Grandpa," Asa said. "I'm back."

"Oh, my God, you are. Come here, boy. I've been worried sick."

Asa crossed the office area and hugged his grandfather.

"Where've you been, boy?"

"It's a long story," Asa said. "Mr. Gold found me and brought me home."

Daron let go of Asa and walked over to me.

"Mr. Gold, I'm in your debt. It's nice to meet a man who keeps his promises. Was the boy in much danger?"

"Enough," I said. "It's not entirely over yet."

"I don't understand."

"Asa, why don't you fill in your grandfather while I keep an eye out for visitors?" I said.

"Yes. Of course," Asa said. "Let's go into your office, Grandpa. I have a lot to tell you."

They walked back to Daron's office. I could hear the murmur of their conversation from my post, but I couldn't understand much of it. From my vantage, I could see much of the long drive up to the manor house from the guardhouse at the fork in the entrance road, and I could make out the front gallery of the manor house itself. The lights were on in the gallery, and I could see the two guards standing watch there.

I pulled my 3x binoculars from my duster pocket to get a little closer look at the guards. One of them was talking on either a cell phone or a two-way radio. I couldn't tell from the distance. I figured he was probably just checking in with the guardhouse.

Then I recalled that the guardhouse was empty when we drove up to the manor house. I had figured at the time that the guard there was just off taking a whiz somewhere. Now I wasn't so sure.

I pulled out my cellphone and called Full Moon Security. Sheldon Moon himself answered the ring.

"This is Eamon Gold," I said. "I'm at Corona Farms."

"Yes, Mr. Gold. What can I do for you?"

"How many people do you have scheduled here tonight?"

"We always have three people out there. One for the guardhouse, and two at the manor house. Why?"

"The guardhouse guy didn't call in sick or anything today, did he?"

"Not that I know of. If he had, we'd have assigned a substitute. Mr. Corona is one of our best customers. We like to take care of him. What's wrong?"

I tried to keep an eye on the front porch guards through the binoculars while I talked with him on the telephone.

"When Asa and I drove up a half hour ago, the guardhouse was empty. There are two guys on the porch, but I don't know where the third is. Just a couple of minutes ago, I saw one of the guards on the front porch talking to someone on a two-way or a cell."

"Maybe the fellow in the guardhouse stepped out for a moment."

"That's what I thought. I can't see the guardhouse from here, though. Is there some way for you to check in with him?"

"Of course. Hold on a moment."

There was a click, and my ear was filled with canned music.

Then I heard a *beep*.

I pulled the phone away and looked at the screen. The battery was almost dead. I'd been so busy over the last couple of days that I'd forgotten to recharge it.

The phone beeped again, and then the display went black.

"Shit," I said.

Asa poked his head out from the office.

"What's wrong?" he asked.

"Cell phone's dead," I said. "I was talking with Sheldon Moon. Can I use your office phone here?"

"Sure."

I walked over to the nearest desk and picked up the receiver on the phone. There was no light on any of the lines, and the only noise that came from the earpiece was an echo of my own rapidly accelerating breath.

"Mr. Corona!" I called.

Both Daron and Asa answered, "Yes?" at the same time.

"I'm not getting anything on this phone. Would you check yours?"

A second later, Asa walked out of the office, followed closely by Daron.

"Maybe the storm..." Asa said.

"Maybe not," I said.

"What is it?" Daron asked.

"The lines might be cut. The front guardhouse was empty when Asa and I drove in a little while ago. I was on my cellphone talking with Sheldon Moon, who said that he had three men scheduled this evening."

Asa and Daron looked at each other. Then Daron walked over and took the binoculars from me. He peered through them at the two guards on the front porch of the manor house.

"Those are the two who showed up today," he said. "I never saw the third guard. What's going on, Gold?"

"I don't know. I'm going back down to my car. You keep an eye on the front porch and the drive up from the guardhouse."

I left the binoculars with him and jogged down the walk toward my car. I had the Browning on my belt, but I wanted a little more security in case everything turned to total shit.

The rain whipped at my face as I took the last steps down to the tiny parking lot two at a time. I peered over the roof of my car, to see where the guards were. They were still on the front gallery. One of them was now sitting in one of the rocking chairs.

I opened the trunk of the car and pulled out the Mossberg and the Python. I also stuffed a half dozen extra double-ought stainless shells in my duster pocket, along with three full speed loaders. I didn't have a spare clip for the Browning, but it was full, and if I needed more than fourteen nine-millimeter bullets with all the other firepower at my disposal, I was already screwed anyway.

When I closed the trunk lid, I looked back toward the manor house, and saw a pair of headlights bouncing up the road from the guardhouse.

I crouched behind the far side of the car and watched the headlights through the windows. The car swung around the circular driveway and pulled up in front of the gallery. In the spill of light from the gallery, I could see that it was a dark Ford. I didn't need much light to recognize Jack Delroy when he climbed out from behind the wheel.

He lumbered up the front steps and spoke to the guards there. As he spoke, he pointed back down the drive toward the guardhouse. His posture was animated, but the guards just seemed to shrug and shake their heads. Delroy pointed at the two gallery guards then and turned to walk back down the steps to his car. I saw him pull what looked like a cell phone from his pocket.

The guard I had spoken with on the porch pulled his pistol and shot Delroy in the back. The other guard pulled his pistol and joined in. The force of the shots drove Delroy into the side of his car, and then he slumped down to the ground in a motionless heap.

I had seen enough.

I dashed back the steps and sprinted along the walkway to the processing plant. I could see Daron Corona barking orders to Asa. He held the door open for me as I reached the building.

"You saw?" I gasped.

"I sure did. They shot that boy dead."

"It was Jack Delroy. I don't know what's going on, but those aren't Full Moon guards."

"And we can't call the police," Asa said. "All the telephones are dead."

I pulled the Python and the Browning from under my coat and handed each of them a weapon.

"I have the shotgun," I said. "We have to presume they'll come up after us in a few minutes. I can only hope they don't know how well we're armed."

"What in hell is this thing?" Daron asked, looking down at the Browning. "I got something much better than this."

He handed the Browning back to me and walked back to his office. Seconds later, he came back with the oldest firearm I'd seen in years in his hands.

"Springfield 1903 thirty-ought-six," he said. "Same one I used in the Battle for Corona Farms back in 1933."

"What in hell, Grandpa?" Asa said.

"I've had this rifle for seventy years," Daron said. "I can knock the nuts off a butterfly at a hundred yards with this piece."

I would have been surprised if he could *see* a hundred yards, but I wasn't in a mood to argue.

"You have ammo for that antique?" I asked.

"Two whole boxes."

"Okay. No time to discuss it. You pull together your gear. We're sitting ducks here in the office. I think we need to get out where we can find some natural cover. I don't think they know we're on to them yet. We might be able to surprise them."

As Asa and Daron pulled on rain slickers, I went back to the door, turned off the office lights, and pulled out my binoculars again.

Delroy was still lying next to his car, but now another set of headlights appeared on the entrance road. I didn't need to look twice to know it was the Lexus, probably with stolen tags.

Enfante pulled the car into the circular drive, and he piled out with Greg Freund, Barney Navvo, and Chris Driscoll. Enfante took one look at Delroy and started yelling at the guards. I could almost see the cords stand out on his neck from an eighth of a mile away. The guard who had fired the first shot waved his hands, apparently arguing with Enfante. They went at it for a couple of minutes, and then both of them threw up their hands, and the fight was apparently over.

"They're going to come straight up the hill," I said to Daron, who had joined me. "If we can get to higher ground, we might be able to get the drop on them."

"I count six," Daron said.

"Six against three," I added, wiping the rain away from my face. "We need to take out at least half of them in the first several seconds, or they'll be all over us. How do you get up the hill behind the processing plant?"

"This way," Asa said.

We followed him out the back door of the plant, where Corona had installed a set of stone steps leading up the hill to the vineyards. We scrambled up the steps. At the top, I turned to Daron.

"You know the lay of the land here. Where should we set up?"

"I'll go this way," Daron said, pointing to his right. "There's a shallow irrigation ditch about fifty feet from here. You and Asa can hide behind the first couple of rows of vines over there. That way, we can catch them from two directions."

I looked at him with what he obviously saw as admiration.

"Classic military pincer movement," he said. "It multiplies our firepower, and they'll think we have a hundred guys up here."

"All right," I said. "Come on, Asa."

Asa and I ran toward the vineyards, while Daron went in the other direction toward the irrigation ditch. We crouched down behind the second row of vines. The ground was soggy and sucked at our shoes. I pulled out my binoculars and peered back down the hill. Enfante had driven the Lexus up to the parking lot and had pulled in beside my car. The guards were inside Delroy's car. They killed their headlights and rolled out of the cars as a group.

"You tell your grandfather everything?" I asked.

"Not quite everything," Asa said. "We didn't have time. He knows I was held by Enfante, but I didn't get to the whole story. He was really impressed with the way you got me out."

"What about the..." I started.

"No. I couldn't tell him."

"Well, let's make sure you get another chance."

Enfante and his gang ran straight up to the processing plant and drove through the door. I saw a spill of light fall from the main entrance of the plant as someone hit the lights, and then there was a series of muted pops as they shot up everything in sight.

Several seconds after the firing ceased, they ran out the door and looked around, everyone looking in a different direction.

"Goddamn it!" Enfante yelled at one of the guards. "You probably spooked them when you wasted that guy from the security agency!"

"What was I going to do?" the guard said. "He knew I wasn't with Full Moon. I could see it in his eyes. We were blown, and he was going to call the cops."

"You don't know that!"

"Nothing we can do about it now. They have to be around here somewhere."

The group huddled, and then walked away from the stone steps, toward the shipping docks.

"They think we're in the aging cellars," Asa said, quietly.

"It's a good hunch. You'd have to be crazy to hide up here in the rain and the mud. Is there an entrance to the cellars from up here?"

"No. The main entrance is through the shipping docks, and there's one on the other end at the processing plant."

"I knew about those. Daron showed them to me a few days ago."

"Well, that's all there is."

"They'll be back then."

It took about ten minutes, but the group again collected near the front entrance of the processing plant. I couldn't hear Enfante, but he apparently told the fake guards something they didn't want to hear.

"Like hell," one of them said. "Why don't I just paint a target on my chest?"

Enfante slapped him and pointed in our direction. For a second, I thought the guard was going to pop him, but after glaring for a respectable moment he started around the building. He was followed by the second guard and Chris Driscoll.

"Get ready," I told Asa. He pulled the Python out and braced it in front of him. "I'll shoot first. You nail anything I don't hit."

The group slowly started up the stone walk. By that point, it was the only way up the hill, because the rain had turned the grass into a slick glossy sheet.

"We'll let them get to the top, and wait for them to fan out," I whispered. "If we try to trap them on the steps, they might be able to run back and take cover, and we'll be here all night."

One by one, the invaders made their way up the stone steps and crouched as much as possible, trying to blend in with the shrubbery on either side of the steel handrail. I could see by then that they were packing military rifles, mostly Chinese knockoffs of the Russian AK-47. I didn't doubt for a second that they had been modified to fully automatic fire.

Just as Enfante pulled up the rear and crested the top of the steps, I heard a whipcrack from my right, and a bullet spanged off the steel handrail. Daron had decided to take the first shot, and he had missed.

I had about a half second to act, before Enfante's posse turned tail and rolled back down the steps. I stood, pointed the Browning in the general direction of the top of the steps, and pumped out three rounds, moving the gun just a little between shots.

Asa stood beside me and emptied the Python. Off to my right, I heard another crack from the irrigation ditch, and the first guard clutched at his chest and fell backward. Driscoll screamed and grabbed at his thigh, but only for a second before one of Asa's rounds caught him high in the chest. He sat down clumsily and clawed at the wound for a few seconds.

I thought I heard him crying.

I had hit one of the rifles, but I didn't think I had struck flesh, until Barney Navvo stood and pulled his jacket back.

"Bastard hit me, Tobe," he barked. He leveled his rifle in my direction and emptied the magazine into the rows of chardonnay grapes. I was already flat against the ground, and I could hear Asa hyperventilating next to me.

"Give me the Python," I said.

He handed the gun to me and I reloaded it using the speed loader before handing it back.

"Don't use all your ammo in one volley," I told him. "Pick your targets. This isn't a cowboy revolver."

I took the Browning in hand, stood quickly, and dropped two slugs into Barney's easy target of a torso, as he tried to cram a second magazine into the rifle. I heard him expel an *ooph* sound, and then he grabbed the handrail to keep from falling over. A second later, he staggered away from the rail, both hands clutched to his chest, and then fell over.

"Okay," I said, "we're halfway there. Time to change positions."

Asa led the way as we crouched and half-ran, half-crawled through the rows of grapes toward the end of the vineyard. As we ran, I kept our attackers at bay by spraying their location with the better part of one of the Browning's magazines. I hoped that Daron was smart enough to move too. We made our way across two drainage ditches and flattened against the soggy earth.

Behind us, I could hear the high-pitched burp of automatic weapons chewing up our previous position. We had made our dash just in time.

I looked back and saw the remaining three split up and lie down to prevent being the easy shot Barney had become.

"They're learning," I said, as I pocketed the empty magazine and slammed a new one into the Browning.

"Can we still take them?"

"We have the advantage that you and Daron know the terrain."

"You talking about me?" Daron said, as he crawled up behind us.

"Jesus!" I said. "I almost shot you."

"Damned decent of you not to," he said. "I count three left. What about you?"

"That's the way I see it," I said. "We're too far away for the pistols. You think you can pick off one more with that cannon?"

Before he could answer, three streams of supersonic automatic fire split the air above us. We bellied up against the loam and waited for it to end.

"How many more cartridges do you have?" I asked Daron.

"Just a couple."

I turned to Asa.

"Unless you have another speed loader, I'm almost empty," he said.

"Damn. All I have is what's in the Browning, and my Mossberg. Not much against those rifles."

I thought for a moment..

"I have an idea," I said. "But I need you to get one more of them, Daron."

I turned toward him and discovered I'd been talking to myself. During the fusillade, he had slithered away.

"Still a little life in the old guy," Asa whispered.

"I'll say."

Something wet and clumpy flew over our heads in Enfante's direction and landed about twenty feet from him. The second guard stood and fired toward it. It was a fatal mistake. I heard the sharp bite of the Springfield, and the guard's head snapped back. He stood, mostly by reflex, for half a second, and then crumpled.

By then, Enfante and Greg Freund had slammed new cartridge magazines into their rifles and ripped off two bursts in the general direction from which Daron's shot had come.

I heard a rustle behind me several seconds later, and Daron reappeared.

"Will that do?" he asked.

"That will do. Give me a hand, here," I said.

I peeled off my oilskin duster and pulled my pocketknife from my jeans. I ripped the right shoulder with the knife, and then rubbed it in the mud.

"Here's what we're going to do," I said. Then I told them.

A couple of minutes later, I had crawled several rows over from Daron and Asa and took a deep breath. It was showtime.

"Hey, Tobe!" I yelled.

For a moment, I heard nothing back.

"What is it, Gold?" he called back.

"I'm all shot up," I called. "I need medical help."

"That really sucks," Enfante yelled.

"I mean it. You got the old man with the last volley. The kid's got one in the leg and one in the chest, a sucking wound. I got hit in the arm, and I can't move it. I want to come out. I'll give you Asa if you let me pull out."

"Why in hell would I want to do that?"

"He can testify against you. I can't. He's all I have to bargain with."

"Show yourself!"

I slowly stood, my Browning in my right hand. My left arm hung stiff and lifeless against my side.

"I'm losing a lot of blood," I said. "I'm getting a little weak."

"Come on," Enfante said. "Out into the open."

I let go of the Browning, so that it hung from my finger by just the trigger guard and limped toward Enfante.

"Careful with that gun," he said.

"It's empty," I said.

"I don't trust you. Toss it away."

I pulled back my hand and tossed the Browning about fifteen feet away. It landed in a mud puddle. I hated that. I would be a couple of hours cleaning it.

If I lived long enough.

The rain beat down on the top of my head and ran in rivulets down each side of my nose. I blinked several times to get it out of my eyes. I reached around and held my left arm against my side tighter.

"Hurts like a son of a bitch," I said. "I'll trade the kid for a pass."

"What about the old man?"

"I already told you. You killed him. Asa's back in the grapes, about five rows. He's out of ammunition. You can go get him. Just let me walk."

I saw Enfante and Greg Freund slowly get to their feet. They had their AK's braced in front of them. Enfante sneered at me. I could see his white, even teeth in the near-dark.

"Pretty brave now, aren't you?" he said.

"I never claimed to be brave. Just let me go."

"Call Asa out."

"He's shot up, I told you."

"Call him out!"

I sighed and shook my head.

Slowly I turned, with my stiff left arm hidden from them by my duster.

"It's no good, Asa!" I called. "They have us. Come on out, and I'll guarantee it'll be quick."

As I spoke, I relaxed my left fist, the one which had cradled the muzzle of the Mossberg, and let it slide out the tattered left sleeve of my duster. I caught the trigger guard as it almost slid by, and I flipped the safety off. The rest of it fell out the sleeve, and I grasped the pistol grip.

"I don't think he's coming," I said, as I turned back around. By now I had the Mossberg up and ready. I pulled the trigger, and the left side of Greg's neck exploded under the impact of the steel shot. He dropped the rifle he was carrying. They both hit the ground about the same time.

Enfante pointed his rifle in my direction. He got off a shot just as I jacked a second shell into the chamber. It glanced off the center in my bulletproof vest and drove all the wind out of my lungs. As I rolled toward the ground, I took a quick snapshot in his direction, and put a load straight into his stomach.

At the same time, I heard Daron's Springfield bark once, back in the grapes. The impact made Enfante drop his AK, but not before I pumped up a third double-ought shell and caught him right at the point where his collarbones joined. I could see a fine pink fog collect and then slowly disperse behind him in the light from the processing plant. He fell backward and rolled down the hill.

I sat down in the rain and tried to quench the fire in my lungs with a deep breath that just wouldn't seem to come.

We had won the Second Battle of Corona Farms.

FORTY-FOUR

I sat in the muck, with the rain pouring down on my head, for what felt like half an hour.

I felt a hand on my shoulder.

"It's over," Daron told me. "I checked. We got them all."

"Uh huh," I mumbled, my voice wheezing a little. "What about Delroy?"

"Haven't gone down to the house yet."

"He had a cell phone with him when he was shot. We're going to need it."

I slowly rose to my feet and stumbled on rubbery legs down the stone steps, past the entrance to the processing plant, and on to my car. I drove down the hill to the manor house.

Delroy was sitting up against the baluster at the bottom of the steps. He had his jacket off and was struggling to pull off his shirt. His breath came in quick, shallow gasps.

I pulled the car into the drive and stepped out. I still had the Mossberg in my hand, and I leveled it at him.

"Don't you think I've been shot enough for one night?" he asked.

He kept working at the shirt.

"You had a vest?"

"When you're dealing with mobsters, it's always handy. You want to give me a fuckin' hand here, or do you enjoy watching people struggle in pain?"

I set down the Mossberg and helped peel the shirt off his back. I could see the multiple slugs flattened against the Kevlar vest that had saved his life.

It took a few moments to undo the vest, and Delroy tossed it onto the front steps of the manor house. I helped him put his shirt back on, though there was very little left of it in back. He picked up his jacket.

"Well, that's the end of that coat," he said, as he surveyed the holes in the cheap wool.

"Cheer up," I said. "I hear WalMart's having a sale next week."

"Fuck you, too."

He tried to stand. I helped him to his feet.

"You leave anyone for me to kill?" he asked.

"Sorry. What in hell were you doing up here?"

"Tracking the Lexus. I saw it was headed toward Napa, so I decided I'd get here first. Thought maybe they were bringing Asa."

"The other GPS tracker under the car was yours?"

"One of Full Moon's. Sheldon suspected Enfante over a week ago. Had a hunch that a mob guy running the place where blackmail photos were being taken might just have a hand in taking them."

"You could have told me."

"I tried to, remember? You threatened to shoot me and fourteen other guys. I know when I'm not wanted."

"You got here ahead of Enfante, but then you realized the two guys on the front porch weren't from Full Moon."

"Yeah. I tried to play it cool, but as soon as I pulled out my cell I was burned. Damned white of them not to pull the ol' *coup de grace*."

"They were busy. Your car's up the hill."

He limped around the corner to look up the hill.

"Killed 'em all, huh?"

"There were six. Enfante, Chris Driscoll, Greg and Barney, and the two guys who posed as Full Moon guards."

"Driscoll? I was betting on Chiklis."

"So was I. Sometimes you're wrong."

He wheezed a couple of times and coughed up something thick and roux-like. He spat into the bushes.

"We got a problem," he said.

"I know. My cell's dead, and they cut the telephone wires. I came down to get your phone."

"Glad you were so concerned about me."

"I saw them empty two revolvers into you. What was I supposed to think?"

The last two words were undercut by the sound of a large diesel engine roaring to life. We both looked up the hill as Daron Corona drove a backhoe loader from behind the processing plant.

"What in hell is that old fart up to?"

"I think he just decided to plant a new stand of grapes," I said. "Come on, we'll take my car."

———

When we got up the hill, Daron was out of the backhoe and had been joined by Asa Corona. Daron and Asa had already dumped Greg Freund's body into the front shovel of the machine and were working on picking up Chris Driscoll.

"This boy's a mite hefty," Daron called out to us. "I'd appreciate a little assistance. I'm right happy to see you aren't dead, Jack."

"Day's not over yet," Delroy said. "What are you doing, here, Daron?"

"What's it look like? You gonna help us or not?"

"We need to call the police," I said. "This isn't 1933 anymore, Mr. Corona."

"And what are you gonna tell them when they get here?" Daron asked, gasping a bit from the exertion. "You got six dead guys lying around here, and there was three of us. That guy over there, the one you shot last? Hell, his head's damn near blown clear off. Way I see it, these guys aren't gonna be missed."

Delroy looked at me, and then walked over to Daron and Asa. He bent over and grabbed Driscoll's legs. Together, the three of them heaved the body into the maw of the shovel.

I watched and tried to work through the ethical problems of it. Somehow, it seemed wrong to just dig a hole, dump a bunch of guys in, and plant a vineyard over them. If Enfante and his cronies had managed to kill the three of us, though, I had a feeling they wouldn't have left much behind to mark the event.

Turning it over to the cops would prove to be a problem in the long run. There would be endless questions, paperwork out the wazoo, and eventually we'd also have to deal with JuneBug, who likely wasn't inclined to take kindly to us offing six of his made guys.

I ran through a lot of thoughts like that, bouncing back and forth from grace to perdition. In the end, it all came down to the realization that nobody was going to believe that an old man, a gay kid, and a burned-out private dick could take on six mobsters and survive, unless we had done something dirty and underhanded. It didn't matter that the six assholes had been malicious. It didn't matter that they had come to Corona Farms with the express intent of wiping us off the face of the earth. In the end, it came down to a single concept.

History is written by the victors.

———

We buried them at the far corner of a field that Daron had recently marked off for a new planting. The hole was deep, deeper than any normal grave. One by one, Delroy, Asa, and I lugged their dead weight over and heaved them into the dark musty excavation, until we were through. Then Daron shoved all the dirt back into the gap, ran over it a couple of times with the backhoe and it was over.

"A lot easier than last time," he said, after shutting down the machine. "Spent all night with hand shovels."

"What are you thinking of planting here?" Delroy asked.

"Muscadines. I hear there's a call for muscadine wine back east," he said.

He climbed down from the backhoe and bummed a cigarette off Delroy, who also took one for himself. They shared a conspiratorial smile as they fired them up.

Daron drew in a long drag from the cigarette, and immediately started to cough. The fit passed quickly, though. Then he walked over to Asa.

"I'm going to say this in front of the men, Asa. I want someone to hear this. What we did tonight was terrible, but it was the only way. I don't know what you've done that gave these people the means to blackmail you, and I don't want to know. I don't want to hear anything that will diminish you in my eyes, because after tonight I couldn't be prouder of you if you were my own son. You did a man's work this evening. You have to carry that with you for the rest of your life."

Asa nodded, his head bowed, as he stared solemnly down at the settling mound of earth which would remind him for decades to come of the Second Battle for Corona Farms.

"Hey," Delroy said. "It's stopped raining."

We all looked up. The clouds were parting, allowing a spear of moonlight to pierce the sky. It seemed to fall over the hills to the east. Through the dispersing billows, I could begin to make out the pinpoints of stars.

It appeared that the storm was over.

I followed in my car as Delroy drove the Lexus into San Rafael. We parked it behind a convenience store, made certain that it was wiped down, and I took him back to Corona Farms to retrieve his Ford. When we got there, Asa and Daron had uncorked a bottle of zinfandel and were sitting on the porch rocking and sipping from Corona Farms crystal goblets.

I climbed out of my car and walked up the steps.

"I'm going to leave now," I said.

"Just a moment," Daron said.

He pulled himself up from his rocker and walked over to me. He reached into his jacket pocket and handed me a thin envelope. I kept one eye on him as I opened it. The check had a couple more zeros on it than the bill I had prepared for Asa.

"Take it," Corona said.

"Are you buying my silence?" I asked, warily.

"Consider it a bonus for bringing my grandson home safely. From what he's told me, you earned it."

I folded the envelope and stuck it in my shirt pocket. Then I reached out, grasped Daron's hand, and shook the way men are supposed to – hard enough to show you mean business, but not so hard as to brag. We had an understanding, this old man and I, and it went a lot farther than six moldering bodies in a makeshift grave up the hill.

I shook Asa's hand, and even Jack Delroy's. We had formed a conspiracy of silence, forged in a bond known mostly only to soldiers and astronauts. What had happened here, would stay here.

I drove back down the long drive toward Napa.

I never saw Daron Corona again.

My car somehow willed itself to Heidi's apartment. I parked on the street, turning my wheels toward the curb in about the only act of civic responsibility I'd managed all night. I stowed my weapons in a safe in the trunk.

Then I walked up to her apartment door and rang the bell.

She came to the door moments later. I think she gasped when she saw my haggard face and torn duster. I was still coated with mud from digging a mass grave, but she didn't know that.

She didn't say a word. She stood aside as I walked in, hung my mangled coat on the coat tree in the foyer, and stumbled straight back to the refrigerator, where I grabbed a bottle of Anchor Steam.

Heidi was waiting when I came to the bedroom.

I sat on the side of the bed and twisted the cap off the beer. Silently, I drained half of it in a single draft. Then I placed the bottle on the bedside table.

I turned to her. She looked frightened.

"I'm ready to talk," I said.

ABOUT THE AUTHOR

Retired college professor and forensic psychologist Richard Helms has been nominated six times for the SMFS Derringer Award, winning it twice; five times for the Private Eye Writers of America Shamus Award; twice for the ITW Thriller Award, with one win; and once for the Mystery Readers International Macavity Award. He is also a frequent contributor to *Ellery Queen Mystery Magazine*, along with other periodicals. Mr. Helms is a former member of the Board of Directors of Mystery Writers of America, and the former president of the Southeast Regional Chapter of MWA. When not writing, Mr. Helms is an avid woodworker, and enjoys travel, gourmet cooking, and rooting for his beloved Carolina Tar Heels and Carolina Panthers. Richard Helms and his wife Elaine live in Charlotte, North Carolina.

Made in United States
North Haven, CT
16 April 2022

18320458R00178